HAIGHT ST.

PIERRE OUELLETTE

HAIGHT ST.

A CRIME NOVEL

ISBN: 978-1-7331007-0-0

Library of Congress
Control Number: 2020937217

Cover design and formatting: Keith Carlson

First edition

JORVIK PRESS

5331 S Macadam Ave., Ste 258/424,
Portland OR 97239

JorvikPress.com

ABOUT THE AUTHOR

Pierre Ouellette lives in the Portland Metro Area and is the author of six previously published novels that span a diversity of subjects and settings. He served for two decades as the creative partner in an advertising and public relations agency focused on science and technology. Prior to that he was a professional guitarist and played in numerous pop bands and jazz ensembles, including Paul Revere and the Raiders, Jim Pepper and David Friesen.

ALSO BY PIERRE OUELLETTE

The Deus Machine

The Third Pandemic

The Forever Man

Bakersfield: A Crime Novel

WRITING AS PIERRE DAVIS

A Breed Apart

Origin Unknown

"Have you ever dreamed about a place you never really recall being to before? A place that maybe only exists in your imagination? Some place far away, half remembered when you wake up. When you were there, though, you knew the language, you knew your way around."

"That was the Sixties."

"No, it wasn't that either. It was just '66 and early '67. That's all it was."

Peter Fonda
in the role of Terry Valentine
in *The Limey* (1999)

1965

LOS ANGELES

1.

DOWNTOWN
AUGUST 13, 1965

Watts was burning. James Stone had a clear view from the sixth floor of Capitol Records in Hollywood, twelve miles away. Billows of black and grey thrust up into a sky stained a dismal brown by chronic smog. Too many cars, too many raging black people. The Negroes were having their say, and this time, the whole country tuned in.

Here at Capitol, the riots cast an anxious hush. The company had numerous black artists and a lot to lose from an all-out rupture in race relations. While there might be a trace of latent bias around here, it was relatively mild compared to the world at large. Everyone understood that without the Negro contribution, much of American music was pretty much a lost cause.

Stone stared at the smoke and its dark ascent into a dubious heaven. He could almost hear the random pop of small arms, the brilliant sprinkle of shattered glass, the primal bursts of shouting and cursing. He wondered how the cops were handling it. He'd once been one of them, an LA cop. His last gig was Vice in Hollywood, just before that ugly business that exiled him up to Bakersfield, where things got even uglier. In the end, it turned out to be his salvation, of course, because it got him into the music business. Guys he'd heard up there in dive bars had punched through into the big time, people like Buck Owens and Merle Haggard. He'd caught the wave when it was still a tiny swell, and rode it on back to Hollywood, where he was making about ten times his former police salary.

His old cop partner Murphy had phoned him this morning and weighed in bluntly: The niggers down in Watts have finally gone and done it. It's time to crack some heads and get this thing settled up for good. Stone knew that Murphy represented the prevailing sentiment within the department. Stone thought otherwise, always had, although quietly. He himself came from a minority, a white one. He was an Okie from a family of refugees that migrated here during the Great Depression. The LA Police Department had sent a large contingent of officers to confront them at the state border. Suspicion and resentment soon followed them right on into town.

Stone stared slightly to the left of all the smoke. South Gate. It was where he grew up. Alameda Avenue divided it from Watts and the black community. Two migrant groups, one from the middle of America, the other from the heart of Africa. One fueled by economic desperation, the other by outright enslavement. Neither wanted to be there, but both knew there was no way back. And so it was that they turned on each other.

Stone remembered the start of it, when he was a kid. The brutal economic fist of the Depression had laid South Gate low, and the Saturday matinee dropped to twenty cents, which bought you both a serial and a feature at the Vogue Theater on Long Beach Boulevard. The hard times stopped at the turnstile, and a big screen reached out and regaled you with rockets, ray guns, monsters, and bearded villains.

His family lived in a tiny house with two postage stamp bedrooms and one slightly larger space that served as both kitchen and living room. His dad had built, plumbed and wired the thing all by himself. His dad was smart that way. Most people heard his Okie drawl and probably wrote him off as just another dumb drifter in off the Plains, but they got it all wrong. He'd moved here two years before the Depression even started, when James was six and his brother four. It wasn't really desperation that drove the old man to South Gate, it was a chance to leverage his considerable skill as an engine mechanic. In a slightly different world he would have gone through college and become an engineer. Given this practical bent, he never centered his life on the stand-up-and-shout brand of religion favored by most Okies. As he told James and his brother, "You can't yell and think at the same time, and as soon as you stop thinkin' you got a problem."

"He come a long way in his life," his mother later said of his father. "And he was always good to you boys. Lotta men weren't. Don't you ever forget that, hear?"

Stone had not.

"Always had his own mind about things," she said. "Kinda like you."

His own mind. It brought the Spook Hunters roaring back, closing the distance between now and then in a single heartbeat.

South Gate High School. He was seventeen, strong and quick, incredibly quick. Football looked to be his social salvation. In his younger years, he'd been ridiculed and teased about his Okie origins, his rural sensibilities, his signature drawl. "Hey Okie boy," they said, "your family must be really rich: You got an extra mattress tied to the top of your car." Or "Sorry, my mom says I can't hang around with hillbillies." Which puzzled him greatly. He was six when they left Oklahoma, and he didn't recall any hills at all. Only the earthen planar fighting a brilliant blue sky.

Over time, a simmering mix of sadness and anger settled in, the kind common to all who dwell outside the mainstream and the impossible norms it imposes.

Then came football. He made varsity in his sophomore year and became a full-fledged member of the school's jock aristocracy. His Okie mannerisms withered away in the newfound light. Girls became readily available. Teachers shepherded his academic progress. Boys deferred to him.

Then, the Spook Hunters. It happened on a fall afternoon after football practice. The sky was dull from smog and long shadows streaked the playing field. A half dozen players approached him as he walked toward the lockers. Key players, the best on the team, the most highly regarded both on and off the field.

"Hey Stone," one of them said. "We want you to join up. We need a guy like you." It was Walters, the quarterback.

"Join what?"

"Spook Hunters. You in?"

Stone instinctively followed the legacy of his father. "Don't know. Got to think about it."

He scanned their young faces. They appeared both puzzled and bemused. He'd just been invited to join a secret society of the highest order, an elite within the elite. How could he possibly hesitate?

"Well don't think too long," the quarterback said, and the group walked off.

So there they were, with the whites on one side of Alameda Avenue and blacks on the other. The white side had led off by crossing over and randomly assaulting black targets of opportunity. Thus, the Spook Hunters came about, mostly young men in their teens and twenties, racist shock troops who had the tacit support of the community at large.

Stone's dad noticed that he seemed quiet and troubled at dinner that night. He joined his son on the porch steps in the evening light.

"So what's got your goat?" he asked.

Stone told him about the invitation. It has an honor to be asked, but he just didn't feel right about it. He didn't know why. He just didn't.

They sat in silence for several minutes before his dad spoke. Not unusual. He always seemed to give carefully measured replies.

"Well, y'all gotta make up your own mind," he said, "but there's a little more to this thing than just spooks and school. Us here in South Gate are a little piece of a lot bigger pie, and the people that own that pie are callin' the shots. And the way they look at it, we're the white niggers and the folks across the way are the black niggers. But in the end, we're all niggers. So what we are fightin' for? To tell you the truth, I really don't know."

As he lay in bed that night, Stone decided his dad had it right. Their family had been put down his whole life for their Dustbowl origins. One slur, one insult after another. He imagined it wasn't much different on the black side of Alameda. In fact, it was probably worse. It was one thing to have your drawl go against you, and quite another your skin color. The next day he told the quarterback he'd decided not to join, and that was that.

"So what do you make of it, Mr. Jimmy?"

Earl Benton had come in and joined Stone at the window. Stone wasn't happy with the moniker, but it had stuck solid. He'd come up the country side of the business, and 'Jimmy' had a downhome ring to it that was apparently irresistible.

"Not good," Stone said.

"You used to be a cop here, right?"

"Way back."

"Can you see yourself down there, busting heads?"

"Nope, I can't." Stone didn't like Benton. Never had. He was a pure promo man, with no genuine feel for the music. Stone, on the other hand, was considered to have a golden ear. In the studio, he could pick up on small changes that made an enormous difference. The players liked him because they felt like he was making things better, not just bending them to his will.

"Oh well," Benton shrugged. "Doesn't matter. It's gonna be what it's gonna be. You heard about the bitching from the Beatles?"

"Yep." Capitol had the US distribution for this British band that had taken off like an unleashed Doberman running down a mugger. But the group wasn't happy with the way Capitol was messing with the tracks on their albums. The company was adding and subtracting songs from the British versions to squeeze every American dime they thought they could make.

"They just don't get it," Benton mused. "This is America. It's a different deal."

"You sure about that?" Stone asked.

"Well...yeah," Benton trailed off. Like most of the hype people, he had no idea what the fuck he was talking about. He cast a diversionary glance at his watch. "Gotta go. Check you later."

Stone smiled to himself. In truth, he favored the other British contender, the Rolling Stones, who were on a competitor's label.

The music felt a lot closer to the street, more like what he'd encountered up in Bakersfield. Their latest release had a tune entitled
"The Under Assistant West Promo Man" that cleverly mocked the
likes of Benton. He was sure that if he'd brought the Stones to
the brass at Capitol, they would have issued a resounding thumbs
down. But they also knew Stone had a knack for finding gems in
the rough, like up in Bakersfield. He was their hedge against missing out on the latest whatever. They had to give him room to roam.

Like with so-called surf music. A few years back, he'd been
down in Huntington Beach and stumbled across this guy named
Dick Dale, who was playing a weekend dance hall gig. Dale played
guitar through the biggest amplifier Stone had ever seen. On a
break, he told Stone that it was powered by a 100-watt amp driving an enclosed 15-inch speaker to the edge of chaos. The music
pulsated with a primitive simplicity and energy that was absolutely
captivating. Stone knew intuitively that the only way capture its
essence was to record it live. He took the idea to Capitol and of
course, they applied the brakes. You only made live recordings of
groups that already had a string of studio-produced hits. Wrong.
Shortly thereafter, Dale independently recorded an album in front
of 3000 writhing dancers at a big hall in Balboa. When Capitol
heard it, they finally came out of their stupor and acquired the
rights.

Stone scanned the smoke plumes one last time and returned to
his desk. Outside, the city plowed on relentlessly like a huge ship
moving through the sea of time. Nothing he did was going to alter
its course. It made him fear that he might lose his touch, might feel
his finger slip off the pulse of the moment, might lose his instinct
for the zeitgeist. He'd turned 43 a month back and Christine had
taken them to Taylors to celebrate with a world-class steak. After a
couple of glasses of Bordeaux, he turned slightly sodden and wondered aloud how long he'd last. The Rat Pack was out, the Beach
Boys were in. The thrust of it all knocked him a little off balance,
like a fighter who'd taken a big hit but stubbornly held on.

Christine smiled quietly and heard him out. She was good at
that, most likely due to her training as a physician: Unless you

listened carefully, you might miss a key symptom. When his lament finally spun down, she reached across and put her hand over his. It felt warm and soothing. After nearly ten years, he was still hopelessly attracted to her. "I think you've still got a few miles on you, big guy," she said. And that was all it took.

Stone got up, crossed to the credenza, started up his tape deck and played a version of the Beach Boys' latest album on Capitol taken directly off the master. First time he'd heard it, his ear quickly told him that the entire group was in orbit around Brian Wilson. The guy was a flat-out fucking genius. Wilson had totally short-circuited the established recording protocol and acted as his own producer. Management could only stand back and watch in slack-jawed wonder. If the kid had been born in Europe of the 1700s, he would have given Mozart a run for his money.

Stone closed his eyes. The deck's rotating reels had a hypnotic effect, and he felt Capitol, Watts, and promo men gradually recede to a manageable distance. Brian Wilson was just the start. The whole industry was going to get upended. Something was coming, something big. He just needed to figure out what it was before it hatched.

2.

CENTRAL LOS ANGELES

The King parked his rental car two blocks from his destination. He could hear the snap of gunfire in the distance and see the columns of black smoke boiling up out of the Watts business district. A strange calm held sway out here in the neighborhoods, which always seemed immune to this kind of thing. He had the sidewalk to himself as he started down the block. The street and yards were empty and the scent of burning wood hung heavy in the air.

He wore a tailored silk sport shirt, pleated linen slacks and suede Oxford shoes. An outfit designed to disguise the twenty extra pounds he currently carried on a muscular frame. All done in colors that complemented his black skin. The King had an eye for this kind of thing, as well as the financial resources to pull it off.

A big thud rolled down the street from the commercial strip to the west. Very disappointing. He'd sensed genuine opportunity here, but now he'd have to postpone his plans indefinitely. Civil unrest was bad for commerce. The business model he'd carefully constructed on the East Coast was no longer applicable in LA. It demanded a finely tuned dynamic between suppliers, processors, distributors, customers and government. No matter. There were four other major cities on the west coast to explore and develop.

As he strolled leisurely down the block, the King put each location through a rigorous mental test. He ran an intricate set of numbers, projected consumption levels, profiled potential partners, extrapolated supply chains and assessed the competition's relative strengths. Finally, he cross-correlated the entire matrix to extract the necessary decision-making data.

If the King had been white, he would have been the CEO of a major US corporation.

If the King had been white, his visionary approach would have revealed vast markets unseen by others.

If the King had been white, he would have resided in Westchester County, or the Gold Coast, or Brentwood.

If the King had been white, key politicians would have sought his counsel and his monetary favor.

But the King seldom dwelled on such things. He regarded racism as a given, something permanently baked into the American culture. Better to move within it than to try to break out of it. It put him in a world with its own economy, its own values, its own justice system. All of which he understood in a way that a white man would never fully grasp. Over the last 20 years, he'd leveraged this competitive advantage to crown himself king of an empire hidden in the shadows of this great and powerful nation.

He soon reached the house he was looking for, a one-story bungalow done in pink stucco. Its lone occupant would not be expecting him, and that was the whole point. He opened the screen door and rang the bell. "I'm comin', I'm comin'," he heard from within. It prompted him to draw a Walther PPK automatic out of his pocket, a compact weapon easily concealed by the folds in his slacks.

The door opened to a middle-aged black man in a bathrobe. "Hey..." the man started to say.

The King didn't wait for the terror to fully form in the man's eyes. There was no need to savor the fear nor to bask in revenge, like they always did in the movies. Speed and efficiency were the practical concerns of the moment.

He raised the pistol and fired a bullet into the middle of the man's forehead from a range of two feet. A mist of gore shot out the back of the skull, and the body toppled over backwards.

The King pocketed his weapon and used a handkerchief to shut the front door. Out on the street, it was pickup day for the trash, and the cans lined the curb. Several houses down, he wiped the gun and threw it into one.

On the way back to the car, he reflected briefly on the dead man's role in his empire, and how he had entrusted him with a position of power, which the man grievously abused. It left him no choice but to personally dispense justice as an example to others within his inner circle.

By the time he slid behind the wheel of his car, he'd put the whole matter behind him. Based on his analysis, he knew precisely which West Coast city he would approach next.

A young boy, maybe ten or so, rode slowly by on a bicycle. The King rolled down his window.

"Where you goin', son?"

The boy stopped. "Don't know. Just ridin' around."

"Well you get yourself on home. This ain't no time to be out and about."

"Yes sir."

The boy pedaled off down the empty street. The King sighed. What was wrong with parents these days?

3.

EAST LOS ANGELES

Larry Boyd. Young, blond, and burned brown by yard work and beach cruising. He pressed his calloused palms on the pawnshop's glass counter while the owner lifted the guitar out of its tweed case.

"Jazzmaster, huh?" The owner, an Indian, gave it a critical once over and trained his almond eyes on Larry. "Used to be a big seller. Not anymore. The market's moved on."

"Yeah, well maybe. So what can you give me?"

"I can't give you anything," the owner said. "I loan you. I keep the guitar as collateral. That's the way it works. You don't pay me back, I sell it."

"Alright, so what can you loan me?" Larry grasped the essence of the transaction, but not much more. Money management was not his thing, never had been.

The pawn guy ignored him and slowly rotated the instrument. He had the upper hand and they both knew it. They also knew that Larry would take the cash and never be back. Another golden boy gone all wrong.

"Twenty-five bucks. That's the best I can do."

"But it's almost brand new," Larry protested. His mother had bought it for him just last year. Right before she moved to Palm Springs to spend the rest of her life sipping gin and tonics poolside while the parched air sucked whatever moisture was left out of her faltering skin. She'd quickly joined a gaggle of like-minded friends given to cursing the malevolence of their ex-husbands. Each a fiend in his own special way. In her case, the ex was Larry's father, a dentist who practiced in Brentwood and wound up performing complex procedures on one of his hygienists.

Larry had missed all the domestic fallout because he'd moved out to attend junior college, where he was supposed to atone for his miserable SAT scores. Didn't work. His father cut off his funding, which reduced him to a pitiful string of handouts from his mother. But none of these reversals kindled any anxiety within him. He lived under the brilliant sun of southern California as it arched high overhead and cast no shadow of doubt nor darkness. It illuminated a landscape of unlimited possibility. You simply dreamed your way forward. Money would inevitably follow, like a mindless disciple of some kind.

Out in the parking lot, he climbed into his prewar Ford pickup with its failing clutch and asthmatic carburetor. A buck's worth of gas would easily get him down to Huntington Beach. He shared a budget-level apartment there with two roommates, both given to long stretches of unemployment. Not unlike Larry. All three forever waded through a perpetual stew of fast food, beer and odd jobs.

Twenty-five bucks. He felt good. He was on a roll.

"Weed at the Box. Make the scene."

The cryptic note was scrawled on the backside of a vacant pizza box, one of dozens littering the apartment's cramped kitchen. His roommate Jethro had written it. Larry stepped over a fatally gouged surfboard on his way out. They had all aspired to the surfing life, but it turned out to demand a lot more persistence and practice than any of them could muster. Better to cruise along its fringes and affect the look but not the trade. Any number of hot young babes failed to understand the distinction.

At the Jack in the Box, Larry quickly spotted Jethro's tousled blond mane in a booth near the back. A wiry guy in a faded T-shirt faced him, a bearded fellow with a tangled mass of receding brown hair. Jethro slid over to make room for Larry. "Hey dude, meet Mr. John Griggs of Laguna Beach."

Griggs reached a hand across to Larry, who was startled by the man's pale eyes. They had the look of a becalmed sea right after a great storm has passed. "Peace, man," Griggs told him. The greeting puzzled Larry. He'd never heard the word 'peace' used in this particular context. "What say we go over to the beach," Griggs suggested. They piled out of the booth, leaving behind a couple of Cokes and a limp pile of French fries.

"You guys surf?" Griggs asked as they walked across the street into the parking lot of a state park fronting the ocean.

"Yeah, sort of," Larry replied. "We're working on it."

"Good," Griggs said as they reached his vehicle, a '53 Ford station wagon with wooden door panels. "Come on in." He opened a back door and Larry and Jethro climbed in while Griggs went around to the driver's seat.

"Better," Griggs commented as he unlocked the glove box. "No narcs with binocs." He pulled out a plastic baggie of cannabis buds and dangled it in front of the pair. "So how many?"

"We can go ten bucks' worth," Jethro said tentatively. Neither were veteran pot customers.

"Don't have a scale," Griggs told them. "You trust me?"

"Yeah, sure."

"All right then." Griggs produced an old pill bottle and stuffed four buds into it. Jethro paid with a ten-dollar bill and Griggs put the baggie back in the glove box. Larry went to open the door and Griggs said "Hang on, man. We're not done yet."

Larry felt the fear, felt it bad. This guy was a dope dealer, a certified criminal.

"What's left?" Jethro asked nervously.

"The love."

"The love?" Larry asked. Now he was worried that Griggs might be queer.

"Yeah, the love." Griggs smiled softly and rested his tanned arm on the top of the seat. "I used to be a really bad motherfucker. Can you believe that?"

"Yeah, I guess."

"A while back, I robbed this guy in a parking lot. Scared the shit out of him. Looked like a rich dude, but he was pretty light on bread. I had him empty his pockets and this little tin full of pills fell out. I figured they were either bennies or downers. Either way was okay, so I popped one on the way home."

He paused, brushed back his unkempt hair and smiled to himself. "It took about half an hour, and then I went over to the other side." He looked up. "And I've never been back."

"The other side? What's there?" Larry asked.

"Love. Pure, perfect love. It's the real world, the one where we're all truly brothers. You see, man, we're all connected, and in ways you can't even imagine. You gotta understand that all this fighting, all this stealing, all this cheating: It's all a con, a shuck, an illusion. The real thing is right here, all the time, but you just can't see it. Not without a little help."

He reached down and came up with a folded piece of paper. He carefully parted the folds to reveal a half dozen small pink pills. "Lysergic acid diethylamide. LSD. It'll set you free. And if we can get enough people to try it, it'll set the whole world free."

The power of Griggs' conviction was nearly overwhelming. A Laguna surfer turned messiah. Who would have thought it?

"Wow," Jethro exclaimed. "That's too bad. We just gave you our last ten bucks."

"No charge," Griggs said as he folded the pills back into the paper. "This isn't a product. It's a sacrament. You'd don't sell it. You share it. It's a gift from the brotherhood of eternal love. Take it and go in peace." He handed the paper to Larry, who said, "Well yeah…Thanks."

Griggs turned the ignition and the old engine reluctantly rolled over. "Gotta get going. Spread the love, dudes. Good luck."

"Same to you," Jethro replied as they stepped out and Griggs drove off.

"Wow," Jethro remarked. "That's one powerful dude."

Larry stared down at the folded paper with the pills. "You gonna try it?"

"Maybe later," Jethro said. "Right now, I'm going for a toke or two on this weed."

Back at the apartment, they ground up one of the buds and rolled a fat one with Zig Zag paper. Larry took a single hit and left the rest for Jethro, who tossed off his sandals and flipped the TV on to a rerun of Gilligan's Island. While they sat on the couch, Larry opened the folded paper containing the pills.

The other side, Griggs had said. The right side. And there was something about the way he said it, with a ring of absolute truth that precluded any debate.

The other side, the right side. No bitter mom. No two-timing dad. No academic apocalypses. No more dumping endless grass clippings into plastic barrels. Most of all, no impediments to playing massively cool surf guitar.

He plucked one of the pills off the paper and swallowed it.

4.

IA DRANG VALLEY, VIETNAM
NOVEMBER 1965

She'll be okay. We'll get through it.

Pfc Randy Poke stared up into a sky of pale blue. The elephant grass danced and swayed all around him to the churn of nearby chopper blades. A silent dance. His ears registered only a silver rage that damped out the world beyond. The onset of shock had erased most of his pain. And it mercifully shoved all the fear and terror into the far distance.

Only Rhonda came through.

He'd tried to roll over to get up, but it didn't work. His right arm was gone, severed six inches below the shoulder. His right leg was also missing, blown off halfway up the thigh.

Randy Poke didn't know it right now, but he was a silent partner in a catastrophic US defeat at a place called Landing Zone Albany in the Ia Drang Valley. Here, US and North Vietnamese forces met head-on for the first time in a major engagement. Nobody won. Everybody lost. An ominous preview of things to come.

Last thing he recalled was wading through the elephant grass and anthills when the enemy suddenly opened up. Chaos, gunfire, explosions, men dropping, men dying in their tracks. He never felt the explosion that maimed him. He never knew what kind of weapon caused it. A mortar? A grenade? A mine? It no longer mattered as he lay stunned in tall grass the color of straw.

Rhonda would want to hear the story, and he would tell it to her as best he could. He would start with the big military transport plane flying in from Hawaii and disgorging his unit at Da Nang airbase. He would then describe their overnight stay in framed tents and the dawn assembly where their battalion commander announced that they would be in battle by the end of the day. He would relate his premonition that, for the men of Alpha Company, this was very bad news.

As the wall of grass rocked to and fro, a fellow soldier came into view and looked down at him in alarm. The man knelt and began applying tourniquets to his arm and leg. He had the two stripes of a corporal and his name tag said "Carson." His lips kept moving, but Randy couldn't hear a word. Another soldier came into view and together they put a poncho down and gently lifted Randy onto it.

"Rhonda's going to be okay with this," Randy told Carson.

The corporal's lips moved in reply, all of it lost on Randy. The poncho served as a makeshift stretcher and they began moving him through the grass, which grew more agitated as they neared the chopper.

Randy saw the blur of the rotor blades appear overhead, beating frantically against the jungle air. He felt the chill of the metal floor as they slid him in. He turned one last time to Carson, the corporal.

"She won't care if I'm missing a few pieces. It'll be okay."

Tears streamed down Carson's face as he raised his hand to say farewell.

Randy tried to return the gesture, but without his right arm, it was impossible.

As the chopper rose, Corporal Matt Carson sank to his knees in a profound state of despair. The kid looked like he should still be in high school. The kid had hoped the hope of the innocent, that everything would be alright, that his girlfriend would embrace his mangled body, that his future shone bright and true, that it hadn't been brutally snuffed out in this weeping green furnace.

Carson covered his ears to blot out the screaming of the wounded. He hung his head and sobbed for the longest time. No one bothered him. They all knew the score.

When he finally raised his head, the revelation came to him. This war, this stupid war was a monstrous conspiracy brewed from far above by righteous old men in tailored suits who spewed out vacuous phrases like "domino theory" and "counterinsurgency" as they traveled about in comfort and safety.

When Carson looked up, the chopper was gone, the sky empty. He would never know that Pfc Randy Poke quickly expired on that cold metal floor, wrapped in a shroud fashioned from visions of Rhonda.

But what he did know was that something near the center of him was grievously damaged and threatened to collapse the entire edifice.

5.

LOS ANGELES

Rhonda Savage stood before the mirror in the restroom of The Skeet and Shoot, a bar of modest caliber on Burbank Blvd. in Van Nuys. She idly assessed her reflection and saw a reasonably attractive woman of 24. Blue eyes, with natural blond hair falling to her shoulders in a light curl. Skin still smooth and unblemished. A slightly voluptuous figure belittled by women and beloved by men. It all added up to a net surplus of social bargaining power.

Outside, "Wooly Bully" blared from the juke box. Rhonda recalled that Randy really liked that song and wanted it played at their wedding reception. Her time with him had been sublimely happy and extraordinarily foolish. Given the course of her life, he was the guy she could never really have. Not after Bakersfield. It had left her with a glaze of arrogance inherited from the rich and powerful men she had consorted with at age thirteen. Luxury cars, big houses, abundant dope, piles of cash and a penchant for ruthless predation. Both repulsive and intoxicating. She came to feel as an equal, a major player outside the bounds of conventional morality.

She knew instinctively that as long as she maintained this position, she would remain inoculated against the anguish that festered somewhere near the core of her. After three foster families and six years of counseling, she held firm. Men wandered in and out her life, with no lasting impact. Sex, yes. Love, no.

And then, Randy Poke. He had an ineffable innocence about him and a capacity for affection that simply overwhelmed her. A good kid from a normal family, with manageable dreams and reasonable aspirations. He dwelled in what seemed a magical kingdom, previously inaccessible but now suddenly within reach. Her heart finally pulled her over the threshold.

Even then, she thought it wouldn't last. Sooner or later she would have to come clean about her past. She finally did so on a hot evening as the air conditioner whispered and sighed in the background. He nodded thoughtfully while the sad string of revelations gushed out of her. When she was done, he briefly reflected, and told her it really didn't matter. That was all a long time ago. It had nothing to do with what they had together now. They would simply move on.

It was one of the few times she ever cried. Joy or sorrow or both? She couldn't be sure.

The letter from the draft board came a week before he finished his apprenticeship as an electrician. They should have seen it coming but were lost in each other and largely oblivious to the world beyond. He put a positive spin on it. Most guys never saw combat and worked behind the lines. His electrical credentials would put him in an engineering battalion of some kind. Meanwhile, she could find a female roommate to save money from her job as a cashier at a nearby grocery store.

She recalled the last time she saw him, boarding the bus with all the other inductees bound for basic training at Fort Ord. The last thing he did was to give her a wink and a thumbs up. And that was the end of it.

Forever.

Since he and Rhonda were not legally bound, the telegram went to his parents. She got the call from Randy's mother, who dispensed with all compassion and condolence. She simply read the contents:

THE SECRETARY OF THE ARMY HAS ASKED ME TO EXPRESS HIS DEEP REGRET THAT YOUR SON, PRIVATE FIRST CLASS RANDOLPH H. POKE DIED IN VIETNAM ON 15 NOVEMBER 1965, FROM WOUNDS SUFFERED WHILE ON COMBAT OPERATION WHEN HIT BY HOSTILE FIRE.

PLEASE ACCEPT MY DEEPEST SYMPATHY. THIS CONFIRMS PERSONAL NOTIFICATION MADE BY A REPRESENTATIVE OF THE SECRETARY OF THE ARMY.

That done, his mother said only "I'm sorry" and hung up. The woman had never liked her.

Rhonda tumbled into a deep pit of grief, a place of no light or hope. But it lifted after only a few days and she knew why. Her passage into the realm of normalcy had been nothing more than wishful thinking. Her fiancé's death confirmed it and set her back on her true course.

But to where? What was the destination?

She recalled the last major passage in her life, at age fourteen, when Detective James Stone extricated her from that nasty mess in Bakersfield and put her on a bus to Los Angeles. In a bitter paradox, it changed everything yet changed nothing.

A pair of insistent knocks on the restroom door interrupted her rumination.

"Hey!" a male voice yelled. "Time to party. Come on out."

She knew the voice. It belonged to a guy who called himself Speedo, a mesmerizing mix of courage and recklessness, of abandon and purpose. He'd hit on her right after she entered the place an hour ago and she brushed him off, preferring to survey the scene. But this time he definitely had her attention. His banging on the door of the women's restroom put him in a class by himself. She shouldered her purse and opened the door.

Speedo looked like he might be Burt Reynold's long-lost brother, right down to the thick black mustache. "Hey babe, let's get this thing in gear," he commanded.

"What thing?" She feigned skepticism, just to keep him in play.

"We get a beer, we sit down, we make a plan."

"What kind of plan?" she countered.

"The perfect plan," he shot back. His dark eyes took on a primal brilliance. "Let's get moving. The universe won't wait."

Rhonda found this last remark intriguing, if a little vague. He took off toward some booths on the far side of the bar, expecting her to follow, and she did.

He gave her his personal rundown as he poured them each a beer. Edward P. Dalberg, best known as Speedo. An auto racer, a stock car driver, an emerging star on the California circuit. Had a fast car, fat sponsors and a decent shot at winning a clutch of trophies. But then came that incident at the end of the downhill straightaway at Riverside Raceway. He hit the brakes too late going into Turn 9, shot into the infield and flipped repeatedly in a violent ballet of steel, dirt, gas and rubber. It reduced his car to a crumpled ball and left him little chance of survival. They carted his comatose body off to the hospital, where he remained for two months. Broken pelvis, punctured lung, fractured ribs, shattered arm. Not to mention the "head injury" that knocked him somewhere outside of himself looking for a way back in.

But in the end, he left the hospital with a new brain, he told her, a much better one.

And what made it better? She asked.

It let the light of all creation shine down on him, he told her. It gave him a universal license to ignore formalities and do as he wished. Near-death had set him free.

And what's it telling you to do right now? She asked.

It's telling me to leave here. With you.

Rhonda thought she saw the hustle coming and moved to expose it. Leave? And go where?

North, he told her. Along a sacred meridian reserved especially for their private use. One that traced the summer solstice through to the Bay Area.

Yeah, sure.

He leaned across the table very close to her face. Ask yourself this, he told her. What's left for you here? Anything? Anything at all?

They descended the Grapevine in the wee hours, high on weed and speed. The headlights knifed the blackness and the highway rolled beneath them in a blur. A hot nocturnal wind blasted in the window on Rhonda's side, where the crank handle was missing. Speedo pushed the '56 Chevy up into the 90s while delivering a nonstop narrative on the metaphysical nature of their journey.

And so it began.

6.

SAN FRANCISCO

Stone and Christine gazed out at the bay from the upper deck of The Franciscan, where they had just finished a dinner of Dungeness crab legs backed by a bottle of pinot grigio. They had a window seat that afforded a spectacular view of San Francisco Bay. A small island with a familiar profile caught Christine's eye. She pointed to it and turned to Stone.

"Alcatraz. You ever send anybody there?"

Stone shrugged. "Might have. I don't know. We were state and they were federal. Sometimes we crossed paths. I might have pinched somebody who also wound up on the wrong side of the Feds. It did happen."

Christine smiled warmly. "Do you ever miss it?"

"Cops and robbers? It had its moments, but not really. It was what it was, and now I have you."

"Good answer. You're a clever guy."

"We'll see about that. I'm not scoring big at work right now."

"And that's why we're here, right?"

"Right." A few weeks back, he'd decided he needed a shift in venue. It would do them both good to get out of LA for a few days. They flew in and installed themselves in the Fairmont up above Chinatown on Nob Hill. He considered making it a working vacation but decided against it. Instead, they went on long walks and took in the local galleries and shops and waterfront.

Outside, a soft white wall of fog crept over the Golden Gate Bridge and swallowed the last of the evening sun. "So you want to go out on the town?" Stone asked her.

"Maybe just a little," she replied. "I'm up for a quick drink."

"Sounds about right."

They paid the bill and caught a cab out front. "Where to?" the driver asked.

Stone was in a mildly festive mood after a half bottle of the pinot. "We want to get a nightcap. Take us someplace we've never been, okay? No tourist joints."

"You got it," the driver replied. He had an Irish accent. Probably fresh off the boat from the old country.

They drove along the waterfront for a few minutes and turned left up Fillmore. About a half dozen blocks later the driver pulled over in front of a nondescript two-story building painted gray. A small sign above the entrance spelled out THE MATRIX in capital letters.

"So this is it?" Stone asked.

The driver responded with an impish grin. "Have you ever been here?" he asked.

"Nope. Can't say I have."

"Then this is it."

The driver's sly wit sealed the deal and Stone paid the fare.

Once inside, Stone immediately saw a problem. The far end of the room housed a bandstand all set up for a performance. Drums, amps, mics, PA gear. It spelled the end of his vacation-based moratorium on live music.

"Uh-oh," Christine said with a trace of humor. "So now what do we do?"

"We go with the flow," Stone replied. "Let's have a drink."

They sat at the bar and Stone looked out over the room. It had obviously been built on the cheap, with several dozen used tables and cheap chairs. The cab guy was right. Definitely not a glittery tourist trap. Christine ordered a gin and tonic and Stone had a whiskey sour. As they sipped their drinks, the place began to fill up, and Stone couldn't deny his professional instinct to assess the audience. Young, casually dressed, educated and most certainly local in origin. Inheritors of the city's famous bohemian past.

The place quickly filled to capacity and developed an energetic buzz of anticipation. Stone looked to the bandstand and had to wonder what the payoff was going to be.

"We're the oldest people here by fifteen years," Christine observed.

"I take that as a good sign," Stone responded. The last thing he needed was to watch people chasing after the likes of Perry Como.

The band took the stage: A drummer, bass player, and two guitar players. After the usual ritual of tuning, knob twisting, and volume checks, a shaggy guy in jeans and a short-waisted leather jacket hopped up to the center microphone.

"Ladies and gentlemen, the Matrix is proud to present Grace Slick and the Great Society!"

A slender, attractive girl came on stage to a robust round of applause. She looked like she could be a fashion model, with bright blue eyes and dark brown hair falling over her shoulders.

Stone already had his doubts. The instrumentation looked like a timely rip-off of the Beatles, with a hot chick added up front to keep things interesting. Quite appropriate for a local bar in a big West Coast city. The first few stanzas of their opening tune seemed to confirm his suspicions. It was "Sally Go 'Round The Roses," a one-off hit from a few years back by a girl group called the Jaynetts. It looked like he had yet another cover band on his hands. Oh well, it was only going to cost him a couple of drinks.

But hold on. By the third line of the lyrics, the group had his attention. This was far from a literal copy of a worked-over pop tune. Slick, the singer, took a jazz-like approach and bent the original melody with large doses of originality. Her voice lacked the slick professionalism of most mainstream vocalists but had a strangely insistent quality. When they reached the instrumental break, the band shifted into a hypnotic mode with an extended guitar solo built around scales imported from somewhere to the east. Highly unusual. Completely modal, with no chords moving underneath. Your ear just sailed along with it.

"So what do you think?" Christine asked him when the song ended.

"Interesting," Stone answered. "Way too long for AM air play, but there you go." Stone guessed that none of these people gave a rip about AM air play, and that was part of their appeal.

A slew of tunes followed that he assumed were originals. Slick had this unusual rapid-fire vibrato that reminded him of the same effect on a guitar with a tremolo bar. The last song of the set started with a long instrumental break in that same eastern mode that showed up elsewhere. After a full four minutes, Slick came in:

One pill makes you larger, and one pill makes you small...

Wait a minute. What is this?

Go ask Alice, when she's ten feet tall...

Alice? Like in Wonderland? What's going on here?

And if you go chasing rabbits, and you know you're going to fall...

Very strange. Like some kind of abstract poetry.

Remember what the dormouse said...

The dormouse? What's a dormouse got to do with it?

Feed your head, feed your head...

The song ended abruptly while still moving at full speed. The crowd went wild. They know, Stone thought. They know what it all means. They're moving in some synchronous universe with its very own sensibilities.

This song, this singer, this band, this audience. They're the tip of some monstrous musical iceberg still largely submerged.

They're it. They're what he's been waiting for. They're the new thing.

Stone turned to Christine as the band left the stage. "What do you think?"

"I don't know," she said. "I'm not sure I got it, but it definitely kept my attention."

And that's what it's all about, Stone thought. Literally thousands of new songs battle for the public mind every year, and only a handful survive: The ones that get your attention.

"There's something going on here," Stone said. "There's definitely something going on."

Christine gave him a knowing smile. "You've got that look," she observed. "You're out on the runway ready to take off."

She was right. "I've got to talk to them," he said as he got up off his stool. "If anybody bothers you, tell 'em your boyfriend's a cop who's been known to get ugly."

"I don't think that'll be necessary," she said. "Unless they've got an oedipal problem and confuse me with their mom."

"Then tell 'em you're a doctor and advise appropriate treatment. I'll be right back."

The group had filed out through a door to the right of the stage. It led to a small alley out back, where three of the band formed a ritualized circle and were sharing a joint. Stone instantly knew the smell from his days working Vice in Hollywood. Since then life in the music industry had pushed him to a more tolerant attitude toward anything short of sticking a needle in your arm.

His sudden appearance startled them, and the bass player quickly dropped the joint and ground it out. Stone knew it didn't look good. He was twenty years older and conservatively dressed, at least by their standards. A potential cop. He needed to quickly prove otherwise.

"Hi," he said with an easy grin. "Sorry to bother you. My name's James Stone. I'm with A & R at Capitol Records."

The phrase "A & R at Capitol Records" worked like a master key nearly everywhere in the music industry. You immediately had people's attention. Tonight proved no exception. The trio visibly relaxed.

"I've gotta say I like what I heard," he continued.

"Well good," the drummer said. "We like it, too."

Stone ignored the whiff of arrogance. It might simply be a statement of fact. Or maybe an oblique bit of humor. "Have you guys done any recording?"

"Yeah, right here," the bass player said. "A live thing."

"You happy with it?" Stone asked.

"Well, kind of," the bass player said. "We could have had better gear, but it's okay I guess."

"What label you on?"

"No label. We're still working on that. It's gotta be right, you know."

"Absolutely," Stone agreed. "So you guys own the tapes?"

"Sort of," the drummer said. "The owners here paid for the session, so they've got the tapes. But we own the music. So we'll just see how it goes."

Stone sensed a potential legal complication. Experience had taught him that the more people involved, the more complex the deal became. He pulled a card out of his wallet. "Tell you what, I'd like to keep track of how all this goes down." He gave his card to the drummer. "Keep in touch, okay?"

"Yeah, sure," the drummer replied.

"So how did it go?" Christine asked when Stone returned to the bar.

He smiled. "The usual. I don't know them. They don't know me. Right now, all we have in common is the music. But that's how it starts."

Christine raised her glass. "Well here's to a happy ending."

"Amen." Stone was already soaring high above this particular place and band. It reminded of him of ten years ago when he witnessed the birth of the so-called Bakersfield Sound. What had propelled it was a tightly connected network of artists, bands and performance venues. They all fed off each other. Same thing here. He was sure of it. All he needed was to convince Capitol to let him have at it.

1967

SAN FRANCISCO

7.

GOLDEN GATE PARK

Stone's feet told him it was time to take a break. The sheer scale of the park had done him in. He'd started his trek in the Outer Sunset district, about a half dozen blocks from the Pacific Ocean. From their rental he headed east along the park's southern border, which stretched over two miles. A thousand acres of worlds within worlds. A golf course. A horse run. Several small lakes. A polo field. Playgrounds. Athletic fields. Picnic grounds. A major art museum. A pro football stadium. Even a police station.

He took a brief rest on a bench near some tennis courts and watched the marine mist give way to a bright spring sun. Life could be worse, he thought, even if he was late to the game. Back in Los Angeles, he'd lobbied intensely with Capitol to spring him loose and let him troll for talent up here. But they kept stalling. Too radical and bizarre, they said. No clean-cut, industry-designed entertainment packages, like the Monkees or Paul Revere and the Raiders. The entire scene had a whiff of anarchy about it, a lack of predictability and control. A sort of musical Third World.

And, of course, Capitol got it wrong. The woman singer Stone heard at the Matrix joined a new group called The Jefferson Airplane. Her song "White Rabbit" put their debut album on the express elevator toward the top of the charts. Suddenly the media erupted into a feverish buzz about the new "psychedelic culture" and its Mecca here in the city by the bay. Faced with a sea change in popular taste, Capitol had relented a few months back and sent him north to work his belated magic.

Stone got up and checked his watch. He'd told Christine that he'd meet her around two at the Free Clinic, where she volunteered her services as a doctor. She had a strong altruistic streak that dated all the way back to Bakersfield, where she ran a small practice in her spare time that catered to the destitute and disadvantaged.

He started off down a paved path that curved east around a copse of trees. The Free Clinic was beyond the far end of the park in the Haight-Ashbury district, a focal point for the influx of so-called hippies. By now Stone had enough exposure to this emerging tribe to see beyond the media hype to the truth of the matter. Many, if not most, were refugees seeking asylum from a culture that no longer made any sense to them. He had to admit they had a point. After three major assassinations, a war of dubious intent and cities collapsing into civil chaos, the world seemed fractured and the old order doomed to utter collapse. To drive home the point, there was even a pop song out entitled "The Eve of Destruction." They chose to escape rather than stand their ground, which seemed pointless. And this city, this park, this district, became their place of choice to build anew. But build what? Stone was still working on that point.

After rounding a curve in the path, he came upon a large expanse of green lawn, about the length of a football field. And here they were. Many hundreds of them. Some sitting, some standing, some meandering. Young men, almost biblical in appearance with flowing unkempt locks and scruffy beards. Young women dressed in loose cotton, with long hair parted in the middle and held close by embroidered headbands. A few clustered into small knots that sprouted little tribal flags of paisley print or political slogans like "Get the Hell Out of Vietnam." Live music emanated from a few of the knots, primitive and immediate. It played out on beat-up acoustic guitars and wooden flutes, always a little out of tune, which bothered Stone's trained ear. It set a few of the women to dancing, with eyes closed and faces tilted heavenward. They moved in a formless and spontaneous kind of way, with no detectable pattern, limbs tracing random tracks through the air.

Stone had seen this before. Instead of following a rhythmic template, they treated the music as a point of departure into spaces unknown.

Off to one side a film crew set up at the direction of a reporter from a national network. He pointed out into the field when something struck his fancy. A cameraman hoisted a 16-mm film camera onto his shoulder and adjusted its telephoto lens to get the shot. They worked as though they were filming wild animals on the African plain: You don't want to intrude and interrupt the natural flow of things. With a little luck they might even get some bare breasts. When they returned to the cutting room, they would assemble their footage to conform to a story of hope and innocence mingled with unbridled hedonism. Perfect for public consumption.

Stone had learned that the binding principle behind this entire phenomenon escaped the cameras, which captured the effects but not the cause: drugs. Marijuana, hashish, peyote, mescaline, psilocybin, cocaine, methamphetamine, heroin. And above all, LSD, the premier chemical of psychic liberation. It entered into almost any conversation you had here in the park. Acid, as they called it, served as a rite of passage into the tribe.

Stone had to wonder. In his days as a Hollywood cop he'd been exposed to all kinds of illegal drugs. In the end, they all came down to cheap thrills, cerebral joy rides in the shadows of American life. As a matter of principle, he'd steered clear, so he had no point of personal reference as to where they took you. Nor did he care to find out. He'd passed forty, and the exhilarating recklessness of youth had faded into the remote distance. A few drinks out on the town with Christine gave him all the buzz he needed. Still, he noticed a certain reverence surrounding the subject of LSD among these kids. You didn't consume it for a hedonistic hit, not at all. In fact, it might take you to some very disturbing places before it delivered you to some kind of higher plain. A group of self-styled gurus like Timothy Leary saw it as a sacrament of personal realization and preached its virtues to an eager congregation.

Halfway across the field, Stone paused beside a circular group of about half a dozen. A shirtless kid strummed an old Silvertone guitar tuned to an open chord of some kind, which obviated the need for any fingering with the left hand. He beat out a steady rhythmic drone that set the others to nodding in time. Nearest Stone, a boy still in his teens carefully painted a primitive flower on the cheek of a young girl whose head tilted up toward the sun. He sensed Stone's presence and paused.

"You a cop?"

Stone could see why the kid wanted to know. He was adult in every sense of the word, including his short hair and civilian clothes. "Not anymore," he replied. "Not for a long time."

The kid seemed nonplussed by his answer. "Oh yeah? So why'd you quit?"

A very good question. One that he could expound on at great length, but this was hardly the setting to do so. "Let's just say I couldn't figure out how to be honest and a cop at the same time."

"Wow," the kid said with a trace of awe. "That's pretty heavy, man. Must've been a bum trip."

Stone had to smile. "You got it. Anyway, that's a long time back."

The painted girl spoke up without opening her eyes. "There's only one time that counts and that's right now. There is no other time. Just go with it."

"I'll do that," Stone promised. "You from around here?" he asked the boy.

"Hitchhiked up from Fresno. Had to get out."

"How come?"

"Got in a big fight with my mom's boyfriend. He kicked me out."

"And what did your mom say about that?"

"She didn't say shit. See, that was the problem. She never said shit. So I had a choice. Either I could waste him, or I could take off. So I left." He held up two fingers in a V. "Peace, brother. It's the only way."

The cumulative weight of Stone's cop years made him think otherwise, but he kept it to himself. "Let's hope so."

"My mom couldn't even find a boyfriend," the girl piped up. "She's a total bitch. She used to say she was going to the Laundromat and then she wouldn't be back until the next day. It took her a week to even notice I was gone because that's when the school called her."

"What about your dad?" Stone asked. He operated under the naïve assumption that there was still a male presence in most families.

"What's a dad?" she asked, without the slightest trace of irony.

"Good question," Stone said. "I've got to be going. Take care."

"Same to you," the boy said as he reached for his paintbrush to finish the flower. "Follow your bliss."

A lone figure stepped out of the shade and onto the path directly in front of Stone at the east end of the park. Stone's years on the street in LA gave him an intuitive sense of real trouble and he sensed no immediate danger. An army field jacket hung limp on the man's malnourished body. Spectral eyes of pale green looked out from a dirty face framed in a ragged beard and wild hair.

"Hey man," the figure said. "I've got to catch the bus downtown and I'm a little short. Could you help out?"

"Sure." Stone reached in his pocket for some change. Ten to one said this guy was a veteran from the conflict in Vietnam. You saw them here and there around the city. Hollowed out and spent. A little change was the least he could do. But first, a quick test.

"What was your unit, soldier?"

"First Air Cavalry. Ia Drang. It was fucked up, man. I mean really fucked up. Don't let 'em tell you different."

"I won't," Stone said as he dropped some coins into the man's outstretched palm. A name tag on his field jacket above the left breast pocket read CARSON. The foggy gray letters were fading into oblivion, along with the man himself. Stone had witnessed some ugly shit during his cop time but never the kind of sustained violence this person had likely endured.

"Thanks," the man said. "Don't believe anything they say. It's all a fucking lie, just a huge fucking lie."

He started off toward the shade but stopped to look back at Stone. "I screwed up, man. I really screwed it up."

"Screwed what up?" Stone asked.

"I should have put the limbs on the chopper, along with the rest of him."

Before Stone could ask him to clarify, he faded away into the trees and was gone.

8.

POINT REYES

The King read the big button on the tie-dyed tunic of Mr. William Thompson. "Superspade. Faster Than A Speeding Mind," it declared.

"Superspade, huh? You must be one smart motherfucker."

"Depends on who you ask," Thompson replied cagily.

"Well I've been doin' a lot of asking. And you come up number one around here. If you didn't, we wouldn't be talking."

The King had chosen a conservative Brooks Brothers suit and Ivy League tie for this twilight meeting in Thompson's apartment. He'd encountered numerous other Superspades over the years. In the end, what mattered most to hyper-inflated characters out on the fringe was a feeling of respect.

"If you don't mind, I'd like to call you Mr. Thompson." The King read Thompson's eyes, which registered a favorable impression. So here they were, two successful black men engaged at the highest levels of commerce. "After all, we're both businessmen. Only difference is you're new school, I'm old school."

"And what kind of business you talkin' about?" Thompson asked.

"You're the major player in a rapidly expanding market. My compliments on that." The King did not exaggerate. Two years back, the righteous white governor of California had outlawed LSD, thereby creating an instant black market of enormous proportion. People like Mr. Thompson here had stepped in to fill the void according to the immutable laws of supply and demand. And now, two years in, he had proven himself a formidable competitor.

"You have not had your eyes opened to see what's beyond," Thompson responded cryptically. "This is much more just a market. It's the key to a higher order."

"I'm in no position to judge. You could very well be right." The King had taken a gamble that appeared to be paying off. Mr. Thompson, aka Superspade, was a product of this new psychotropic drug culture, not its criminal counterpart. It left him remarkably naïve when it came to assessing the true character of people like the King. "Let's step back and look at the business side of things," the King continued. "I'm sure your customer base is growing a lot faster than you can supply it with product. And if you can't then somebody else will. Your market share will shrink. You'll go from Superspade to Formerspade before you know it."

A hint of concern crept over Thompson's features. The potential loss of social status trumped any concerns he had about money. "So, what am I supposed to do about that?"

"Two things. You need reliable suppliers. And the key to reliable suppliers is volume purchases. It may not be fair, but the big guy always gets fed first. What it all comes down to is capital. You need the money up front to make things happen."

"And you just happen to have the money, right?" Thompson was cynical but interested.

"If you were a white guy running a straight white business, you could just go to one of those big white banks and they'd give you loads of money. But that's not what's going on here, is it? You're not even close to straight. Reagan shit all over you guys with these new drug laws. And even if he hadn't, do you really think those white bankers are ready to do business with someone named Superspade? No way."

"Maybe not." Thompson was wavering.

"I'm a banker, see. Only difference is I'm a black banker who knows exactly where black people like you are coming from. Now don't get me wrong. I don't want anything to do with running your business. That's all up to you. I just supply the money when and where you need it. The rest is your very own trip."

"For a price, right?"

"Yeah, for a price," the King admitted. "But I can tell you this: it won't be any more that what those fat cats would charge. And probably a lot less. They'd take one look at your black ass and squeeze you for every dime they could get."

"Probably so." Thompson paused in thought. "So what you talkin' about?"

"Well first off, I need to earn your trust."

"How you gonna do that?"

The King brought up a briefcase he'd brought and placed it on the coffee table next to an ornate hookah pipe. "First of all, I'm gonna prime the pump. There's ten grand in here. Zero interest. No charge. Second, I've found a source. They say he's gonna be the next Owsley. He's over in Marin and ready to do business."

"The next Owsley? How come I haven't heard of him?"

"Because that's the way he wants it. He's a little on the paranoid side and doesn't like publicity. We need to bring him along and the best way to do that is money. I told him that the ten grand is just a start. After that, we'll be good for fifty grand a pop."

"I need to see the lab," Thompson said. "I need to make sure he's not a middleman. There's a lot of shuckin' and jivin' going on out there."

"Right on," the King agreed. "I've already set it up."

"When?"

"This evening. I've got a car and driver to take you over to Sausalito. You're going to meet two guys who'll take you on up to the lab. If everything's cool, you do the deal and you're back here in time for Johnny Carson."

"And if it's not?"

The King shrugged. "Not a problem. We bide our time and find another source."

"Marin, huh? I want to buy a piece of this restaurant over in Tiburon," Thompson said. "See, I got plans beyond all this shit."

"I'm not surprised. You come off as a visionary type of dude. We do this right and you can open a restaurant in the middle of Manhattan if you want."

"Manhattan," Thompson repeated. "Yeah, I like that."

The driver said little as they crossed the Golden Gate Bridge, which was just fine with Thompson because he was busy counting the cash in the briefcase. Sure enough, it totaled ten thousand dollars wrapped into stacks of one hundred-dollar bills. As a complimentary measure, the King had also included a small vial of high-test cocaine. Any doubts that Thompson had about the deal vanished with the third snort. His compact with the King secured his position as a frontrunner in what had rapidly become the largest drug market in the country.

LSD. Lysergic acid diethylamide. A mere 250 micrograms took you halfway across the galaxy without even leaving your couch. At six dollars a hit, it was the trip of a lifetime, a bargain basement excursion to nirvana. Of course, sometimes it could go terribly wrong, but in the end you always came back with spectacular tales to tell. So much for the consumer side; the supply side turned out to be a tricky business. Other illicit drugs started their lives as plant matter. Flowers, leaves, pods, etc. Processing them into psychoactive substances required only a minimal knowledge of chemistry that criminal enterprises could easily master. Not so with LSD. Its progenitor was not a plant, but yet another chemical, lysergic acid monohydrate. You needed an unprecedented degree of chemical expertise to get it right, especially on a consistent basis. Hence production was confined to a small group of individuals, such as the notorious and venerated Owsley Stanley III. A new chemist on the scene was a major event in the madcap world of Superspade.

Thompson closed the briefcase and snorted the remnants in the vial just as the car pulled into a public viewpoint on the north end of the bridge. It came to a stop next to a VW bus, the preferred vehicle of the new counterculture. "I'll be back here in ninety minutes," his driver informed him. "Peace, bro."

"Peace to you," Thompson replied as he got out. A wiry guy about his age came out of the bus and extended his palm by way of greeting. His shoulder-length brown hair shifted gently in the breeze off the bay. One of the tribe, Thompson thought, a good sign. A second fellow got out on the passenger side and opened the rear doors. His hair was shorter, but he wore a buckskin coat and mountain man hat that complemented his full beard. "Welcome to Marin," he said with a soft smile. "I'm Adam and that there is Hank."

"Good to meet you," Thompson said as he climbed in and sat in the rear seat. "So where we going?"

"A little ways north up toward Point Reyes," Hank said as he climbed in and fired up the engine, which chugged and muttered in the rear of the vehicle. "Ever been there?"

"Can't say as I have, Thompson answered. Like many young black men, he was a purebred creature of the city streets.

"Very beautiful," Hank commented. "You should check it out sometime. You'd really dig it. Very peaceful. It'll put you in a good place."

"I'll keep that in mind," Thompson said. The coke high told him that these were a couple of beautiful guys in a beautiful world. Perfect.

They took 101 through the little town of Sausalito and turned north up into the lightly forested hills overlooking the bay. Streetlight gave way to darkness and the van's headlamps cast twin tunnels of pale yellow onto the two-lane road.

"So who's the man?" Thompson asked, obviously referring to the chemist.

The pair grinned at each other. "Can't say," Adam said. "He's real jumpy about stuff like that. He'll tell you when we get there, but it's got to come straight from him. That's just the way it is."

"What about the lab?"

Adam shrugged. "Same thing. Just hang tough. All will be revealed. Good vibes will prevail."

"I think my old man wanted to be a chemist," Hank said. "Always fucking around with gasoline and dynamite and shit. It's a wonder he didn't blow himself to bits."

"Oh yeah?" Thompson said. "And where was this?"

"A little ways outside Redding. Up there, you can just do your thing, and nobody bothers you."

Eventually the lights of Stinson Beach and Bolinas appeared on the left. Thompson could almost feel the immensity of the Pacific beyond in the blackness. "Not too far now," Hank said. "Hang in there."

The lights fell away, and they rolled along through a series of shallow curves lined with underbrush.

"Comin' right up," Adam observed as he slowed the van almost to a stop. A gap in the bushes revealed a dirt road leading up into the low hills spotted with stands of trees. "Here we go."

"Perfect place," Hank commented as the van bounced along the rutted surface. "No cops, no narcs, no nothing."

The van rolled to a stop in the weak light of a half moon. Adam cut the engine and a sudden silence prevailed, broken only by the vague hiss of the distant ocean. Hank climbed out and opened the back doors for Thompson. He pointed to a dense stand of trees about thirty yards off. "Right up there. All nice and tucked away." He motioned Thompson forward and started off in that direction.

"Man, this is way and the fuck away," Thompson said as he fell in behind Hank, briefcase in hand. The coke was wearing off and little shadows of doubt danced out on the periphery of his perception.

He never heard the sharp of report of the snub-nosed .38 caliber pistol. It tunneled a round deep into the center of his head, killing him with astonishing speed. He collapsed in a lifeless heap in the dry grass.

Adam came up from behind, gun in hand, and looked to Hank. "What do you think?"

"One more for good measure," Hank suggested.

Adam hooked his foot under the body, rolled it over and planted a second bullet just to the right of the sternum.

"Done," Hank declared. He squatted down, opened the brief-case and pulled out a packet of bills. "Payday. Just like the man said."

"Yeah, the man. So who do you think he is?" Adam asked.

"Don't know," Hank said. "I'm not that hip to black dudes. Just met him that one time."

"Well he's done with us and we're done with him," Adam added. "So let's get this finished." He looked down at the body, where a moist red blotch grew out the tie-dyed tunic. "Might as well take the jewelry while we're at it." He slid a pair of diamond rings off the limp fingers, removed silver bracelets from each wrist, and a thick chain of gold from around the neck. "Your dad really do that stuff with gasoline and dynamite?" he asked as he worked.

"Sure as shit did. When he wasn't beating the fuck out of us."

"Yeah, well, it's a badass world. Know what I mean?"

"Yep. Unless you're a hippie, of course."

"Right," Adam chortled. He dumped the jewelry in the brief-case and shut the lid. "Let's bag him up and get out of here."

Hank walked back to the van and returned with a sleeping bag. "You like to camp?" Adam asked.

"Not really. My last old lady left it. Wow, what a bitch."

"Yeah I know all about that," Adam said.

They wrestled the corpse into the bag and dragged it down to the van, where they slid it onto the floor between the seats. After retrieving the briefcase, they headed down to the main road and turned north toward Point Reyes.

Along the way they spoke of drugs and highs, and how you could cut the top off an edgy meth trip by snorting a little smack. No needles, no problems.

Upon reaching the headlands at Point Reyes, they parked at the road's end and carried the sleeping bag to the edge of a steep cliff above the surf. It pounded the rocks below in an even and timeless cadence. They each grasped one end of the bag and swung it into a rocking motion. Every rock increased the amplitude until Adam yelled "Now!" and they let go. The bag sailed over the edge and bounced and tumbled down the rocky face. Twenty feet above the surf, it wedged between two outcroppings.

"Good enough," Adam observed. "We're outta here."

They rode in silence back to the city while the coals of hell festered in the pit of their souls.

The phone rang thrice then stopped in the King's suite at the St. Francis Hotel on Union Square. The signal. The deed was done.

He sighed and put down the book he was reading in bed, an account of Napoleon's ill-fated invasion of Russia. His taste had always run to historical non-fiction and biographies. The good ones offered timeless lessons in the exercise of political and economic power.

Phase one of his current campaign was complete. He had removed the largest potential competitor in the local drug trade. A vacuum would ensue. Small dealers would skirmish among themselves to gain market share, creating a substantial amount of chaos. And, like all markets, this one tended toward order and structure. Quality and price must remain stable to maximize consumer demand. And the King intended to do just that. What he needed at this point was a small-time dealer to seed his campaign, someone with a connection to a dependable chemist, someone wrapped in all this mystic bullshit that seemed to go along with these psychoactive substances. Once entrenched, the King would recruit other dealers, and over time he would shift the product mix to include staples of his national trade: speed, cocaine and heroin. They had a timeless appeal that transcended the fashion of the moment.

And what about the police? Where did they fit in all this? The King rolled over, turned off the light, and quickly drifted off to sleep.

The police were not a problem.

9.

HAIGHT ST.

Stone knew better than to try to park on Haight Street. It would be jammed with tourists gawking at the hippies. They even ran tour buses along the avenue now, replete with drivers who gave a rolling narrative over PA systems to plump middle-aged couples from Nebraska.

"On your right, you'll see Love Burgers, which gets its name from the new belief in free love. Notice all the long hair and short skirts out front."

"On your left, we're passing the Print Mint, a poster shop devoted to the wild hallucinations brought on by psychedelic drugs."

Stone found a spot a block south of Fredrick Street on Stanyan and plugged the meter. The day was slightly chilly and overcast but free of rain, so he didn't mind the walk. Most of the faithful who flocked here from around the country had an ill-conceived notion of the local weather. They pictured the sunny clime of Southern California, with its surfers gliding over the waves under clear skies. Not here. The city was a peninsula at the mercy of the ocean. A sunny day could be rapidly smothered by an invasion of fog that drove the temperature well below the comfort level.

He walked north up Stanyan, which bordered the far end of Golden Gate Park. Three blocks later, he took a right onto Haight Street, the central axis of the Haight-Ashbury District. Sure enough, it resembled a carnival midway, with crowds of hippies and tourists treading sidewalks lined with three-story buildings.

Most consisted of a street-level business topped by two stories of apartments with rounded bay windows. Needless to say, business was good.

Four blocks down, he reached Clayton Street, and his destination, The Free Clinic. You couldn't miss the place. Several dozen hippies stood in line down the street, waiting to get in. Many were obviously ill, with pale faces, malnourished bodies, hacking coughs and the sweaty sheen of fever on their skin. A month back, Christine had met Dr. David Smith, who founded the clinic. Ironically, he was from Bakersfield, where Christine had run a similar operation, dispensing free medical services. A large divorce settlement had left her financially secure and she shared her good fortune with those who labored among the oil wells and turnip fields. In other words, Christine and the Free Clinic were pretty much made for each other.

Stone climbed the steps at the entrance past those waiting in line. He expected a few dirty looks, but none came. Of course not. He was way too old and way too straight to be a patient. Inside, more of the sick crowded a little alcove backed by a reception counter manned by a gray-haired woman in her fifties. A sign beside the counter defined the rules of the game: "No dealing drugs, no holding drugs, no using drugs."

"Hi, Marie," Stone greeted the receptionist. "How are you?"

"I'm well, Mr. Stone," she replied with an easy smile. "Which is saying a lot around here."

Stone marveled at how Marie sustained her dry sense of humor amid this perpetual calamity. A baby broke out in a goopy cough behind him. Its distraught young mother nervously rocked the child and stroked its flushed cheeks.

"You can go on back," Marie said. "Dr. Harmon is probably upstairs." She turned her attention to the next patient, an unkempt young man still in his teens. "I got some kinda worms," he reported. "It's a real bummer."

Stone went up the stairs and started down the hall. He had the good luck to catch Christine as she walked out of one of the exam rooms. She wore classic doctor's garb, with a white lab coat, stethoscope, conservative skirt and a clipboard full of notes. He wondered if she'd ever realize how truly attractive she was. Probably not, and that was a big part of her charm.

"Am I interrupting something?" he asked.

"Always," she said. "Don't worry about it. Let me drop off my notes and we're out of here."

Stone and Christine sat in a little coffee house a block or so east of the clinic. Outside, the mixed parade of tourists and hippies rolled by relentlessly. Stone noticed that some of tourists were armed with super-8 movie cameras. They boldly filmed the hippies without permission, as if they were performance pieces of some kind. But the hippies didn't seem to mind and often broke into spontaneous poses to accommodate the action. An amusing fusion of hip narcissism and cinematic voyeurism.

"We're absolutely swamped," Christine told him. "God only knows how many thousand kids are roaming around out there. We see it all. Bronchitis, strep throat, gonorrhea, drug overdoses, diarrhea, psychotic episodes, you name it. And it's getting worse. They're still piling in here. The city has become some kind of beacon."

"A beacon," Stone mused. "Yeah. A really bright one."

"Most people see love as the brightest light of all. Especially when they're sixteen. Can you blame them?"

"No, I can't." He knew that, in his own life, that beacon was nearly extinguished at one point. A ruined career. A childless marriage gone wrong. Then he met Christine and it switched back on.

"Something incredible happened today, but I don't know quite how you're going to take it," she said. "Want me to go on?"

"Please do."

"Rhonda showed up. Here, at the clinic."

"Rhonda?"

"Rhonda Savage."

It took a moment for it to register "Are you sure?"

"I'm sure," she said. "It was definitely her. Ten years older, but definitely her. She came in for an ear infection."

"Did she remember you?"

"Oh yes. And you too."

"Wow." It flung him back a decade. Into the summer heat and haze of the San Joaquin Valley. Produce fields sucking the aquatic life out of mountain streams high above. Oil pumps probing the barren hills like predacious insects. All centered on Bakersfield, where he worked as homicide cop. And in the midst of it, Rhonda Savage. Thirteen years old. An import from the dark side of LA. Sexualized far beyond her years. A victim of men who knew better but could have cared less.

She came into his sphere as the byproduct of a homicide he was investigating. It didn't take long to discover that she was enmeshed in a pit of depredation that rivaled anything he'd seen in his years as a Hollywood vice cop. He had no choice. He had to get her out. She'd drifted far beyond the domain of legal protection and justice in this place. So he sent her back to Los Angeles to start over in a more civilized context. Had it worked? He wasn't sure. He'd heard nothing for many years now.

"Is she out on the street?" Stone asked Christine.

"Apparently not. She said she has a boyfriend that she's sharing space with. Some guy that used to race stock cars."

"Well that's better than nothing, I guess. What did she look like?"

"You really want to know?"

"Yes, I do."

"Tough as nails. She's definitely on the attractive side but with a really hard edge. She must be about twenty-four and looks it. Not your typical hippie chick, for sure."

"Doesn't sound promising," Stone observed.

"She wants to see you," Christine told him.

"What?"

"She wants to see you. She says she owes it to you."

"Boy, I don't know," Stone said after a pause.

"I think you're probably the only adult male in her life that gave her a fair shake," Christine said. "I think that's created at least some sense of obligation."

"Maybe. So how's this supposed to happen?"

"She knows she can find me here to set it up. And I gave her our home phone."

Ten years. Her entire journey into adulthood. A couple of strange twists in Bakersfield had provided enough money to see her through to college. He'd set it up with an attorney in LA, so he was out of the loop. He also called in some favors from people in social services to make sure she landed in a decent family setting. And that was the end of it. He thought of her now and then, but less and less over time. Their only remaining link was a tentative cluster of memories that grew dimmer by the year.

"Well I guess we'll just have to see how it goes," Stone said.

"I guess so," Christine said. "You were a good man then and you're a good man now. That's all that matters."

10.

GOLDEN GATE PARK

Larry Boyd sat high on Hippie Hill, a grassy slope that looked down on the central region of the park. The afternoon sun shone on hundreds of hippies milling about below. Some had assembled in small clusters or couples. Others drifted solo through worlds of their own manufacture.

Soon Larry would leave his perch and mix among them. With a practiced casualness, he would offer his wares to those who seemed receptive. Acid. Pure stuff. Two hundred fifty mics. Six dollars a hit. The proverbial ticket to a new kind of paradise.

He thought of it not as a sales effort but as a divine mission. As the summer wore on, they would all become one and broadcast their oneness to the entire planet. So it was ordained. Timothy Leary deemed it so. At the start of the year he had delivered his psychedelic sermon at a gathering called the Human Be-In:

"Turn on, tune in, drop out."

Over twenty thousand of the faithful heeded his exhortation from where they stood on the park's polo grounds, a short distance from where Larry now sat. It reverberated through the media and became a mantra unto itself, earning an indelible spot in the national memory. And it was embellished, in timeless religious fashion, by music both vigorous and passionate. The Grateful Dead, Big Brother and the Holding Company, Quicksilver Messenger Service and Blue Cheer all took to the stage to reinforce Leary's holy incantation.

Larry fished a roach out of the leather pouch he carried and idly examined the yellow stain on the border between the rolling paper and the hardened ash. He lit it, took a puff and reflected on his pilgrimage to this particular place and time.

It started, of course, with that hit of acid he took in his apartment back in Huntington Beach. As it enveloped him, he had intended to go to the beach but never got that far. Next to his building someone had planted a mixed garden of vegetables, fruit and flowers. He wandered into it and immediately became lost in the colors, the brilliance, the play of life over vines, petals, leaves and stems. After a brief bout of anxiety, he let it consume him and he became one with it; and, by extension, with all beyond.

Later that evening, he sat quietly in his apartment with the TV off for a change. No Gunsmoke, no Bewitched, no Get Smart. Suddenly, they all seemed like facades, like fronts disassociated from the world as it really was. His first acid trip was over, but a new vision of his future took its place. The dealer John Griggs had tasked them with spreading the word, and now he understood why.

Over the next few weeks, he shared his epiphany with others along the beach and learned of a new nexus forming to the north, in San Francisco. A utopia founded upon the very same kind of revelation that he'd experienced. It beckoned with irresistible force. Soon, he was hitching his way up Highway One along the ocean, with only twenty-five dollars and a backpack bearing a few artifacts from the irrelevant past.

He arrived in Haight Ashbury with no job, no home base, no real plan. None of it mattered. The place crackled with energy, a force field you could instantly tap into to make your way. He quickly hooked up with people on the street and became one of half a dozen sharing an apartment at the east end of the district. One day a week he cleaned up in a porno store down in the Mission that paid him in cash. Just enough to keep him off the sidewalk.

It also bought him time to learn the structure of the local LSD market and how the substance worked its way from chemist to consumer to synapses. He developed relationships with a few dealers occupying the lower rungs of the distribution chain, who sold him the substance at a discount of two dollars per hit. A few forays into the park taught him that he could make dozens of sales per day. The porno store job quickly went away. Girlfriends presented themselves. A new apartment appeared. The business side of the acid cult became a moderating force that tempered the purity of his vision but failed to erase it entirely. Trade and transcendence could co-exist and accommodate each other quite nicely. At least for now.

He stood up and did a lazy stretch. Time to get after it. He started down the hill toward a paved path that served as a main thoroughfare through the park. He put out a quick scan for potential business. He'd become quite good at this. You didn't want to waste your energy on those drowning in mystic insolvency. By the time he reached the bottom of the slope he'd identified a promising lead. A couple floated along the path, obviously stoned. The girl was a little older than most, but a real fox. The guy had the look of someone locked into a pretty much continuous high.

He timed his to approach to come up on them at an unobtrusive angle, as if by chance. He addressed the guy first to avoid any impression that he was hitting on the girl. While the park harbored a surplus of love, it was not without sexual tension. He pulled out a joint and lit it up as he neared them. The worm was now on the hook.

"Peace, dude. Want a hit?"

Speedo accepted the joint without comment and took a hit before passing it to Rhonda, who inhaled deeply.

"Good shit, huh?" Larry asked.

"Yeah, good shit." The Speedo agreed. His voice had an edge to it.

"Comes from Humboldt County. You can't beat it."

"So you selling?" Speedo inquired.

"No, just sharing. That's all. Peace."

"Peace," Rhonda replied with a cunning smile, which made her doubly attractive to Larry.

"You guys into acid?" Larry asked.

Speedo's eyes came into sharp focus. The fog lifted. "Yeah, we're into acid."

"I might be able to help with that," Larry volunteered.

"Oh yeah?" Speedo asked somewhat abrasively. "How's that?"

This guy's got some bad karma hiding in his basement, Larry thought. So what's the chick see in him? You never knew. Anyway, best to close the deal and move on.

"I got a few hits I could spare. Really good shit. Two hundred fifty mics. They cost me six bucks each, and that's what you can have them for. I'm not into profit. That's corporate bullshit."

"Yeah, corporate bullshit," Speedo repeated. "You got four hits?"

"Yes, I do." Larry pointed to a nearby stand of trees. "Let's go over into the shade."

Once there, Larry pulled a small aspirin tin out of his pocket and carefully pried it open to reveal four plastic capsules. Each contained a powder of pale lavender. "Here you go. Pure shit. Uncut. I know. I did some."

"Better be," Speedo said as he handed Larry the money and took the tin.

"I wouldn't jive you, man," Larry assured him. "I wouldn't do that."

Larry glanced at Rhonda. She had watched the transaction attentively but said nothing. "You trip out too?" he asked her.

"Not my thing." Once again, she beamed this strong erotic presence that narrowed the world to just the two of them. Too bad she had this crazy guy in tow. In the hippie world, males substantially outnumbered females. The media always framed their shots to suggest otherwise, but in truth, young women fetched a premium. Given this demographic, free love was something a lot less than free.

"We gotta split," Speedo intervened. "See you around."

"Peace," Larry replied.

"Yeah, right," Speedo said as they turned their backs and headed back toward the path.

Larry stood in the shade and fondled the ten other aspirin tins in his pocket. They would get him through a day or two, but not beyond. He had an inventory problem, but not for long. Up until now he'd dealt with mid-range dealers who doled out limited quantities to keep you on the hook. But a little while back he made the biggest score of all.

He connected with a chemist.

It happened by pure chance. He was at a free concert right here in the park, listening to the Grateful Dead and Jerry Garcia in particular. He knew just enough about guitar playing to realize that this guy was the engine that powered the entire band. Garcia had this incredibly fluid style unlike any other among the legions of bands popping up around the city. Larry noticed that the guy next to him shared his enthusiasm, nodding his head every time Garcia launched into one of his improvised excursions. The guy had relatively short hair, rimless spectacles, shorts, and a T-shirt with a giant skull on the chest. At the end of a particularly inspired solo Larry turned to the guy. "Far fuckin' out. Garcia's a real monster."

And they were off from there. The guy's name was Bruce Hadley, or least that was the name he went by. Said he was from a bucks-up family in Michigan, with a dad in the upper strata at Chrysler. Had a flare for science and became a chemistry major at Berkeley. First heard Garcia playing in a pickup band with a keyboard guy named Howard Wales. Went psychedelic and applied his chemical knowledge to the synthesis of lysergic acid. Had a lab in a house on a secluded lot in the Berkeley Hills. Not a big lab, but a quality lab. Bruce was all about quality.

After an informal vetting period, Hadley had Larry come up to see the operation. It occupied a large basement with naked cement walls and a floor of tiled linoleum. Rows of fluorescent lamps poured down on benches, sinks, and a maze of piping. A tangle of flexible tubes snaked its way through a wooden lattice and connected to an assortment of vials and beakers. Bottles and plastic containers bore the inscrutable names of substances like acetic anhydride, sodium cyanide and hydrochloric acid. All lost on Larry, who understood he was the sales side of things and not the science.

"Time to sample the product," Hadley announced. They dropped three hundred mics each and spent a transcendent afternoon and evening at the house and out on the property, which was studded with large trees and covered better than half an acre. The house proved quite spacious, and Larry realized that life at the top of the acid trade came with some spectacular perks.

On the trip back to the Haight, Hadley proposed that it was time for Larry to expand the scope of his operations. He admired Larry's dedication to Timothy Leary's directive to spread the love, to start your own religion, to cast off the shackles of the straight life. In effect, he was offering Larry the chance to become his main dealer. A fantastic opportunity. It was well known that the major chemists settled on one main dealer to be their interface with the distribution side of things. It was equally well known that they were notoriously fickle and frequently rotated this position. Apparently, Larry had dropped into this cycle at just the right time.

Just one problem remained, the oldest problem of all. Money. A main dealer was expected to prop up the cash flow to cover things like the house in the hills, the lab equipment, the chemical components, and a lifestyle commensurate with the chemist's status in the community. In return he received a generous cut of all the downstream profits.

Larry climbed back up Hippie Hill to his original perch as Speedo and Rhonda retreated into the distance. Yes, money. Of course, it was an issue but not an insurmountable one, not given the purity of his mission. Higher powers would conspire to take care of it. And right then and there, they did just that.

"Watched you do the deed down there, my man. You're smooth, real smooth. I like that."

Larry had failed to notice the arrival of the black man, who sat down next to him. A big Panama hat put his face in shade, and aviator sunglasses further obscured his features. He wore a sport shirt, khaki shorts, and leather sandals.

"You a cop?" Larry asked. The man appeared to be in his forties. Way too old for an idle afternoon in the park. Anymore, the place was swarming with narcs.

The King let out an exquisite laugh. "Far from it, friend. About as far as you can get."

"So if you're not a cop, then what are you?" Larry asked.

"Let's just say I'm an investor. I look for talent and skill and figure out how to turn it into money. And if I do say so, I'm pretty damned good at it. That's why I'm talkin' to you, brother."

"Oh yeah?"

"Oh yeah. You might not know it, but you're a truly exceptional human being. You got a real way with people. You can't buy that. Either you got it or you don't. You're a lucky man."

"You're jivin' me."

The man took off his sunglasses. "Yeah, I can see where you might think that." He looked out over the field below. "There's a whole lot of jivin' goin' on around here. But I gotta tell you I just don't have time for that kind of thing. And neither do you. You're a busy man."

"Busy doing what?"

"You young dudes are on to a whole new thing with these psychedelics. It's not just about gettin' high, it's about a whole new way to live, a better way. Am I right?"

"Yeah, you're right."

"Kinda like a new religion almost. But just like the old religions, you gotta have some scratch to make it happen. You can't just wait around for it to rain loaves and fishes. Know what I mean?"

"Pretty much, yeah." Larry wasn't sure about the biblical allusion, but he was sure about the money problem.

"Now, I've been talkin' with people around here and I've got a pretty good idea how this scene works. A guy like you, you're pretty much stuck at the bottom." The King carefully avoided the use of words like dope, drugs, and dealer. He didn't want to offend Larry's sensibilities, which probably saw all of this as a crusade, not a hustle. "You're a long way from the source, and the only way to get close to the source is cash money. Just like any other business."

"So you want to give me a bunch of bread, is that it?"

The King winced slightly, as though offended. "No, no. You got it all wrong, friend. I want to invest in you. There's got to be something in it for both of us. I've got the money; you've got the knowledge and the skills. We put them together and things happen, good things."

"Yeah, maybe." Larry's mind danced through his possible deal with Bradley the chemist. "So if we did something, how would it work?"

"You know any of these chemical guys that make the stuff?"

"I might. And what if I did?"

"If you did, how much would it cost to make you a player?"

"A lot. Maybe forty or fifty grand to fill the pipeline."

The King nodded thoughtfully. "Yes, that could be done."

"Sounds like exactly what a narc might say," Larry said.

The King broke into a broad grin. "I was hoping you'd say something like that, because if you didn't, there wouldn't be any deal." He reached into the pocket of his shorts and brought a news clipping, which he carefully unfolded and handed to Larry.

Larry scanned the story from the *Cleveland Plain Dealer*. "NEW HOSPITAL WING DEDICATED" the headline read. The photo beneath clearly showed the King together with a distinguished white gentleman. "Edward Mather and Dr. Jeffry Wepner celebrate the opening of the new Cardiovascular Center."

"Mather, huh?" Larry said. That your real name?"

"It was then," the King replied with an opaque smile. "And it didn't leave much time to pursue a career as a police officer."

"I guess not."

The King produced a blank business card with a scrawled phone number and handed it to Larry. "Tell you what, you think about it, but not for too long. Right now you're the top dude, but several others have expressed interest. By the way, what's your name?"

"Boyd. Larry Boyd."

The King stood up. He did so with surprising muscular ease for someone his age. "Well young Larry, why don't you just call me King and we'll be square. Okay?"

"Okay."

"I'll be talkin' to you soon." Larry started to rise, but the King motioned him down. "Have a nice day."

The King descended Hippie Hill and took a path deeper into the park. The kid was hooked. He was also perfect. Not dumb, but not very bright either. He'd be easy to control after the proper connections were made. Once the pipeline to a major supplier was in place, the rest would be relatively simple. He would quickly dominate the local market using time-honored techniques.

The King checked his watch. He'd make it on time to the fountain by the de Young Museum, where he and his cohort met periodically. They would sit on the benches near the water's edge, and its rush would conceal their conversation. A prudent precaution. Technical advances in surveillance gear demanded it. Those who possessed such gear were precisely the sort of people they wished to avoid.

11.

HUNTERS POINT

The driver gave Matt Carson a dirty look as he exited the bus on Innes Avenue where Hunter's Point juts out into the bay. The long oily hair, the dirty old field jacket and the unkempt beard tagged him as a lowball hippie of some kind. Not the case. Carson looked the part but belonged to a more troubled tribe, one baptized in the pointless violence of Vietnam. Many now wandered the streets of America in a profoundly agitated state that often grew worse instead of better.

Their plight was compounded by the public's reception to their return, which ranged from guilt to shame to downright animosity. Carson received his first dose before he even got out of the airport. He wore his dress greens because he technically was still in the army for another six months. While he waited for the shuttle, two teenage girls passed by and stared at him. Both had long hair and paisley headbands, and one wore a pendant with a peace symbol. They cast hateful looks his way, and one hissed "killer pig" as they passed him.

Their attitude blindsided Carson. He knew the country was in torment over the war, so he hadn't expected a hero's welcome. But not a naked confrontation like this one. He wanted to run after them, stop them and tell them that he hated the war far more than they could even imagine. He wanted to share with them the true horror, the unmitigated carnage, the nonstop fear that plagued so many of his peers. He wanted them to realize that their sheltered existence in the sunny subdivisions of California bore no relation to the slaughter playing out on the far side of the world. Instead, he stayed put and recalled a biblical phrase: He came unto his own, and his own received him not.

Back then he still had nightmares about the maimed kid on the floor of the chopper. A psychic wound that refused to heal. It festered within him like a chronic infection, waiting for the opportunity to go systemic. It came a few months later. He'd been assigned to a basic training unit as a supply clerk, a non-job to pass the time until his discharge. A young sergeant ran the supply room, a righteous and officious individual who treated it like his personal empire. Carson hated him instantly. The guy was a pompous façade. He had never seen a day of combat. One day he insisted that Carson redo a big stack of requisition sheets because of a petty mistake that made no real difference. As the clerk, Carson had access to the arms vault. He retrieved a .45 caliber pistol, shoved the guy up against the wall and pointed the pistol against the bridge of his nose. He calmly explained that if the sergeant ever bothered him again, he'd kill him. Fortunately, the sergeant kept the incident to himself: If he reported it, he would come off as a coward for backing down, which in fact he was.

The episode only reinforced the damage Carson had already suffered. He'd passed the point of no return. He'd discovered a special kind of rage within him, one that extended to all forms of authority. Police, military, bosses, judges. A steady job became impossible.

Carson pulled his pack onto his shoulder and watched the bus rumble off down Innes Avenue. Fuck you, Mr. Driver. Anybody made you go out and kill people today? Any of your buddies showing up with big holes in them? Didn't think so.

He hiked two blocks down the street under an overcast marine sky to a dive bar that shared space with a transmission repair shop. A small red neon sign identified it as The Ball and Chain. He pulled the door open to a blast of Link Wray belting out of the jukebox, along with the smell of stale beer and urinal disinfectant. The man he'd come to meet sat sprawled in a wooden chair beside a pool table. His belly bulged under a dirty T-shirt, and a black leather vest hung from his beefy shoulders. Carson knew that the back of the vest was emblazoned with a skull sprouting feathered wings, the logo of the Hells Angels. The man went by Pig Eye and resembled Carson in his disheveled state. He drained a pint of beer as Carson sat down opposite him.

"Hey dude," Pig Eye said with a bestial grin. "You made it. Wanna beer?"

"No beer," Carson said. "It bends me the wrong way."

Pig Eye chuckled. "Well we don't want that, now do we?" He turned to two men playing pool to his left. "Hey guys, meet my man Carson. He's the real fucking deal." He looked back at Carson. "That's Hank and Adam. Righteous dudes." The pair gave Carson a sullen nod and went back to their game.

"They ride with you?" Carson asked.

Pig Eye darkened. "Nobody rides with me that ain't got the patch," he declared. And they ain't got the patch." He lightened. "But they got great dope. Uppers, downers, and everything in between. Want to buy in?"

"Don't think so. You ready to do it?"

"Ready as I'll ever be." Pig Eye hoisted his big frame out of the chair, and they headed out the door.

An alley wound around to the back of the repair shop where Pig Eye's big Harley Davidson sat parked in solitude. He reached behind a scarred metal dumpster and pulled out a quart-sized cylinder with a screw-on cap. He undid the cap to reveal a cluster of colorless quartz crystals. "It's enough to blow you and everyone you know all the way to Jesus and back again."

His claim went beyond marketing hyperbole. He worked at a large construction supply firm that carried a wide assortment of explosives, including one called Semtex. Certain coke-driven arrangements had been made for it to disappear from the inventory.

"So let's see what you got," Pig Eye continued.

Carson took his pack over to the dumpster and began to place its contents on the flat metal lid. A plastic stock, a bolt assembly, a barrel, a recoil spring, and so on. That done, he went about assembling them in a highly practiced motion. Pig Eye looked on with great interest. "You're pretty fuckin' good at that," he commented.

"Better be," Carson replied laconically. "If I wasn't, I wouldn't be here." He had mailed the components of an M16 combat rifle from Vietnam one by one over a period of several months before he left. The bureaucratic fog of war made it relatively easy. Too many packages, too little time. They all sailed right on through to his sister's house in Long Beach. She kept them in a neat little pile in the garage until he returned.

Carson cocked the weapon. Metal glided brutally over metal. He pulled the trigger. The firing pin clicked. Without warning, he pulled an old military trick and tossed the weapon in a vertical motion to Pig Eye. The biker barely had time to grab it out of the air. Pig Eye just smiled. He appreciated the implicit violence of the act.

"We're done," Carson announced.

"We're done," Pig Eye agreed.

The sun burned through the overcast while Carson waited for the bus. He basked in its newfound light. The transaction with the biker gave him the means to make a statement. He had no idea what that statement might be, but the simple knowledge that he could do so was sufficient.

At least for now.

12.

GOLDEN GATE PARK AND BEYOND

The water bubbles violently. The ship fights to make headway. Far ahead, the shoreline curls and bends and threads into a massive green wall of vegetation. It lives a life all its own and answers to no one. We can't land here. If we try, we will be consumed, digested and expelled as pink dung. And the dung will cause us to grow once again, and again and again. On and on into a perfect forever. The air shivers with a blast of sounds, children laughing, beasts crying, heroes crowing, villains cursing. It kicks up a wind that blows us off course. But what course might that be? Time to take the helm, time to control our destiny...

"What are you doing?" Rhonda asked Speedo.

"We need new direction," he told her. "We need new purpose."

She came close to telling him how weird he was acting but refrained. In fact, he was always weird, but not like this. It was the acid. Had to be. He'd dropped it right before they left for the park. That was maybe thirty minutes ago, and now suddenly he was going right over the top. It probably didn't help that she was high on hash, but that didn't change the fact he'd shifted into some cosmic gear she'd never seen.

So here they were, in a pedal boat they'd rented to cruise on Slow Lake. With Speedo suddenly pedaling them like a madman toward the shoreline. "There's nothing there but a bunch of bushes," she protested.

Speedo's eyes bulged. "Oh my God, the bushes! Cannibal plants! Quick, take the helm!" He brought his feet up off the pedals. She took over and steered them out into the middle of the channel, where several other boats leisurely cruised along.

The fleet presents itself on a glittering surface of a million daz-zling diamonds, all children of an omnipotent sun. Each craft riles the waters into a soapy foam full of bubbles that wink and pop into another place, another time. The flesh of their crews pulses with life in a perfect blush of radiance. Who are these people, this aquatic herd plying the waters of this sacred lake?

Until now Rhonda had never seen him high on psychedelics. Very disturbing. Not like the blissed-out hippies. She thought back to his account of the big crash, the hospital, the head injury, the coma, the slow recovery. It seemed a stretch at the time, a typical tale of braggadocio told by a male in heat. But maybe not. Does a damaged brain beget a damaged mind? Maybe the acid acted as a second layer of scrambling.

Rhonda was clever in this way of grabbing insights a layer or two removed from the obvious. With men she held it in reserve, since many found it threatening or unsettling at best. But not Speedo. At first his enigmatic persona had been a source of fas-cination. The wild flights of fancy, the primal sexual encounters, the impulsive adventures. They had taken up residence in a little apartment at the far end of the Haight and lived off the sale of his car and the pawning of her engagement ring. She felt no shame in doing so. Her time with her departed fiancé was an anomaly, a relic from an impossible past, and carried with it no sense of obli-gation. But now the money was nearly gone, and Speedo didn't seem to possess any marketable skills. Too bad, because she had no intention of becoming their sole source of support.

She navigated their craft down the main channel and pulled up to the docks in front of the rental building. Speedo beheld the scene in wondrous silence. He kept nodding his head in some mys-terious affirmation.

We sail into the harbor, the gateway to the city beyond, the city that breathes its own wind. Great white ships pulse and glow at their moorings, awaiting passage into the emerald sea. A bustling crowd strolls along the piers, replete with beasts of all shapes and sizes.

Rhonda stepped onto the dock and held out her hand to guide Speedo out of the boat. "I've got to use the restroom. Wait for me here on the bench."

The virgin goddess reached down from above the clouds and offered her hand to him. A perfect hand in a flawless gesture of love. Its warmth washed through him and exploded into wondrous color. But she quickly withdrew, and the milling crowd swallowed her whole. He tried to reach out, but his arm turned into soft rubber and wilted. It didn't matter, because he would now mount a throne of brilliant green and rule for eons to come.

Rhonda looked back as she entered building and saw that Speedo had made it to the bench. He leaned back, spread his arms, and slowly surveyed the waterfront with a preternatural confidence. Ruggedly handsome, oddly charismatic and completely unhinged. She shook her head and continued to the restrooms. Time to cut loose, to get out, to move on. There was no use beating herself up over the decisions that landed her here. Expedience trumped guilt as a survival tactic. It would take a little planning to extricate herself, but she was thoroughly familiar with the process. Speedo was not the first.

No more governing the harbor. Time to descend from the throne and become one with the masses. Time to feel them, smell them and inhale them into himself. He glided along the waterfront and out into massive gardens beyond. Flowers waved petals of red flame in salute as he passed. Some turned carnivorous and fed on airborne insects that grated and whined like runaway buzz saws. The noise chewed a hole in his spine that spilled down into his innards. It massaged his spleen. It caressed his liver. It embraced his entrails. It filled him to the brim with life everlasting.

Rhonda returned to the boats and shaded her eyes against the sun. No Speedo. Just an empty bench. She walked the length of the docks and past the boat they'd rented. Not a trace. Maybe this was the end of it; maybe he would simply wander off and be lost to the urban void. Wishful thinking. In a few hours he was going to come down off his high and head home from wherever he landed. Despite his demonic energy and impulsive thrusts into the unknown, he'd not been violent with her. Not yet. But her intuition told her there was a boiling pocket of rage not far below the surface. Her best move was to devise an escape plan that avoided a direct confrontation.

A wave of loneliness consumed her as she looked out at the couples cruising along in their pedal boats. How did they do it? What was the magic that bound them and kept them dear to each other? She cut herself short before her lament consumed her. Her best move right now was to get back to the apartment, pack up her few belongings and get out. She left the lake's edge and took a path that headed east back toward Haight-Ashbury. By the time she passed the de Young Museum, a strong sense of relief set in. She was relatively young, unquestionably attractive, and loose in a city overflowing with wealth and power. With a little luck and a measure of shrewdness, some of the spillage would be hers for the taking.

The sun warmed her back on its westerly arc, and she stopped to examine a large monument that thrust up out of the green lawn. It towered over a background of trees and was topped by a powerful woman wearing a winged helmet and holding a flag that signified some kind of victory in a battle of ancient wills long forgotten.

Was that Rhonda up ahead on the infinite highway? And just who was Rhonda? Who knew? And who was the woman cast in stone looking down upon her? The figure held a chiseled flag that fluttered in spite of its stone origin. And now the tower where she perched began to writhe and twist in a profane dance. The serpents on the woman's helmet came alive and hissed and sputtered through hypodermic fangs. They caught the rhythm of the tower's dance and arched and lunged at invisible prey. The woman smiled approval through granite lips. Whose cartoon was this anyway? And where did Rhonda go? That was the key, the mission. Follow Rhonda, the mother of all.

Rhonda left the monument and moved onto a path that became thickly wooded, nearly tropical. Lush ferns, palms, exotic flowers. Somewhere up ahead a duck quacked. It took her back to Family Two, when she was fourteen. She sorted her four foster families by number rather than name. She had averaged about one per year, all with the same result. The household's mother quickly found her to be an eminent threat to domestic stability, more because of who she was than what she did. Since the dawn of her sexuality in Bakersfield, she'd run free of the usual constraints imposed by family, school and church. Her libido had nowhere to hide. For the most part, the foster fathers behaved honorably but couldn't conceal their fascination with her latent eroticism. Each banishment set off a twin blast of pain and anger. She'd played by the rules and it made no difference. So why bother?

The path opened up to expose a large, stagnant pond topped by yellow scum and an abundance of lily pads. Each formed a green disc with a small wedge cut out, and a pink lotus flower floating along its edge. The dense vegetation shielded the pond from the breeze and turned the scene into a perfect still life. Rhonda paused at the far end and smelled the perfume of constant rot and rebirth. A lone duck quacked its approval.

The horn of the angels blew its fanfare to announce her presence. She levitated on the far shore with a curl of vines anchoring her feet. Dressed in a hooded robe of blue gossamer, she extended her arms and blessed the armada of green discs assembled before her. That done, she drifted off into the chaos of leaves, branches and flowers beyond. The armada took this as their cue and lifted off the water in unison. They hovered overhead in silence, awaiting an unknown cue.

Rhonda continued her odyssey through the park, passing the tennis courts and turning right onto a broad meadow of freshly mowed grass. Ahead rose the gentle slope of Hippie Hill. A flock of birds formed a noisy cloud that descended toward the meadow's floor.

The armada has sailed. It departed the pond, followed the path, and floated out over an ocean of green. But what of the goddess who guides them? Is that Rhonda? Is that what Rhonda has become? But wait, the armada is under attack! Giant birds tear through their ranks, claws at the ready. The ships scatter and dissolve into the clouds. The birds settle onto the ocean's surface, which splinters into a billion squirming blades of grass.

Rhonda stopped to rest halfway up Hippie Hill. She pulled her legs up, gathered them close, and rested her chin on her knees. She wore a cotton blouse and snug jeans – a little too snug for the hip world around her. She looked out at the young girls in their breezy cotton dresses and long hair parted in the middle. It made her feel more isolated than ever. Where was her place in all this? Who knew?

"Hey, long time no see."

She looked up. It was Larry, the guy that sold Speedo the acid. Confident, casual and self-possessed. He sat down next to her. "So where is your old man?"

"Don't know. He's tripped out."

"Oh yeah. On what?"

"On the acid you sold him."

"So is that a good thing or bad thing?"

She gave Larry a closer look. Maybe there was more here than she thought. "Depends on who you ask."

"I'm asking you," he said with a relaxed grin.

"Let me put it this way," she answered. "He's tripped out even when he's not tripped out."

Larry nodded. "Yeah, I know what you mean. There's a lot of that going on around out here. So why do you stick with him?"

"I don't. We're done."

"Wow," he said. "Bummer. So where does that leave you?"

"It leaves me right here, talking to you."

"I'm good with that. Where you from?"

"LA."

"Me too," he responded. "Were you in the movies, or modeling or something?" It implied that she was beautiful without saying so. A time-tested ploy.

"Not really. I was engaged, but he got killed in Vietnam."

"Yikes. Super bummer. That why you left?"

"More or less. It's complicated."

He shrugged. "It always is."

"What about you?" she asked.

"I was living on the beach, fooling around with a little surf guitar. No real job. Just taking it light. Then I met this righteous dude who turned me on to acid. It opened my eyes, man. I saw on through to other side."

"And what was there?"

"A new life. I had a mission. I had to spread the word about psychedelics. And what better place to do it than right here? I just packed my shit and split. Never looked back. We're all brothers here. We're all on the same trip."

"Brothers, huh? What about women?"

"Yeah of course. Women too. Coming together, sharing the love."

"You're serious about all this, aren't you?"

Larry went quiet and stared down at the grass. "Well yeah," he said when he looked back up. "I don't know any other way to be. Sorry."

"And it's okay to be a dealer while you're doing it?"

"I've thought about that. A lot. But you know, it's not written anywhere that you can't make a little bread and also be a believer. Can you dig it?"

Rhonda had to smile. Larry was amusing, and pretty cute. "I'll have to get back to you on that."

"Look," Larry said. "You're just hanging loose right now, so why don't we hang together for a while. We can go back to my place and smoke a little hash and just mellow out. No big deal. You can split whenever you want."

"Whenever I want?" Rhonda teased.

Larry picked up on it and smiled. "Whenever you want."
Rhonda stood up. "Okay then, let's hit it, Mr. Dealer."
"I'm Larry," he offered as he rose. "And who are you?"
"A surprise," she answered.
"A surprise," Larry pondered. "I like that. Let's go."

The grass refuses to calm. Its blades wiggle and consume my feet.
They pull and tug on my legs and advance up to my knees. Para-
lyzed. They hold me from going to her. Just when she needs me the
most. The devil guides her away, his clawed hand over her elbow. His
naked scalp explodes into electric arcs that fill the air with the stink
of ozone. He grins the grin of a thousand carnivorous teeth. Red oil
drips from the corners of his mouth. He slobbers in anticipation. He
can hardly wait. My lower legs are gone now, they live elsewhere. No
matter. I'll find a way to follow her at any cost.

"One more block and we're there," Larry told Rhonda as they
walked east on Page Street. He didn't want her to bolt now that
they were almost home. Numerous episodes with other women
had taught him that once they were through the door, they were
pretty much his for the taking.

"Pretty cool," Rhonda said. "You're only steps away from the
park."

"Goes with the trade," Larry explained. By now, he sensed that
she liked the notion that he sat a few rungs up in the hippie hierarchy. Not just another stoned schmuck. Acid had a sacramental
aura about it, and he dwelled close to the source – and the profits
as well.

"How long have you lived here?" Rhonda asked as they crossed
Schrader Street.

"Just a few months. It took me a little while to get my bearings when I first moved here, but then I found my groove." He
neglected to mention the stretch where he worked the janitorial
job in the porno shop in the Mission.

"No roommates?" Rhonda asked.

"No roommates. Funny thing about roommates. Nobody has
'em if they can afford not to."

"What about people living in these communal places?" Rhonda asked.

Larry smiled triumphantly. "They can't afford not to." He stopped in front of a three-story walkup. "Here we go. Single family dwelling at its finest."

Rhonda looked up at the narrow building with its triple stack of bay windows topped by an ornate roof. "Nice." She would never share with him that she'd spent considerable time in houses five times as big. In the grand scheme he was a minnow. In her immediate circumstance he was a sizable catch.

He took her arm and led the way up a concrete stairway to the first floor, where three doors marked the entrance to each unit. He stopped. His street instincts told him something was amiss. He looked down the sidewalk toward the park. No people. Just a row of telephone poles sprouting out of the cement, each supporting several layers of taut wires.

I have my legs back and now they must become sea legs. A great vessel lies buried beneath the pavement, an ancient sailing ship. Only its masts break the surface, stripped of sails. They sway in unison, awaiting the moment when the hull rises once more. The sidewalk bulges and undulates in anticipation. Of course. Because the devil is the captain, the same one that steers her up the stairs and into his fortress. And what will he do to her up there? Will his phallus spout fire? Will his electric tongue glide over her most intimate regions?

Larry opened the door to his apartment on the third floor and showed Rhonda in. "So here we are. Downtown living at its finest. Have a seat."

Rhonda did a quick scan. Concert posters adorned the walls. The Dead, Blue Cheer and Big Brother. All with curved lettering that mimicked the optical warp brought on by psychedelics. A hookah pipe with serpentine appendages sat atop a coffee table fashioned from an old wooden cargo hatch. The furniture consisted of pads and pillows encased in covers printed in busy organics. A tiffany lamp of flowering glass done in red, amber and green perched on a wooden barrel. A big crystal ashtray held a heap of roaches spent yellow with brown rims. Cinder blocks supported a shelf that held a stereo and tape deck on one level, and a cache of albums and tapes on the other.

"Have a seat. I'm not into booze, but I can make us a little tea," Larry offered.

"That works," she responded. She'd already decided she was going to have sex with him but offered no hint that might be the case. Far better to be entertained by his ritualized dance of seduction.

When the tea was done, he threaded a reel onto the tape deck and hit play. "This is the Dead, live at the Fillmore. Not out yet. Got it from a friend. Good stuff."

He sat beside her and reached for a wooden box on the coffee table. Hindu gods popped out of its surface in bas relief. He took out a Moroccan hash pipe and a cube covered in wrinkled tin foil. He opened it to expose a cube of dark brown hashish. "Came straight from Nepal," he told her. "No middleman. It's the real deal."

He produced a lighter and they shared a few puffs as the Grateful Dead played on in the background. Rhonda liked the high. Pot made her drowsy, but this stuff sped her up and set her hormones in motion.

Larry reached over and caressed a lock of her hair. "You're a really groovy chick, you know that?"

"Yeah, I do know that," she said as she leaned back into the pillow behind her. "So what are you going to do about it?"

He needed no further prompting.

Afterwards, she remained nude even after he pulled his clothes back on. She had no sense of shame whatsoever and utter confidence in her sexual self. Many men found this intimidating, but that was their problem. She got up and moved to the center of the three bay windows, which put her on full display up and down the street. Larry quickly followed. He didn't want to share his prize with the world at large. He came up behind her and put his hands on her shoulders. "So, you want to stay for a while?"

"Not really," she said.

There they are, up on the third level. His talon-tipped fingers curl around her naked shoulders. He's had his way with her. He's done unspeakable things. One of us must be destroyed. We can't inhabit the same universe. But what's happening? The pavement is buckling, the sidewalk reeling, the wooden masts rising. The great ship in the city's bowels has awakened and floats up with a vengeance. The earth below my feet starts to give way. Either I move or I'm swallowed. I sprint away on legs of quicksilver. But I know this place. I will be back.

13.

SAUSALITO

Matt Carson descended the embankment off Johnson Street and threaded his way through the tumble of big rocks at the water's edge. The twilight dimmed his progress. No one would notice as he slipped past the rocks and into the dim recess beneath the wooden pier. He tugged on a rope beneath the farthest piling and pulled out a small inflatable raft concealed in the darkness. After climbing in, he brought out a set of small oars and rowed out into the open water of Richardson Bay. A slight breeze spilled down from the hillside above the waterfront, where the evening lights started to wink on.

He was nearly home.

The water quietly lapped at the raft's rounded bow as he rowed at a steady pace. The rhythm of it produced a hypnotic effect that pulled him deeper into himself, into a museum of malignant war-time memories.

Each exhibit held its own special horror, and tonight he found himself in a clearing surrounded by a wooded area near a remote village in the Dong Nai province. He crouched all hot and damp in an irrigation ditch near the center of the clearing. The platoon commander knelt next to him and was stupid enough to rise half-way up and scan the tree line with his binoculars. A bullet fizzed above them as he came back down. What was he trying to prove? Didn't he know he was just another green lieutenant with his fuck-ing head already on the chopping block? Unfortunately, Carson's job as radio operator meant he had no choice but to stay close to this idiot. The other two dozen men in the ditch kept their distance. This guy was bad luck with a capital B.

The radio crackled. Carson grabbed the headset and the company commander came on. He passed the headset to the lieutenant, who listened intently and finally replied, "Sir, I recommend we send second squad out in a probing action. Once we locate the sources of fire, we can call in artillery... Yes sir, I'll lead."

Carson winced. It was insane. A dozen men would have to cross fifty meters of open ground, led by this mindless moron. They'd all be cut down before they got halfway to the tree line where the enemy was dug in. All for nothing. If the enemy had mortars, they would have already zeroed in on the ditch and cut the whole platoon down as they tried to escape. But they didn't. So all the platoon had to do was wait for darkness, which was only a few hours away, and then crawl on out to safety.

The lieutenant put down the headset. "All right, second squad listen up. We're gonna move out toward the tree line. I'm going to lead. First squad will provide covering fire. Do I make myself clear?"

The line of soldiers in the ditch stared at him incredulously. It was pure suicide and they knew it. After an interval of sullen silence, somebody down the line spoke up.

"Hey lieutenant, you ready to give your life for your country?"

The lieutenant managed a grim smile. "You better believe it, soldier."

A solitary round punched the lieutenant's left eye out, and he pitched backward into the dirt.

"Enemy fire," someone yelled. "Get down!"

It wasn't enemy fire, and everyone knew it. Carson also knew what to do next. He grabbed the headset. "Second platoon here. The lieutenant took a hit on the way out. Looks like he's gone. We're standing by."

Carson knew that early in the war it wouldn't have happened this way. Under questioning, at least a few of the men would have fingered whoever fired the shot. But not now. In fact, anybody who blabbed at this point would eventually wind up like the lieutenant.

The forces in the field teetered much closer to anarchy than either the command or the press cared to disclose.

The enemy had stopped firing. All that remained was the oppressive heat and the occasional buzz of aggressive insects. He slipped the radio off his back and waited for sundown.

Carson shipped his oars and let the raft finish its glide to the rusted hull of an old tugboat, a derelict vessel with a pronounced list to port. He grabbed a rope that dangled over the side and hoisted himself onto the main deck. In the dwindling light, he pulled the raft up and stowed it just inside the cabin to ensure his privacy. He unhooked an electric lantern and turned it on to illuminate the stairs down to the lower deck. An odd mix of marine decay and spent machine oil hit him as he descended to the engine room and on back to crew's quarters in the stern. Once in the galley, he clipped a cable onto a car battery terminal, and a series of over-head lights came on.

They revealed shelves stocked with canned goods, quarts of beer and a smattering of silverware. The table in the center held some hand tools and a wiring board. He pulled a small backpack off his back and placed its content on the table, a box that held a pair of walkie talkies. He'd stolen them from a Radio Shack store over in the city, along with a simple musical pitch pipe. He now possessed all the necessary components to complete his system. Its operation was relatively simple, and his military training as a radio operator would ensure that it worked as planned. The pitch pipe's sound would be played into the first walkie talkie, which could send it up to a hundred yards. The second walkie talkie would pick up the tone and send it to the circuit he'd built on the wiring board, which would output an electric current to a blasting cap. The blasting cap would be embedded in a brick of PETN and produce a horrific explosion.

He was tired but anxious to see how well it would work. For testing purposes, he hooked up a flashlight bulb instead of a blast-ing cap. After some minor adjustments, the bulb glowed every time he produced the tone. To make sure, he took one of the walkie talkies to various locations around the ship and played the tone. In every instance the lamp was lit upon his return.

If a war was what they wanted, that's precisely what he'd give them.

14.

PAGE ST.

Larry felt himself stirring just as the buzzer rang. Damn the luck. A very luscious Rhonda reclined next to him on the jumble of pads and pillows. She had slipped her panties back on, but her breasts were still in full view and beckoning. She turned to him. "You going to get that, Mr. Dealer?"

"Yeah." He grabbed his Levis off the floor and pulled them on over his rapidly wilting member. "You want to put something on?" he asked.

She gave him a very neutral stare. "Why?"

"Okay, whatever," he mumbled as he got to his feet. It was all coming back to him now. The hotter the chick, the bigger the trouble. The Grateful Dead tape had run its course and the take-up reel spun freely with its tail making an annoying flapping noise. He turned it off on his way to the intercom, where he pushed the button to speak. "Yeah?"

"Larry, my man!" the speaker barked. It was the King. Had to be. Larry pushed the button to let him up the stairs. Piss poor timing, but business was business. He turned to Rhonda. "I need you to hit the bedroom for a few minutes."

"How come?"

"I got something I've got to take care of. It won't take long, so just hang tough, okay?"

She said nothing and headed for the bedroom at a decidedly leisurely pace to register her annoyance. As she shut herself in, he opened the front door to the King.

"And how are you, young sir?" the King said with an over-whelming grin. He looked at Larry's bare torso and the scattered pillows in the background. "Catch you at a bad time?"

"No, everything's cool," Larry replied. "Come on in. You want some tea or something?"

The King held up his hand as Larry led them to a small kitchen table. "Nothing for me."

"I didn't expect you so soon," Larry explained as they sat down. He'd just phoned the King earlier that day to say he was interested and assumed it would take a while for a concrete deal to form.

"You want to keep up, you gotta move fast," the King declared. "Same as it always was." He slid the briefcase in front of them. "You talked with your chemist buddy yet?"

"Not yet," Larry admitted. "But he's cool. It won't be a problem."

"In that case," the King said. "I think it's time to place an order." He opened the briefcase to expose ten stacks of one hun-dred-dollar bills, each bound with a rubber band. "Fifty grand. Sound right?"

"I dunno," Larry said hesitantly. "I really hadn't thought about the details."

The King took the stacks out of the briefcase and lined them up on the table. "Okay then, first things first. Count the money. Remember, you always count the money. We don't want any mis-takes, now do we?"

"No. we don't," Larry agreed. He took the rubber band off the first stack and started counting.

"This is what the money guys call operating capital," the King explained. It stays sunk in the cash flow. After this, the whole bot-tom line goes into your pocket, with a little left over for me."

Larry couldn't focus on the King's proposition while he was counting. Even if he could have, it wouldn't have mattered. Finance just wasn't his thing. He was a people person, not a bean counter. All he understood was that it took lots of cash to be a big-time player, and he didn't have it.

The King got up as Larry continued counting. He circled the living room, stopping to inspect items of interest, like the big hookah pipe. He came to a small bookshelf, leaned over to scan the titles, and pulled one out. "The Tibetan Book of the Dead," he announced. "You read this one?" he asked Larry.

"Not yet," Larry replied.

The King brought the book back to the table and started reading while Larry worked through the remaining money. "It's all there," Larry announced when he finished.

The King looked up from the book. "You know what it says in here?"

"No. What?"

The King glanced down at the open page. "It says 'There is no difference between the action and the actor. Without focusing on the action, search for the actor. Though one searches for this actor, none will be found.'" He looked up from the page. "Now what do you suppose that's all about?"

Before Larry could respond, the bedroom door clicked open. The King whipped his head toward the sound and his right hand shot under his shirt near his waist.

Rhonda walked out, fully dressed, and looked over at the pair as she headed toward the front door. "I'm outta here," she said to Larry.

"Excuse me a second." Larry got up to follow Rhonda as she headed to the door. "Well yeah," the King said with a knowing smile.

Larry caught up with Rhonda at the top of the stairs. "Hey, we're almost done. Just give me a couple of minutes, okay?"

"We're completely done," Rhonda said. "Check you later." She turned and descended the stairs to street level. As Larry turned back, the King appeared in the doorway. "That's some fox you got there, young dude." He continued out and headed for the stairs. "You got my number. Let me know when we've got a done deal."

"Yeah right," Larry said. He sighed, went back inside, and plopped down in the pillows. He had the money but lost the girl. Yet another zero-sum game.

The King caught sight of Rhonda as he went down the outside steps onto Page Street. Good. He needed to get a fix on her. She'd not only seen him with a known dealer, she'd seen all the cash out on the table.

He trailed her up Page Street, which avoided the surreal carnival a block over on Haight Street. She clearly knew where she was going. They eventually crossed Divisadero into the Lower Haight. A few blocks later she turned right and pulled some keys out of her front pocket. The King crossed to the opposite side of the street and lagged back to remain unobserved.

The girl slowed in front of a three-story building that also had a basement apartment. She descended a small set of steps to this unit, unlocked the door and entered. The King had to smile. Her place was somewhere near the bottom of the rental hierarchy in this part of town. She deserved better. When all this blew over, perhaps he could arrange something more suitable.

15.

NORTH BEACH

"It's not art down there. It's money. Really good money. But now and then I gotta get out and do the real thing. So here I am, in the middle of the biggest tourist trap on the West Coast. It's the only way to make it happen. Now how's that for irony?"

"Hard to beat," Stone admitted. He and Christine were sitting with Barney Kessel at a dime-size table at the Jazz Workshop in North Beach. Kessel was a legendary studio guitar player in LA, and Stone had worked with him several times and always marveled at his playing. Tonight, he was performing in a pure jazz venue with just a bass player and drummer. Stone understood that it took incredible skill to make such a small ensemble work, and Kessel pulled it off magnificently.

Barney looked at his watch. "Time to do it." He shook Stone's hand and faced Christine as he stood up. "Take good care of him, sweetheart. He's got a good pair of ears. Very rare."

"I'll do that," Christine promised.

Stone paid the bill and they left before the next set started. Outside, they waded into the throng on Broadway. Kessel was right. It had to be the biggest tourist trap between here and New York. Drunken convention goers weaved down the sidewalks along with wasted sailors and gawking couples from parts unknown. Hustlers in cheap suits barked at the passersby from their stations in front of sleazy bars: "Come on in! We got the drinks! We got the girls!" They were just getting warmed up. It was still several hours to sundown.

After a few blocks Stone and Christine came upon the grand temple of contemporary sleaze: a club called the Condor, which featured a renowned topless dancer known as Carol Doda. She did twelve shows a night to keep the place permanently packed. Music from her band floated out onto the street and caught Stone's instinctive ear. It wasn't that bad, but playing this gig essentially put them on the road to hell.

Christine looked at a poster of Doda plastered near the entrance. It featured her scarcely concealed breasts and an enormous thicket of bleach blond hair. "Interesting," she commented.

That was the thing about Christine. She never descended into moral outrage when confronted with something like this icon of rampant eroticism. Instead, she viewed it as just another piece in some cosmic puzzle of unfathomable proportions. Like any couple, they had their spats, but they never descended to the level of undiluted righteousness and anger. He ranked this attribute near the top of what bound them together over the long run. Of course, it didn't hurt that he still found her exceptionally attractive. He'd been around long enough to know it didn't always work out this way. He could recall some of the moments when the appearance of former lovers flipped from blissfully romantic to brutally realistic, sometimes in an instant. He could only imagine all the subsurface grinding that brought this on as the world within and the world without folded in upon each other.

"I don't like to say it, but I think our friend Rhonda might be a candidate for something like this," Christine said as she surveyed the scene.

"You mean dancing topless?"

"Or something like that. She came off as being a pretty tough cookie. I'm sure that goes along with the job around here."

"You still think I should talk with her?"

"I do," Christine said, "but it's not going to happen unless she gets in touch. She has our phone numbers and that's the best we can do. We'll just have to wait and see."

"I guess so." It made him wonder. How much damage could a person like Rhonda endure and still emerge reasonably intact?

Back in Bakersfield he'd had several glimpses into the horror she'd lived through. Pornographic pictures of the basest kind from the twilight of her childhood. A terminally alcoholic mother living in utter chaos and filth at a time when her daughter needed her the most. He realized that you couldn't just feed all these things into some analytic machine that generated the probability of a decent life. There were too many unknowns. There would always be too many unknowns. He himself was one of them.

At any rate, he'd given her what he could, considering the circumstances. He'd spent years in a childless marriage and knew the great chasm it left. He could only speculate on how you went about being a real father and often wondered if he could have pulled it off with some measure of grace. In the end, Rhonda was probably as close as he would ever get. He protected her and provided for her but ultimately had to give her up. Their relationship ended in a Greyhound Bus terminal in Visalia when he shipped her off to Los Angeles. He knew they both felt some sorrow in their parting, but he had neither the experience nor the wisdom to process it.

"I think it's time we took the high road," Christine said.

"The high road to where?" Stone asked.

She pointed across the intersection to the City Lights Bookstore. "That ought to do it."

They crossed the street and entered the store with its three floors of literature in many guises. Fiction, poetry, politics, art and beyond. It served as a prime artifact of the beatnik era; a cool, cerebral, jazz-loving, poetry-reading bohemian subculture that created the beachhead for the hippie invasion.

The man behind the counter fit the bill perfectly. He wore a blue beret, a thickly knitted gray wool sweater, rust-colored corduroy pants and work boots. He smiled at them through a goatee of silvered gray that put his age up into the late sixties. "A good afternoon to you," he said. "Need any help?"

"Not really," Christine said. "We're just seeking a little shelter from the madding crowd."

The beatnik's face lit up at the utterance of "madding crowd." It placed Christine in a literary context far beyond Stone. His preference ran to short stories in the *Saturday Evening Post* and *True Detective* magazine. He had no idea that the phrase came from a poem written two hundred years ago by an English scholar named Thomas Gray.

Stone took a more direct approach. "So how long you been here?"

"Since way back," the beatnik said. "Like when it was still hip to read." An obvious allusion to the hedonistic hippies, who placed no premium on intellectual pursuits.

"Must have been a different kind of place back then," Christine speculated.

"Yeah I suppose it was," the beatnik said with a trace of melancholy. "There were a lot of coffee houses where you could spend a buck, sip some coffee and listen to a little radical poetry. Not a bad way to go."

"Sounds pretty mellow," Christine observed.

"Yeah, but not all the time. Things got kind of wild now and then. Saw a blind man win a fight."

"You saw what?" Stone asked.

"Saw a blind man win a fight," the beatnik repeated.

"From 'The Battle of Otterburn,'" Christine said. "A sixteenth century British poem."

The beatnik's jaw went to half-mast. "Wow. Far out." He turned to Stone. "Your lady has got some heavy chops. But that was then. I'm talking about right here on Green Street around 1956."

"Were you there when it happened?" Stone asked. He felt the need to reach for a notebook, just like in his cop days, but squelched it.

"No but I heard about it the next day. Everybody heard about it. It happened at a coffee joint called The Torn Page. The blind man was a guitar player, a cat named Jimmy Pine. Had some really solid chops. Didn't like drunks, so he played coffee houses."

"And what about the other guy?"

"Bellows, yeah Bellows. Don't remember his first name. Wore turtlenecks and smoked a pipe. He fancied himself a poet. Spent a lot of time reading and brooding, as I recall. Kind of like he was one up on the rest of us, know what I mean?"

"Sure do," Stone said. "What was the beef that set it off?" He was now in standard cop mode, trying to construct a timeline to keep things in order.

"Well, what you've got to understand is that while Bellows was a grumpy guy, Jimmy was a pretty emotional guy. Not a bad thing, man. Gave his playing a lot of soul. But it did make him a little testy now and then. Now, I wasn't there, but here's what I heard. Jimmy had just finished his set and put down his guitar. He felt his way over to a table next to Bellows and sat down to take a break. Seems that Bellows asked him what the last tune was. Jimmy told him it was a piece by Chet Baker. Now, you have to understand that Bellows was one of those people that had a big opinion about everything. He told Jimmy that Chet Baker was a junkie piece of shit and his music worthless. So there's the beef for you."

Stone nodded. "And now the fight."

"The way I heard it, Jimmy went atomic and jumped to his feet and so did Bellows. Jimmy said take it back and Bellows said fuck you. Well Bellows' voice gave Jimmy his bearings and he swung. The punch landed high and hit Bellows toward the top of his head. But it really pissed him off and he threw a wild punch that hit Jimmy on the neck below his ear. After that, they just started wind-milling at each other. Finally, they fell over and wrestled on the floor until they were completely done in. Jimmy sat up and told Bellows to take it back or they were going to do it all over again. And you know what? Bellows took it back. And you know why? Because somewhere along the way, he realized that you can't win a fight with a blind man. If he beats you up, you look like a total loser; if you beat him up, you come off as the biggest bully of all time. Either way, you lose. So that's how it ended."

"Sounds about right," Stone said. He turned to Christine. "What do you think?"

"I think they're really lucky no one got seriously hurt," she said.

"Amen, sister," the beatnik added. "Anyway, those days are gone. Bring on the hippies."

16.

LOWER HAIGHT

Rhonda sat cross-legged on a block of foam rubber covered by an old army blanket. A slightly bigger piece served as a bed over in the corner of their one-room apartment. It occupied the basement floor of three levels and was starved of daylight. Essentially a cave with only a single window covered by ancient gossamer curtains.

She arranged her possessions on a dirty shag carpet of soiled gold. They didn't amount to much. A few sets of lingerie, a couple of pairs of jeans, some shorts, a light jacket, some sneakers, a pair of high heels and cap of light wool. Her purse held her makeup, a wallet with ten dollars and her birth control pills. When it came to managing fertility, she was what would later be called an early adopter.

Only one item remained, something she always stowed in a secure place wherever she lived. She got up, went to the kitchen, grabbed a chair and stood on it, which allowed her to reach the top shelf in the cupboard. She probed along the back until she felt a tin box secured by a rubber band and pulled it out.

Once seated back in the living room, she removed the band and opened the box. The photos were all still there, maybe a dozen, some in color, some in black and white. She wanted to sort through them because she always did so at the end of each chapter in her life. In some inexplicable way they served as an atlas that pointed to the next direction she should take.

But there was risk in those pictures. They had the capacity to set off major subsurface tremors. Great geysers of sadness, grief and regret might punch through and run rampant. It seemed so pitiful that her entire legacy consisted of just a handful of images. Other people's photos filled entire albums and bonded them to the world without, to family, friends, marriages, holidays, pets, beaches and ballgames. But hers were orphaned ghosts with no grounding left in the greater scheme of things.

She picked them up and went through them one by one. A black and white picture of her mother at about twenty, not yet a hopeless drunk. A color shot of herself around six at an unknown beach with a little sand pail and a red shovel. A dinner table portrait of a foster family, with her nearly lost at the far end: She no longer remembered who they were. A snapshot of her mother, now considerably rougher, leaning against the fender of an old convertible. A teenage pic of her in a photo booth at a bus station on the way to God knew where. And on it went, image by image, depicting a life on the far periphery of the mainstream.

She put them down and closed her eyes to steady herself. Experience had taught her that self-pity was corrosive and devastating. Survival depended on keeping it at bay. She put the pictures back into the tin box, a little metal sarcophagus full of dying memories, and returned it to the top of the cupboard.

Back in the living room, she put her purse in the backpack with her other belongings and strapped it shut. But wait. A small bottle of her favorite shampoo remained in the shower. She crossed to the little bathroom just off the kitchen and fetched it.

The knob on the front door rotated noisily. Again and again.

She froze. Speedo? Why didn't he just let himself in? Too stoned?

She spotted the answer on the kitchen counter. His keys. He'd forgotten them when they took off for the park this morning.

The knob movement stopped. A series of violent thuds ensued, one so forceful it moved the hinges. "Let me in!" came a muffled shout from outside. Speedo for sure.

She crossed to the door and reached to twist the deadbolt open. "Alright! Alright! Quit pounding!"

She had no choice but to let him in. If he kept it up, someone was going to call the cops.

She turned the lock. A powerful kick swung the door open, narrowly missing her face. Speedo stood motionless with bulging eyes and balled fists. "You fucked him," he hissed. "You fucked the agent of hell on earth. You, the mother of us all."

"What do you mean? What are you talking about?" she said. "You're all screwed up right now. You know that?"

Tears leaked from the corners of his eyes. "Yes, yes, I know that. But the fear is gone. The power is upon me!"

He did an abrupt pivot and strode off down the sidewalk at a frantic pace.

Rhonda ducked back inside and grabbed her backpack. Time to go. Right now. She hustled out the door and took off down the sidewalk in the opposite direction from Speedo.

After several blocks, the adrenaline abated, and her current situation clarified. She was out on the street with nothing but ten dollars and a small backpack full of her stuff. If she'd had more time, she could have engineered a more graceful exit. One that landed her somewhere safe for at least a few days a while she devised some kind of plan to establish a new home base.

She looked around to see if Speedo had doubled back and picked up on her trail. Apparently not. She had to keep it that way. She had to keep moving.

17.

PAGE STREET

Larry sat at the table and counted the money one last time. It stood at the center of the biggest deal in his life, and he couldn't be too careful. For some inexplicable reason, he thought of his father, the dentist in Brentwood. The man had built a successful business and amassed considerable wealth. But now Larry might be in a position to financially eclipse him. He pictured himself pulling up to his father's house in a brand-new Mercedes. The hip, unrepentant prodigal son who'd made it on his own terms. He imagined the shock on his father's face, followed by the sorrow of having so badly misjudged his offspring. In all, a supreme moment of redemption.

He gathered up the stacks of cash, each bound by a rubber band, and tossed them in a worn leather briefcase emblazoned with a peace symbol. It didn't seem right to leave it out in the open. He'd have to think of a more secure place to stash it.

The intercom buzzed.

Larry smiled. Rhonda. Back for more. He knew it. She couldn't stay away. He crossed to the intercom and pressed the talk button. "Yeah?" he said in a very nonchalant tone.

"You hide in your keep. You think yourself invulnerable. But you must answer for what you've done. I demand entrance."

"What?" Larry stared at the speaker. The voice was male and vaguely familiar. "Who the fuck is this?"

No answer. Larry crossed to the bay windows and looked down. A small overhang of roof hid the door to his unit. He couldn't see the caller.

But he did hear the calamitous crash of glass erupt from below. "Jesus!" He ran to the front door and out to the stairwell, which looked down on the entrance. Fuck! It was Rhonda's old man, stepping through the shattered glass in the middle of the doorframe.

Larry's heart rocketed into triple time. He turned, ran back inside, and locked the deadbolt. Would that be enough? Maybe not. Should he phone the cops? No way. They'd see it as a drug deal gone wrong and haul him in, along with the money in the briefcase.

He backed off into the kitchen area, which put him as far as possible from the door.

Thump! A huge fist pounded its wooden surface. Again and again.

A weapon. He needed a weapon. He yanked a kitchen drawer open and drew out a butcher knife.

Wham! The front door shuddered in its frame. Wham! It began to tear loose from its framing. Wham! It pitched down into the living room with startling violence.

Speedo stood there motionless, his eyes incandescent with rage.

"You have betrayed our trust. You have become the representative of an evil beyond mortal understanding. And now you must be judged accordingly."

"What the fuck?" Larry yelled. "You're stoned, man. You're over the top. Get real!"

"The history of a man is in his hand. And so it shall be in yours."

Speedo began an inexorable advance toward Larry, who brought the knife into plain view. "Back off, dude. Right now!"

"You fucked her. You violated the essence of the earth itself."

Speedo closed to within striking distance. Larry brought the knife up into a stabbing position. A final warning. Speedo paid it no heed. His arm shot out and grabbed Larry's wrist just below the knife.

Larry gasped. Speedo's grip held him with almost robotic strength. It forced the knife down to his shoulder and bent his back against the sink. A sharp burst of pain shot up Larry's spine, causing him to drop his weapon. Speedo let him go, lunged forward and grabbed the knife as it clattered against the porcelain inside the sink.

As Larry rotated away, Speedo brought the blade up and planted it deep into Larry's right shoulder. Larry screamed and stumbled along the kitchen counter, trying to keep his balance. But he failed and pitched down onto his back on the linoleum floor. Speedo came down on him and plunged the knife into his chest just to one side of the sternum. Larry's eyes sprung wide and his mouth formed a scream with no exit. Speedo repeated the motion with a second stab that stopped Larry's heart forever. He removed the knife and straddled Larry's dead chest.

"You have been delivered to a higher cause. But your history remains within you, and it must be preserved for all to see."

He raised the knife once again.

Rhonda sat on a bench in the Panhandle, a block-wide finger of park that ran along the northern flank of Haight-Ashbury. She'd sorted through her options and kept coming up short on workable ideas. For the first time, she seriously considered phoning Stone and Christine for help. Not any easy choice. She'd always been averse to anything that compromised her independence; and in Bakersfield she'd been utterly dependent on Stone for an extended period. It left her with mixed feelings. Over time he'd proved to be the one exception to a dismal formula that equated dependence with betrayal, disappointment and bitterness. If she reached out to him again, it might be one time too often.

She put her ruminating aside and checked her purse to make sure she still had the ten dollars in her wallet. She did, but something was missing.

The tin box, the meager sum of her entire identity over twenty-five years on this earth.

She retraced her run-in with Speedo and realized that in the chaos of the moment she'd never retrieved it from the cupboard. Her stomach sank. She had to have it. She gathered up her things and set off back toward the Lower Haight.

A gift from a god who dwells at the greatest of heights, at the far pole of the universe. A reward for destroying the primal seed of evil before it takes root in the world at large. Compensation for deliverance of divine justice.

Speedo sat at Larry's kitchen table and carefully arranged the stacks of hundred-dollar bills. He'd found them here in an old leather briefcase inscribed with a large peace symbol. They had some kind of mystic significance he couldn't quite comprehend but which would be soon revealed to him. He'd also discovered a set of keys on the coffee table. They hung on a keychain of hand-tooled leather engraved with interlocking vines.

He stepped carefully around a large pool of blood to get to the cabinet under the sink. He marveled at how the surface of the pool caught the light from the kitchen window and lent it a curvature of breathtaking perfection. Inside the cabinet, he unrolled a single plastic trash bag off a big spool and pulled it out. It proved big enough to house the briefcase and the gift of compensation he'd so carefully prepared. In the bedroom, he'd discovered multiple sheets of a kind of velum or parchment. He meticulously installed the gift under several layers of the material, taking care to align each sheet in perfect symmetry with the last.

I gather the spoils of conquest, the living tokens of justice so righteously dispensed. I depart the devil's keep and journey forth into a world made whole once more.

Speedo descended the stairs and stepped through the broken glass. He walked down the outside steps and turned to a street-level garage under the apartments. He fitted one of Larry's keys into a door adjacent to the garage, pushed it open and felt for the lights in the darkness. When he flipped the switch, an older Ford Econoline van appeared. He walked through the musty air to the driver's side, hopped in and tried the key. The engine came alive, so he carefully placed his loaded trash bag on the passenger's side. After getting back out, he gave the garage door handle a firm yank and it rolled open. The sudden rush of light dazzled his optic nerves and he staggered backward and shielded his eyes.

The light of a thousand suns shines upon me and blesses me with its immortal glow. It beckons to me and tells me to depart this place before the resurrection of the devil and the seed that dwells in his balls of naked stone.

Speedo returned to the van, put it in gear, and rolled slowly out onto Page Street. He had become one with the light.

Rhonda leaned out from around the corner of an old apartment building constructed of brick and stucco on Rose Street. From here, she could see the entrance to her basement rental in mid-block across the street. No sign of Speedo either coming or going. She cautiously crossed the street into the shadows of late afternoon, watching while she went, and got her key out. She needed to retrieve the tin box as quickly as possible.

Arriving at the door, she unlocked the deadbolt and tentatively peeked inside. No one home. She entered, pulled off her backpack and quickly crossed to the kitchen, where she grabbed a chair and climbed up to the level of the cupboard. After a little anxious probing, she felt the box, brought it out and climbed down.

Speedo came in the front door just as her foot touched the floor.

Rhonda was not easily given to fear, but right now she felt it ballooning up from her gut and lodging in her throat. She froze.

Speedo closed the door behind him. The deadbolt clicked shut. He carried a black trash bag bearing the outlines of two objects within.

"That's close enough," she commanded.

He ignored her and crossed to the kitchen table. The previous madness in his eyes had subsided. He pulled an old leather briefcase out of the bag. Rhonda immediately recognized the peace symbol inscribed on its cover. Larry. It was Larry's. Oh God, oh no.

Speedo reached back into the bag and pulled out a roll of leather or thick paper of some kind, which he carefully placed in the center of the table. "What we have here is the difference between heaven and earth," he declared. He pulled a bound stack of hundred dollar bills out of the briefcase and pointed it at her.

"This," he announced, "is what binds us and enslaves us in a struggle that is not our own."

He returned the money to the briefcase and placed his hands on the leather roll. "This," he continued, "is what we discover when we sit at the right hand of God."

He said it with utter conviction as he unrolled the first thin sheet of leather. "One chapter at a time," he went on as he unrolled the next sheet. "One perfect chapter at a time."

Rhonda remained silent and frozen in place. Any wrong move or utterance might set him off. She could only look on as he unrolled successive layers.

The final layer came off. A human forearm rolled out, hand included. A male arm, with a forest of soft hair sprouting from the dead skin. An arm severed right below the elbow, with cakes of dried blood crusting the stump.

Speedo smiled as he examined it. An almost sentimental smile. "A man's hand is his history. It holds all that he is and all that he will ever be."

Rhonda's stomach convulsed. It forced her to vomit, but nothing came up.

Speedo gave her a knowing nod and began to roll the arm back up in the leather, sheet by sheet. "In time you'll come to understand," he said. "But for now you can just think of it as the right hand of God. The rest will come to you after you seek forgiveness for copulating with the devil." He finished and put the roll and the briefcase back into the trash bag. "I'm through here. I'll be going now."

He picked up the bag, walked to the door and was gone.

Rhonda remained locked in place on the chair by the cupboard. She feared that any motion might cause him to return and deliver unspeakable retribution.

Eventually she climbed down, went to the window and parted the curtains to scan the block in both directions. No sign of him.

But for how long?

18.

SUNSET DISTRICT

Stone settled into his favorite chair to take in the television news on ABC. Walter Cronkite was narrating a segment on protesters in LA raging against President Johnson, who was in town for a political dinner of some kind. He looked back over his shoulder to Christine in the kitchen. "You going to watch this?"

"Don't think so," she said as she tossed a salad of lettuce, tomatoes, cucumbers and mushrooms. "I need a night off from all that."

"Know what you mean," Stone sympathized. He took a sip from his can of Budweiser and watched as the news cut to a commercial for the Ford Falcon, a curious little car that seemed like Ford's answer to the Volkswagen Beetle.

He and Christine had just returned from the Monterey Pop Festival, with its dazzling lineup of new players. Everything from an Indian sitar player to a South African trumpeter to Janis Joplin with her ragtag hippie band. It had been both exhilarating and frustrating. The music verged on revolutionary, but nearly all the acts had already been signed. For Stone, it looked like the gold rush was over and the claims all staked. His biggest regret was not having a shot at this young black guitar player named Jimi Hendrix. He was nothing short of phenomenal. By leveraging the monstrous power now available in a new generation of amplifiers, he took his instrument into a previous unexplored realm of shrieks, howls and screams unlike any before. But the real trick was how he combined it with a solid musicality and an instinctive feel for core melodies that stuck in the listener's mind. Who would have ever thought that something called "Manic Depression" might become a major hit?

The phone rang on the kitchen counter and Christine picked it up. "Hello." She put down the salad bowl. "Rhonda? Yes. How are you?"

Stone twisted in his chair to pick up on their conversation. A frown came over Christine as she listened. "I see. Can you hang on a minute? Thanks." She put her palm over the handset and looked to Stone. "It's Rhonda. She doesn't sound good. She's in some kind of trouble."

"What kind?"

"Didn't say. She doesn't want to talk about it over the phone."

"So what's she want to do?"

"She wants to talk to us in person."

"Is she alone?" A fair question. If she had a rogue boyfriend in tow, it changed the whole dynamic.

Christine took her palm off the handset. "Are you by yourself?" Christine nodded an affirmative to Stone.

He sighed. Rhonda had become a binary proposition. If he helped her, God only knew what he was stumbling into. If he didn't, he'd probably never see her again. Once again, he pictured her climbing onto that Greyhound bus over ten years ago, so brave and alone. He couldn't say no.

"Find out where she's at. We'll send a cab."

Christine took down the address, hung up and called a cab. She came over, sat in Stone's lap, and gave him a warm hug. "Good move, big guy."

"I sure hope so. We'll see."

"That we will," Christine said as she got up and went back to the kitchen. "I wonder if she's had anything to eat. Maybe not."

"We've got some Chinese left over from last night," Stone suggested.

"I'm going to tidy up the guest room and change the towels," Christine said. "Just in case."

"Just in case." Stone smiled. The mom in Christine was floating to the surface. It was nice to see.

A knock came twenty minutes later, just as the news was ending. "I'll get it," Christine said, and headed to the door. Stone felt a small measure of relief as he stood up. He wasn't quite ready to meet Rhonda head on after all this time. Better to have Christine act as a buffer. She opened the door to an attractive woman in her mid-twenties. Rhonda for sure. The eyes, the nose, the shape of the mouth all fit with his memories. Her hair appeared longer and fuller and her makeup accentuated that same strong sexual presence she'd had even back then at the outset of her womanhood.

"Rhonda, come in," Christine said.

Rhonda looked over to Stone as she crossed the threshold. "Hi," she said with only a faint trace of a smile.

"How are you?" Stone asked.

"Not so good. That's why I'm here. Sorry to intrude."

"Not a problem," Stone said and gestured toward the couch. "Have a seat."

"Would you like something to drink?" Christine asked.

"I'm fine," Rhonda said as she sat down. Stone returned to his chair and swiveled it to face her. Christine took a seat at the opposite end of the couch.

"It's been a long time," Stone said.

"I know. I should have stayed in touch. I'm sorry. I just didn't want to disturb you."

"Let's not worry about that," Stone said. "It's good to see you."

"I was too young to appreciate what you did for me," Rhonda explained. "And by the time I did, it seemed like it was too late."

"Well we're past all that now," Christine said. "What can we do for you?"

"I think I might be in a lot of trouble, but I'm not sure."

"What kind of trouble?" Stone asked.

Rhonda sighed. "It's kind of complicated."

"Take your time," Stone said.

"You see, I've got this crazy boyfriend. He used to race stock cars, but he crashed too much. He started taking acid and now he's crazier than ever. I think he just killed somebody."

"When?" Stone asked. As a former cop, he was conditioned to put aside personal reactions and go for the facts.

"Today. This afternoon. Over in Haight-Ashbury."

"Did you see him do it?"

"No."

"Do you know who it was?"

"Yeah, it was this acid dealer named Larry that we met in the park a couple of times. This morning, Speedo took a hit of what he sold us, and we took off to the park."

"Speedo? That's your boyfriend?"

"Yeah, but not anymore. Not after this. At the park he got so stoned I lost track of him. Then I ran into Larry and we went back to his apartment and hung out for a while. After that I went home and Speedo showed up, all crazy and jealous. He figured out that I'd been at Larry's and was totally flipped out."

Stone nodded attentively. He was fairly certain that "hung out for a while" was an oblique reference to having sex. Speedo might have had genuine cause for concern, although not for violent retribution.

Rhonda paused and sighed. "Anyway, he took off. Didn't say where he was going. By now I was pretty freaked out, so I packed up my stuff and split. I didn't want to wait around and find out just how far he might push things."

"Where did you go?" Stone asked.

"Just over to the Panhandle. Then I found out I had to go back. I left something really important behind. Personal stuff."

"So you went back," Stone said. "And then what?"

"He shows up before I can get out. This time, he's got a brief-case from Larry's full of money."

"You think he killed this Larry guy to get it?"

"I think he killed him because he was stoned on bad acid and went bat-shit crazy."

Stone silently summed up the facts and came up short. "How can you be sure that Larry's dead? Did Speedo admit that to you?"

"No."

"Then how do you know?"

"The arm."

"The arm?" Stone asked.

"The lower arm and the hand. Speedo brought it with him. It's the grossest thing I've ever seen. It scared the shit out of me."

Stone turned to Christine, who somehow retained her composure. "Could somebody do that? Could they cut off an arm without surgical equipment?"

"It wouldn't be easy. They'd have to be pretty strong. But yes, they could."

"I'm sorry, but I'm going to have to see this for myself," he told Rhonda. He had to consider the possibility that Rhonda herself was stoned and deluded. Or that Speedo had engineered this whole thing as some kind of sick joke to get revenge for her infidelity. However, for now, he decided to give her the benefit of the doubt "We need to go to this Larry guy's apartment and check it out. Are you up to that?"

"If I have to be," Rhonda said with considerable hesitation.

Stone stood up. "Okay then, let's go."

The drove over to Page Street in Stone's VW sedan, which had proven a perfect size for negotiating the crowded streets of San Francisco. Neither said much on the way. Both were silently processing this extremely bizarre incident in their own manner. If true, it was the kind that would bounce around a cop station for years thereafter.

Stone got lucky and found a parking space on the same block as the alleged apartment. They got out and walked down the sidewalk through the fading summer light and came upon a three-story structure in the middle of the block. Stone noted that it was free standing, so there could have been considerable commotion without attracting much attention from the neighbors.

"What about the other tenants?" Stone asked.

"I don't know," Rhonda replied. "I didn't see anybody."

Stone knew something was seriously wrong when they reached the stairs up to the entrance. At the top were three doors, one for each unit. The glass on the right-hand door was missing, with just a few jagged splinters protruding from the wooden frame. It was also slightly ajar, but you wouldn't have noticed it from the street.

"Was it like this when you were here?" he asked Rhonda.

"No."

They heard a male voice coming from up above as Stone opened the door and started up the stairs.

"Oh my God! Oh my God! Oh my God!"

Halfway up, Stone caught sight of a thin, pale hippie. Barefoot, bell bottoms, tie-die T-shirt. A gray cat sat cradled in his arms.

"Oh man, what a fucking bummer!" he exclaimed as Stone reached the top, with Rhonda a few steps behind. He looked over the young man's shoulder. The apartment door was wide open. Not good. "You live here?" he asked.

"I live downstairs," he said. "I just got home. My cat was gone. It used to come up here to visit this dude. When I saw the busted glass and figured it was a rip-off and maybe my cat got ripped off, too. So I came up and found the door open and... Oh fuck! Oh Jesus!" His slender arms shivered, and the cat squirmed.

Stone noted that the kid had no idea who Stone was, yet freely doled out all kinds of information. In this world Stone was automatically an adult authority figure, whether he liked it or not.

"Stay here," he instructed. He turned to Rhonda. "You too."

He did a quick scan of the place as he walked in. Upscale psychedelic. Lots of hip stuff, but newly purchased. Just what you'd expect from a dealer.

He stopped scanning when he reached the kitchen floor. The bottom half of a corpse and a pool of coagulating blood were clearly visible.

So this was Larry, the archetypal dope dealer brought to an all too familiar end. Nothing new to Stone. His time as an LA vice cop in Hollywood had taught him to expect nothing less. Speed, meth, heroin and now LSD: It didn't really matter what drug was in play. The end game was always the same.

He crossed to the kitchen and looked down on Larry's corpse. Sure enough, the forearm had been severed right below the elbow. Given the extent of the procedure, there wasn't that much blood. Two stab wounds in the chest explained why. At least one had pierced the heart and dropped the blood pressure to zero some time before the limb was cut off. The dead eyes of the victim had that mystical look of resignation you sometimes saw in violent homicides. As if the soul had departed to some distant place where it could calmly observe what had happened and ponder the irony of it all.

"It's him, isn't it?"

Stone turned to Rhonda, who stood in the doorway. "Yeah, it's him. Oh shit. What do we do?"

"That's an interesting question," Stone said. "Anything you know that you're not telling me?" Like, did you help do this?

"No," Rhonda said resolutely. "I've told you everything."

"Everything?"

"Yeah, everything."

"Did you have sex with him when you came back here from the park?"

Rhonda closed her eyes and exhaled deeply. "Yes."

"You didn't tell me that, did you?"

"No, but I didn't think it mattered."

"Next time you don't tell me everything, you're on your own. Got it?"

Rhonda nodded sheepishly. "Got it."

"Good. Let's go."

Once they reached the bottom of the stairs, they found the slender hippie nervously petting his cradled cat.

"I need you to do two things," Stone told him. The hippie nodded in assent. "First, call the cops and tell them what you found.

Second, don't tell them or anyone else that we were here. Can I count on you?" The hippie nodded once again. Stone reached out and gave him a gentle pat on the cheek. "Good. Because I don't want to have to come back."

19.

SUNSET DISTRICT

The trip back to Stone's rental house started in sullen silence. Rhonda evidently thought that Stone was being heavy handed and dominant in his treatment of her. He decided it best not to let it fester.

"Look, here's the deal," he told her. "I don't really know you. Not anymore. All that stuff was a long time ago. Back then I did what I could for you, and that turned out to be quite a lot. But this is now, and I'm not sure where you're coming from. So we need to start over. You're in a real jam, and I understand that. I also understand that we're going to have to do things my way if you want to get out of it. Otherwise I'm no good to you. If you're not straight with me, you're the one who's going down, not me."

"Right." Something in her tone indicated that while she got it, she didn't really accept it.

"And just so you know," Stone said, "I did check up on you a few times, through the attorney."

"You did?" She seemed genuinely surprised.

"Yes, I did. Everything seemed to be on track, so I let it go at that." He sighed and downshifted for the light up ahead on 36th. "Maybe that was a mistake. I don't know."

"Maybe, maybe not," she said. "Either way, I had to start from scratch, and it was a real bitch."

"I'm sure it was," Stone agreed. "So did things get better?"

"A little, but not much."

"I'm sorry to hear that." Stone fought off the urge to accept some degree of responsibility. He kept gravitating toward this parental role that was never really his to assume.

"I had a fiancé for a while," she volunteered. "Did they tell you that?"

"No, they did not. What happened?"

"He was killed in Vietnam."

"Wow. That's terrible."

Her eyes began to tear up. Stone read it as lingering grief over the death of her loved one. He read it wrong.

"You never came and saw me," she blurted out. "You never called and you never wrote. It was like you just disappeared. You were all I had, and then you were gone. Just like that."

Stone was dumbfounded. Once again, he was back in that bus station in Visalia, watching her climb aboard and wondering if this was what it was like to have a child of your own. At the time he'd thought it pure speculation. It never occurred to him that the reverse was also in play, that she was wondering what it was like to have a father of your very own.

"I'm sorry," he told her. "I didn't realize I mattered that much. I would have done more. I just didn't get it. I'm sorry."

"It's okay," she said. "It was a long time ago. It was all different then."

"Yeah I suppose it was." Stone sensed that the sudden fissure in her persona was rapidly closing. Rhonda the child was receding and Rhonda the street warrior was back in charge.

"Am I going to be arrested or something?" she asked.

"Not likely. For starters, you don't have any direct connection to the crime. You won't need legal representation unless you're arrested and charged with an offense of some kind. But that doesn't mean you won't have to talk to the police."

"Why?" she asked.

"Because from what you told me, you'll wind up being a major witness for the prosecution. The cops are going to want to get every detail they can dig out of you."

"That freaks me out. Really bad. And you know why."

Stone nodded. "I do." Rhonda's experience with law enforcement dated back to Bakersfield, and a thoroughly corrupt legal
system that left no one safe, even a thirteen-year-old girl. "I'll tell
you what, let's do this. I'm going to go to the police and explain
the situation. My time as a homicide cop will buy us a few favors.
I'm pretty sure they'll let me be there when you talk with them.
Will that work for you?"

"Yeah, that'll work." She stared vacantly out the windshield.
"You know there's one thing I forgot to tell you about what went
down." She looked over and glared at him. "I didn't lie, I just forgot. Okay?"

"Okay."

"I was hanging out in Larry's bedroom, and when I came out
to leave, this black guy was there. The two of them were counting
stacks of money. He was older and nicely dressed."

"Thanks," Stone said. "I'll make sure that gets passed along.

Her eyes closed and she slumped in the seat. "I'm really tired
now."

"We're almost home," Stone said. "You can stay with us for a
while if you want."

"Thank you."

"No problem." Stone pulled onto 39th street where their rental
was located. Like it or not, Rhonda had moved to the top of his
list. He'd have to forget about discovering the next Jimi Hendrix
for a while.

"I caught up with him in Calcutta," the white man told the King. "I
took him out in what you people would call a bad neighborhood."

"A bad neighborhood," the King repeated from their seat on
a bench near Rideout Fountain. "Yes, I do know a thing or two
about bad neighborhoods."

The sculpture of a lion locked in mortal combat with a serpent topped the fountain. In previous meetings here, both men had
expressed their admiration of the piece. It harmonized nicely with
their shared worldview.

"I used an Army issue .45. Very underrated as a handgun."

"I agree," the King said.

The white man shifted his thick frame, and his belly rolled under his short sleeved white shirt with its loosened tie. "I first picked up on the guy when he was scouting Singapore before the invasion. Had a really nice camera. The Japs really loved their cameras. Still do."

"That's what I hear," the King said. He watched as the man absently rubbed the sparse little island of hair on his broad forehead.

"So is the money in play now?" the man asked.

"Yes indeed," the King replied. "And soon to deliver a substantial return."

"Good to hear. I'll pass that on to the appropriate people."

A sudden gust of wind blew a fine spray off the fountain. It caught the King's eye as he viewed the serpent and the lion. He wondered which one was supposed to win.

You always had to have a winner.

20.

GOLDEN GATE PARK

Stone drove into Golden Gate Park though a bejeweled mist, the child of moisture off the ocean and morning sunlight from the east. He entered the parking lot of the Park Police Station, which served Haight-Ashbury and the surrounding areas. It appeared rather modest in scope, with a small parking lot and a two-story stucco building as the principal structure.

Stone smiled to himself once inside. The desk sergeant looked like he came straight from central casting, with a big bulldog face creased into a perpetual scowl. He offered no greeting and stared at Stone expectantly.

"I need to talk to someone in homicide," Stone said.

"You reporting a crime?"

"I'm pretty sure it's been reported, but I've got some additional information."

The sergeant pointed to a worn wooden bench near the door. "Have a seat." He picked up the phone. "Is Burke around? Yeah… I got a guy out here wants to talk to him." He looked up. "Stand by." He went back to his paperwork.

A few minutes later Detective Sergeant Joe Burke lumbered into view. Mid-forties, blue eyes, flat top haircut. He wore a cheap suit that scarcely concealed an overweight physique. He had a genial air about him, and Stone couldn't help but picture him in a lowball diner with a fried chicken leg in one hand and a big mug of beer in the other.

He shook Stone's hand. "I'm Burke. What've you got?"

"You had a homicide over on Page Street yesterday. I've got some information that may be useful."

"Oh yeah? Like what?" Stone discounted Burke's skeptical attitude. He knew from experience that the lunatic fringe came out in force in a situation like this, especially in a place like Haight-Ashbury.

"I'm in touch with someone who can ID the killer."

Burked pointed down a hallway behind the reception desk. "Come with me."

Stone followed Burke's substantial backside down the hall. "In there," the cop instructed Stone without turning to face him. He was pointing to small room with a table and a few folding chairs.

Stone took a seat and Burke reappeared with a pen and pad. "Now let's start with you," he said. "You are...?"

"James Stone. Five seventy-eight Thirty-ninth Street here in the city. I'm in the record business."

Burke looked up. "The record business, huh? Lot of that going on around here lately." He grinned. "Just check out the park. Pyscho-dellic, man. So how'd you wind up doing records?"

"It's a long story. Used to have the same job as you. I worked homicide in Bakersfield."

Burke's face instantly rearranged itself. He was talking to a member of the tribe, and that changed everything. "Were you down there when all that weird shit happened?" he asked.

"Yep. And then I quit,"

"Yeah, I'd like to quit myself. This hippie stuff is driving me nuts. But I haven't put in my twenty yet."

"You'll get there," Stone reassured him.

Burke picked up his pen. "So what's going on?"

"If I'm not mistaken, you had a homicide yesterday over on Page Street, right?"

"As a matter of fact, we did," Burke responded. "Somebody stabbed this hippie acid dealer and whacked his arm off. Un-fucking-believable. You think you know who did it?"

"No but I know someone who does. I guess you'd call her a friend of the family. It's pretty much a sure bet that the killer is this guy she's been living with."

"Wow," Burke said as he scribbled. "Why don't you give me the short story now and we can get the long story later. What's her name?"

"Savage. Rhonda Savage. She's been living with this guy in a little dump over on Webster Street. He goes by Speedo, but she's never mentioned his real name."

"And how does she know he's the killer?"

"They went to the park and he dropped some acid. Pretty soon he was seriously stoned, and she lost track of him and went home. A few hours later he showed up acting bad crazy and pulled out this severed arm and a bagful of money, then he left again. Anyway, that's the short version."

"Definitely sounds like our guy. Does she have any idea where he might have gone?"

"None."

"Well I'm definitely going to want to talk to her."

"I've got a favor to ask."

"What's that?"

"She's really upset right now. No surprise. She'd like me to be around when you talk. Just a fly on the wall. It'll make things easier for everyone."

Burke gave his hairline a thoughtful scratch. "Yeah, I don't see why not." He put down his pen. "You know, there's somebody else we should bring in on this. Let me go get him."

He shuffled out and returned with a lean, compact man well on his way to baldness while still in his fifties. He had Irish written all over him, and Burke's introduction confirmed it. "Mr. Stone, this Tom Linehan from Narcotics. Some of this may spill over into his pond, so I thought you should meet. Mr. Stone used to work Homicide down in Bakersfield," he added.

"Bakersfield, huh?" Linehan said as he shook Stone's hand. "Tough beat."

"Yes, it was," Stone confirmed. "But at least I didn't have a park with a hundred dope deals going down all at once."

Linehan smiled. A wry smile. He flashed the peace sign with his fingers. "Love, peace, dope. Lots and lots of dope."

"What kind of line do you guys have on this Larry, the dead dealer?" Stone asked.

"As far as we can tell," Linehan said, "He was a bottom feeder. One or two hits at a time. Turning on the tourists, that kind of thing. Go over to Hippie Hill right now and you'll find a dozen of him. Wait a couple of months and you'll probably find a hundred of him. Things are completely out of control. We don't even bother with routine enforcement anymore. Want to light up a joint? Be our guest. We don't have the time, we don't have the people."

"And where you have bottom feeders, you have a food chain," Stone commented.

"You got it," Linehan said. "And it's starting to get nasty. It was different when this LSD thing first started up. You had a lot of dealers who were also true believers. It wasn't about money or power. It was more of a spiritual thing." He paused and snorted. "But guess what? Times have changed and here come the big fish with the big teeth. You read about the Superspade murder?"

"Just the headlines," Stone said.

"Here's this black guy who's become a major acid distributor. Nice guy. Righteous guy. People liked him. Anyway, he goes over to Sausalito to do a major deal and winds up dead in a sleeping bag hanging off a cliff. Now how does that work? We don't know. We're still trying to figure it out. And maybe the case of one-armed Larry will help."

"Well here's something else that might help," Stone said. "The girl told me she saw an older black guy at the victim's place. And guess what? They were counting stacks of money."

Linehan smiled. "How about that? Now maybe she got it all wrong. Maybe they were just playing Monopoly."

"Sure thing," Stone said. "Get out of jail free."

21.

SEBASTOPOL

I *navigate by slant of the shadows cast by the sacred light of eternal salvation. They point my vessel of steel and oil to the north, away from the tortuous blaze that roils the air and the water behind me. I hear it speak in silken tones and it instructs me to apply full power to hasten a glorious reunion that awaits me just over the horizon.*

Patrolman Ronnie Grover sincerely hoped the van was not exceeding the speed limit. The end of his shift came up in just a couple of minutes, and he was meeting two of his pals to go fishing up north on the Russian River. Still, duty called. He sighed and raised the radar gun and aimed it down the Gravenstein Highway, which got its name when Sebastopol was still big into apples. Those days were long gone, and the town had leveled off at about three thousand people. Still, you need a few cops. In his rookie years, he'd considered migrating down to San Francisco, sixty miles away, but never got around to it.

I feel the throb and hum of a thousand explosions. I revel in the surge of power as the vessel seeks its way through this troubled land. The buildings bend and wobble and speak of greed gone rampant. Deliver me, for I carry the history of the hand and all that it represents.

Grover checked the readout on the radar gun. Shit. The van was actually accelerating. The asshole was topping sixty in a zone marked forty. Grover flipped on his flashing lights and pulled out in pursuit just as the van whooshed by him. He quickly closed the distance and sounded his siren. No response. Damn. The van rolled on at close to sixty, weaving slightly as it headed toward the town proper up ahead.

He grabbed the mic. "Dispatch this is Unit One. I've got a speeder on Gravenstein near Redwood headed your way. Doesn't respond to lights or siren. Request assistance from Unit Two."

"Stand by, One." Up ahead, the van slowed slightly but continued. Oh boy, this could get ugly, Grover thought.

"Unit One, Unit Two will intercept at Palm and you can box him in."

"Copy that, dispatch." Grover hit the siren once again. No response. The van rocketed on toward the center of town. A quarter mile ahead, he could see the flashing lights from Unit Two as it raced down Palm to intercept them here on the highway. Unit Two was Jordan, a good man in a tight spot. It would be close, but they could make it work.

It did work. Unit Two swerved onto the highway up ahead of the van and gradually slowed down. The van made one attempt to pass Jordan but was blocked. Grover closed in from behind and all three vehicles rolled to a stop in the middle of the road.

Grover got out and drew his pistol, something he hadn't done for several years. Ahead, Jordan did the same. They closed on the van's driver side with weapons trained on the figure inside. The door slowly opened. "Down flat! Do it! Now!" Jordan screamed as a disheveled and dirty young male came out and went to his knees. He raised his hands high in surrender.

"I dispense divine justice. I forgive you for disrupting the holy journey of the hand to its rightful place atop the firmament."

Jordan kicked him onto his stomach and Grover cuffed him. Traffic began to build up. People got out of their cars to gawk. "Everybody back!" Jordan yelled as returned to his vehicle to call in. You couldn't blame them. This was more excitement than Sebastopol had seen for years.

"Dispatch, this is Unit One. We have a suspect in custody and request backup for traffic control."

"Copy, Unit One. We need a license number on the van."

"Roger that. It's California SZP 582."

"Copy. You guys just hit the big time."

"How's that?"

"There's an APB out on the vehicle from San Francisco."

A third patrol car, the last one available, showed up and began to direct traffic around the scene. Grover and Jordan walked the suspect to Jordan's car and installed him in the back. That done, Grover went to the van to check it out. The rear was empty, but there was a black trash bag on the passenger seat. Normally he would have left it there, but because of the APB, he was curious. He walked back to Jordan's vehicle, where the window was down in the rear. The cuffed suspect stared at him placidly through the open window.

"So what's in that bag on your passenger seat?" he asked.

"Everything that ever was and ever will be," the suspect replied without hesitation.

Grover turned to Jordan, who stood next to him. "I think we got ourselves a genuine certified psycho."

Back at the station Grover watched as they installed the suspect in the holding cell. His driver's license pegged him as one Edward G. Dalberg with an address in Riverside. The guy had caused so much commotion that the chief wanted to find out what the APB was all about. It took just a couple of calls. It seemed that Mr. Dalberg was a suspect in a drug-related murder down in the city and had stolen the van from his alleged victim.

Grover fetched the black bag, which he'd brought to the station in anticipation of something like this. He and the chief took it to a small meeting room and donned rubber gloves before opening it. It held a bulky old briefcase and what looked like a roll of soft leather. They opened the briefcase first and removed five thousand dollars arranged in bundles of hundred-dollar bills. After verifying the count, they returned the money to the briefcase and directed their attention to the roll of leather.

"You smell something?" the chief asked Grover.

"Yeah," Grover replied. "I'm starting to get a bad feeling about this."

"Let's get it done," the chief commanded. He unrolled he first layer and held it up. "What is this stuff?"

"Looks like some kind of leather or parchment," Grover suggested. "Like what you see on ancient scrolls."

"Could be." The chief worked through more layers. The smell got worse. He reached the final layer. "Hang on," he told Grover. "This ain't gonna be pretty."

The forearm of Larry Boyd rolled out onto the table, palm up. Shriveled and mushroom gray. Rigor mortis had stiffened the index finger, which pointed directly at Grover.

"Oh, my fucking God," the chief exclaimed. Both men backed off from the table and stared. "I better call the SFPD and let 'em know about this," he said, and started for the door. Grover was right behind him, trying his best not to vomit.

He should have left the black bag right where he found it.

Stone got the call in the early evening. Christine and Rhonda were watching television on the couch. The Monkees were grinding their way through some corny comedy act set in Malibu. Stone disliked the group intensely. He saw them as pure entertainment engineering, with no roots in the real world. They didn't even know how to play, not really. They wouldn't last.

"Stone here," he said into the receiver.

"Mr. Stone, this is Sergeant Burke from Park Station. "I wanted you to know we found this Speedo guy. He got busted on a traffic violation up in Sebastopol."

"You sure it's him?" Stone asked.

"Absolutely. He was driving the victim's van. Brought the sliced arm and the money along for the ride."

"Not too bright," Stone commented.

"More like stark raving mad. He confessed to a couple of reporters while he was being booked. Said it was bad acid. Kept saying that a man's history is in his hand."

"Sounds like you've got an insanity plea in your future," Stone commented.

"Sure looks like it. Anyway, I still need to talk to the Savage girl. At this point she's the icing on the cake, but we still need her story to cement this thing."

"Understand." He put his hand over the receiver and turned to Rhonda and Christine. "That's the cops. They've got Speedo in custody and the evidence goes right along with what you told me."

"Good," Rhonda said softly. "Good."

"They still need to talk to you," Stone added. "Are you up to seeing them tomorrow?"

Rhonda shrugged. "If I have to."

Stone got back on the phone to Burke. "Can we do it tomorrow sometime?"

"It's kind of crazy here, but yeah. I'll give you a call in the morning and we'll set up a time."

"You got it." He hung up and turned to the women. "That's enough of that. Let's go get some Italian."

They took a cab to the Fior d'Italia on Union Street. Stone's tolerance for the city's traffic had its limits and he was more than willing to buy his way out of it, especially given the current circumstances. Rhonda evidently felt better, which brought her appetite front and center. She went through several courses, including calamari, soup, pasta, salad and steak sautéed in cream sauce. They shared a bottle of Chianti during dinner and a bottle of Liano afterwards. All the while, Christine did a superb job of keeping the conversation moving in a positive direction. She and Stone both knew that Rhonda's history was a veritable minefield, which made the usual banter about family and friends pretty much off limits. They stuck to music, movies, fashion and the like.

It proved helpful because it gave Stone a better measure of who Rhonda had become. On the one side, she presented herself as knowledgeable, intelligent and insightful. On the other, she came off as cynical, tough and emotionally distant. That said, the brief outburst in the car today spoke of a soft side carefully stowed out of sight.

The second bottle of wine lubricated the conversation somewhat. Stone had just started checking the bill when, out of nowhere, Rhonda set off a major detonation.

"So, did you guys ever get married?"

Christine couldn't hide her consternation. They'd been through this before. Too many times. Her face collapsed into a minor frown before it quickly recovered. Rhonda immediately picked up on it. "Sorry, I didn't mean to pry. I just remember you guys seemed really tight back then. So, I thought one thing would lead to another and, well, you know..."

Stone knew he had to intervene and do so quickly. "For starters, we're doing alright just the way we are. We both had other marriages that didn't go so well and weren't looking for a repeat. Also, we were lucky, at least I was." He reached over and took Christine's hand. "I found myself a truly extraordinary woman, and there aren't that many to go around."

Christine spoke up with calmness and conviction. "A lot of women wind up married because they feel they need a man to truly define themselves. I'm not one of them. Never was. It took a while, but I built my own place in the world. And that scared off a lot of men, but not Jim. Anyway, it's not that we're against getting married, we just don't want it to get in the way of everything else."

"Wow," Rhonda said. "I never thought about it like that."

"Most people haven't," Stone added. "But we're not most people."

For the first time that evening, a fully realized smile appeared on Rhonda. "No, I guess you're not."

22.

PARK POLICE STATION

Detective Sergeant Burke's stomach knew it was being cheated. He had promised it a delicious dinner no later than six o'clock. His wife phoned earlier and spoke of roast beef and mashed potatoes with a big slice of apple pie to top it off. Excellent. He also looked forward to a generous glass of Jim Beam and as a pre-dinner reward for his devotion to duty.

But six o'clock had come and gone. Seven was coming right up and he was still here, typing up all the crap on the Larry Boyd murder, him of the severed arm. They had the killer dead to rights, a nut case named Dalberg, but that in no way reduced the titanic volume of paperwork. The DA's office was already on his ass and demanding everything except the victim's dick length.

He'd sent a pair of officers up to Sebastopol to fetch Dalberg, but he wouldn't be booked down here until later this evening. That meant no interrogation until sometime tomorrow. He wanted to talk to the Savage girl before Dalberg, so that pushed his interrogation out into the afternoon sometime. And so on, and so on.

He slid the carriage on his typewriter over to the return position and removed a report in triplicate concerning chain of custody. That was it. He was out of there. His stomach applauded in anticipation.

About twenty feet above Burke, a photoreceptor on the roof of Park Police Station patiently waited for the daylight to drop below a certain threshold. Once this happened, it would trigger the lighting in the parking lot below, making life safer for those working within, at least in theory.

Matt Carson raised his bolt cutters and began to snip away at the chain link fence on the west side of the police station. A profusion of vegetation and trees concealed this section from public view, which gave Carson the time to work carefully and deliberately. It also allowed him to review a litany of offenses that the SFPD had visited upon his person. A kick in the ribs. A boot to the butt. A smack in the face. All designed to remind him that he and his kind were not welcome on the streets of this beautiful city.

After one last snip he peeled back a section of fence large enough to allow his passage. He reached down and picked up a burlap bag that held the explosive device he'd so meticulously constructed. A few simple calculations had informed him that less than a pound of its main ingredient, PETN, would produce a truly devastating explosion. One with enough power to atomize a whole wall into a blast of shrapnel that would shred the entire lower story and bring down the remainder of the building.

He made his way through the fence and crept along the side of a second building that served as a garage. In the failing light, he was barely visible. He stopped at the corner of the garage and peeked around to his target, the main administrative building. Now the risky part. He needed to cross about ten yards of open pavement in the parking lot to place the bomb flush against the building's wall. He had to act quickly while the partial darkness still offered at least some cover. He stepped into the open. The lights out here had yet to come on. He started across.

As Burke shuffled out the front entrance, he was followed by one of the station's patrolmen, a guy named Reeves. They both turned left toward the parking lot. Burke simply nodded at the man. He was tired and hungry and didn't feel like talking.

Carson reached the wall and took a quick look around. No one in sight. He crouched down to place the bag next to the trunk of a small decorative tree.

On the roof the photoreceptor finally ran out of daylight. It activated a relay that created a sudden blaze of illumination around the outside of the building.

As they entered the parking lot, Burke and Reeves spotted this guy in a crouch alongside the nearest wall. He held a bag of some kind and appeared startled. "Hey!" Burke yelled. The guy dropped the bag and took off toward the garage. Burke started after him. "Check the bag!" he yelled to Reeves. No telling what was in it.

The guy sprinted toward the back of the garage with Burke in pursuit. The residual power in Burke's legs surprised him. A sudden boost of adrenaline put them into high gear. Up ahead, he saw the suspect run through a gap in the security fence. He speeded up to match the suspect's pace. In the parking lot Reeves tentatively opened the burlap. He recognized the blasting cap, which was embedded in a brick of white stuff and connected to a small circuit board of some kind. "Aw shit!" He sprang up and ran back toward the front entrance, yelling "Bomb!" as he went.

"Stop!" Burke hollered as the suspect came out of the trees behind the station and darted across Kezar Drive and into the park proper. Burke brought his .38 snub nose out of its shoulder holster as he ran. Up ahead the suspect left the trees and started across an open field. Burke thought the better of shooting. Too many people around. The suspect reached the far side of the field and took off down a paved path, with Burke twenty yards behind. They entered a second field, larger than the first.

And it was here that Burke suddenly felt very funny.

A big ball of pain swelled in his chest and migrated down into his arm. He tried to shrug it off and continue the chase, but it only got worse. Dropping to his knees, he gasped, and the world launched into a violent spin. His skin felt all clammy. Everything went dim. A terrible dread came over him.

Carson looked back as his pursuer collapsed on the lawn. Lucky break. He slowed to a walk and climbed to the tree line at the top of Hippie Hill. From here he could look out across the park to the police station in the distance. He dropped down into the shadows and stared at the collapsed figure in the field below while he caught his breath. The cop had gone down close enough to a streetlamp that he was at least partially visible.

Little points of light entered the far field and moved in his direction. They were on to him. He reached in his jacket pocket and pulled out the walkie talkie and the pitch pipe. The time had come. He pressed the mic button and blew the pitch pipe while looking up to the police station in the distance.

Nothing. He tried several times, with the same result. He was out of range. He'd never intended to detonate the bomb from this far away. It simply wouldn't work. All the while, the lights moved forward, joined by even more lights. There was no way to move back into range.

He tossed the walkie talkie and pitch pipe. Time to abort the mission. Time to evade capture. He hurried to the east, keeping in the shadows until he reached the park's edge and crossed into Haight Ashbury.

A perfect cover. Just another freak among freaks.

23.

UNION SQUARE

The King thought it a fine day and decided to wade out into the downtown bustle instead of having breakfast in his room at the St. Francis. He left the hotel under a cloudless sky and walked a couple of blocks up Powell Street to Sears Fine Foods. As was the custom, two pink Cadillacs occupied the curb at the establishment's entrance to mark its location. The King admired the cars but admired the promotional ingenuity of management even more. He felt that touches like this separated the winners from the losers in virtually any business. His own experience provided a good example. In several eastern cities he'd created a logo that signaled to customers that they could depend on the purity of his product. When combined with sufficient firepower, it virtually guaranteed his ownership of the local market.

He found himself at a table near the window and ordered Swedish pancakes topped with warm maple syrup. Then he took a sip of coffee and opened the morning edition of the San Francisco Chronicle. A story near the bottom of the front page caught his attention, one sensational enough to merit two columns in width. "Suspect Caught in Hippie Amputation Murder," shouted the headline. The King read on with growing dismay. It informed him that one Larry Boyd, a known acid dealer, had been murdered and robbed in his psychedelic pad on Page Street in Haight Ashbury. The killer had cut off Boyd's right arm and fled north in Boyd's van. He made it as far as the town of Sebastopol, where he was stopped by police, who discovered the severed arm along with a briefcase containing $5,000.

The King looked up from the article. Five thousand? What about the other forty-five thousand? What the fuck? He rapidly reviewed the sequence of events in his dealings with Larry Boyd. It didn't tell him who had the money, but it did tell him who would know: the girl, the one who'd seen all the cash out on the table, the one he'd followed home to that dump on Webster.

It wasn't hard to figure. The girl was the killer's woman and she'd told him about the dealer and the money. The guy had gone back, sliced the dealer, grabbed the money and ran.

The King absently twisted a ring of gold and diamonds on his finger. The arm slice wasn't as crazy at it sounded. He himself had been involved in numerous amputations that served as a warning to competitors. But the money thing seemed very strange. What did he do with the forty-five thousand? Did he stash it for some reason? Did he leave it with the girl?

Based on this news story, he was still one step ahead of the cops. He needed to keep it that way. He and the girl needed to have a little talk. Very soon.

Stone checked the clock on the mantle, a ship's clock that had belonged to his father. It required a biweekly winding with a big key and ticked rather loudly, but he somehow found it a source of comfort. Right now, the hands indicated that it was eleven forty-five, and he hadn't heard from Burke about when to bring Rhonda over. He guessed that the Sergeant was buried and simply spaced it out. Given that the morning was nearly gone, it wouldn't hurt to give him a call.

Stone went to the kitchen counter and fetched the San Francisco phone book and consulted the yellow pages to find the number for the Park Station. He shook his head as he did so. Somebody had to find a better way to retrieve information.

He dialed the number. A woman answered. "Park Station non-emergency," she said in voice both bored and middle-aged.

"Yes, my name's James Stone and I'm calling for Sergeant Burke."

"He's not available right now."

"I see. Could I leave a message?"

"I don't think he's taking messages."

"I was scheduled to see him this morning, but I haven't heard from him. Any suggestions?"

"I'd suggest that you phone back later."

"This involves one of his cases and it's pretty important."

"I'm not familiar with the sergeant's caseload so I can't comment. Sorry."

Stone knew it was time for an end run. "Okay then, could I speak to Sergeant Linehan please?"

"About this same matter?"

"Yes. About this same matter." Stone's patience teetered on the verge of free fall.

"One moment please."

Stone had just enough time to recover his good humor when Linehan picked up. "Linehan here."

"Sergeant, this is James Stone. I spoke with you and Detective Burke yesterday about the Larry Boyd case."

"Stone? Oh yeah. What can I do for you?"

"The sergeant was going to phone me to set up a meeting with a key witness, but I haven't heard from him"

After a long stretch, Linehan responded. "They didn't tell you?"

"Tell me what?"

"Sergeant Burke was involved in a pursuit yesterday evening and had a massive heart attack. They took him to SF General. He's in critical care. With a little luck he'll pull through."

"I'm really sorry. I had no idea," Stone said.

"Not your fault. It's part of a bigger issue, so we've kept a lid on it."

"Understand. In the meantime, I've got a key witness in the Larry Boyd murder who's willing to talk. How do you want to handle it?"

"We're going to try to put as much of his stuff on ice as we can, then reassign the rest. I'd bet that the Boyd murder will be benched, at least for the short run. We've got a self-confessed perpetrator in custody and a ton of incriminating evidence, so it's not at the top of the list."

"Makes sense. If you don't mind, I'd like to keep in touch with you on this thing."

"No problem," Linehan said. "Gotta go. Talk to you later."

Linehan hung up. Stone put down the phone. The clock ticked loudly in the silence. Christine was off to the clinic and Rhonda had retired to the guest room. He looked out the window. The marine layer had burned off and left the neighborhood bathed in glorious summer light.

He got up and headed down the hall to the guest room. Rhonda would be relieved to hear she was temporarily off the hook. He knocked. No answer. He waited a discrete interval and knocked gain. Still no answer. He didn't want to intrude on her privacy. Her whole early adolescence had been one massive intrusion on her privacy. He decided to just open the door a crack and see if he could get her attention.

"Rhonda?"

No reply.

"I talked to the cops and you don't have to see them today. Maybe later, but not now."

Nothing. He opened the door enough that he could see the foot of the bed. Empty. He opened it all the way. She was gone, along with her backpack. All that remained was a hand-written note on the bedside table:

Mr. Stone.

I think you are a good person and so is Christine. I really appreciate you taking me in. But as you said, times have changed, and I think I'm way too old to be leaning on you once again. I can take it from here. Please don't try to contact me. Maybe when this is all over, we can get together. Many thanks.

Rhonda

Stone sighed. Like it or not, he kept returning to this parental theme. How would a father react? Probably not very well.

24.

HUNTERS POINT

Pig Eye caught his reflection in the window of Secure Guns & Ammo as he approached the entrance. Hippie-length hair, dirty jeans, biker boots, leather jacket. It all fit, except for the old blanket wrapped around the rifle, the M16 he'd picked up in the trade with the crazy vet. With a little luck it would now be his ticket to a psychoactive paradise.

Earlier in the day he'd stopped by to see Adam and Hank, two guys he hung out with at the Ball and Chain in Hunters Point. They lived in a little dump across from the shipyards and always had good dope. Sometimes uppers, sometimes downers, but always quality shit. Right now, Pig Eye was in the market for a ride on up. He'd lost his job at the construction supply place because of an altercation with this little spic out in the warehouse. It left him both busted and in an ugly mood. Just the kind of thing a hit or two of speed would throw into the back seat.

Hank and Adam bid him welcome and sat him down on a couch riddled with beer stains and pockmarks that matched the cigarette burns in the rug. Turned out they had just the thing, a little meth crystal tamped into a glass pipe. It was new to Pig Eye, so they let him try a sample, and it was an instant hit. His canopy of gloom sailed off into the forever. Out came the beer, along with a rambling conversation about nothing in particular. At one point in the random discourse Pig Eye noticed Hank twisting a gem-laden golden ring on his finger. He asked about it and learned that it was a bonus of sorts, something from a job they'd done recently up in Marin County, a job for some upscale nigger. The dialogue vectored off to somewhere else before Pig Eye could ask what the job was.

Soon the high wore off, rather abruptly. The gloom crept back in. Pig Eye told the pair he'd like another hit, and they told him that the free ride was over. The next one came at a price. Pig Eye explained that he'd just lost his gig and was temporarily strapped. And since they were all good buddies from down at the bar, maybe they could front him a little. Apparently not. They seemed sympathetic but wouldn't budge. Pig Eye stowed his anger. He wanted more of the same and didn't want to queer the deal. He asked them to set some aside for him. He would make some arrangements. They said of course. Anything for a friend.

Pig Eye pushed through the front door of Secure Guns & Ammo with the rifle wrapped under an old blanket. Not a good move. The proprietor, a dour bespectacled man in his fifties, held up his hand. "Stop. Right there." To back up his command, a large automatic pistol resided in a shoulder holster on his left side.

"What do you have in there?" he asked Pig Eye, pointing at the blanket.

"I got somethin' I want to sell," Pig Eye answered.

The proprietor's his right hand slid down toward the pistol. "Hold it out in front of you with both hands. Walk forward. Place it on the counter. Step back."

Pig Eye did as ordered. The proprietor parted the blanket, stared at the M16 and looked up with a scowl. "This is a combat weapon. You know that?"

"Yeah, I know that."

"Where did you get it?"

"From a friend. He was in the war."

The proprietor gave a skeptical nod. "In the war. Yeah." He picked up the weapon, removed the clip, cocked it and pulled the trigger." The loud click caused Pig Eye to wince inside. This wasn't going well.

"How much you want for it?" the proprietor asked.

"I dunno. Let's say three hundred." He drew the number out of nowhere. The firearms market was a total mystery to him.

"You got any ID?"

Pig Eye realized he was about to cross a threshold. He would no longer be an anonymous customer. The ID would forge an indelible link between himself and the weapon. But the lure of the meth pipe intruded and carried the day. Three hundred dollars would buy a lot of dope. He produced his ID and handed it to the proprietor, who copied his name and license number onto a note pad.

"Just in case," he told Pig Eye. "Just in case something isn't right."

"So, we got a deal?" Pig Eye asked.

"Not quite," the proprietor said. "I've got to give it a little thought."

"How about two hundred?" Pig Eye responded with a hint of desperation.

"This is a fully automatic combat weapon. As such, it's illegal. Did know you that?"

"I wasn't sure."

"Well now you are. I'll be taking a big risk, even if I buy it for five bucks. Bring it back tomorrow about this time and if everything seems right, we'll settle up."

"For three hundred?"

The proprietor nodded in exasperation. "Yes. For three hundred. Now get it out of here before someone sees it."

"Tomorrow," Pig Eye said, and lumbered out the door.

The proprietor watched him disappear around the corner. He picked up the phone and dialed the SFPD. He owed the cops a favor. They'd gone easy with him over a couple of recent transactions that were a little less than lawful. This idiot biker gave him a chance to settle up.

Rhonda stood by the stove in the gloom of her basement apartment. Only one burner still worked, and it held a pan of Top Ramen noodles submerged in boiling water. A fleet of bubbles rose and formed shiny little domes that promptly burst into oblivion.

Fascinating. She'd smoked the last of some hashish Speedo had stashed under the sink, and it cast the bubbles in an entirely new light. Such was life in Haight Ashbury during this special summer. Who needed designer furniture, flashy cars and spendy clothes when you could behold things like this brilliant symphony of exploding bubbles?

She turned off the burner and paused to watch the heating element on its journey from brilliant orange to dull gray. Very interesting. After draining the water into the sink, she plopped the noodles into a cereal bowl and sat down to eat. Time to get serious, whatever that meant. She was close to penniless, unemployed and would soon be homeless. At least the threat of Speedo was absent. As a confessed killer, he wasn't getting out of jail any time soon. What had she seen in him? It no longer mattered.

A knock on the front door.

She put down a string of noodles and stared at it. Now what?

Two more knocks, louder this time. Followed by a muffled male voice from the far side. "Hello! Anybody home?"

She didn't recognize the voice. Two more knocks followed. Whoever it was, they weren't going away. She got up and moved close to the door. "Who is it?" she yelled.

"Pacific Gas. We've got an emergency. We need access."

"Why?"

"There's a leak in the feeder line into the building. We're trying to prevent an explosion."

"What's that got to do with me?"

"The line runs in underneath your unit. We need access to check it out."

"All right, hang on." Under normal circumstances, Rhonda might have been more circumspect. But the last thing she wanted right now was a confrontation with authorities of any stripe. She twisted the dead bolt and started to open the door.

The King completed the motion. He pushed his way on through with an ominous smile. "Pretty good imitation of a white guy, huh?" He shut the door behind him, blocking the way.

"Who are you?" she asked, even though she knew precisely. He was the black guy from Larry's apartment, the guy counting the money.

"I don't believe we've had the pleasure," the King said. "We ran into each other briefly just a while back. It was in the apartment of a young gentleman who is no longer with us. And if I'm not mistaken, you're the girlfriend of the party that killed him."

"What do you want?"

The King guided her toward the small table in the kitchen area. "I want us to reach some kind of accommodation where all parties involved feel good about themselves." He gestured toward a chair. "Have a seat."

"You're in a kind of awkward position here," the King said. "And I appreciate that. I'm sure you feel certain loyalties toward your boyfriend, this Speedo guy. On the other hand, he's gotten you involved in a very bad piece of business. So maybe it's best if you go your own way."

"What do you mean?" Rhonda's life had seldom brought her into contact with black people. The one in front of her was destroying all the stereotypes. He was both intelligent and articulate. Also very scary.

"We both know that you saw all that money out on the table at Mr. Boyd's place. Now it would be very natural to assume that you told your boyfriend about it and that he came back to Mr. Boyd's to claim it for his own." The wicked smile returned. "Along with Mr. Boyd's arm of course."

"I never told him anything. He was too stoned to listen. Yeah, he brought the money back here, but then he took off with it."

"You know, I'm not an accountant by trade," the King said. "But I'm pretty good with basic sums. He left Mr. Boyd's with fifty thousand dollars, but when he was arrested, he had five thousand dollars. Now that leaves forty-five thousand floating loose. And I just have to wonder if you don't know something about where it might have landed. I mean, if not here, then where?"

"I don't know. I don't have any idea. Like I told you, he showed up, waved some money around and left. That's the last I saw of him."

The King's hand darted across the table and grabbed Rhonda's. If felt cool and dry. He started to squeeze and stopped just short of the threshold of pain. "That may be, but it's not the last you're going to see of me. I want my money back. I want it returned in full. If not, justice will be done, and not the kind that involves a court of law. Understand?"

"What do you want me to do? I don't know where it is."

The King got up. "In cases like this the best place to start is close to home. Stay put."

He proceeded to methodically search the small apartment, ripping out drawers, clearing the cupboards, emptying the refrigerator, tearing up the bedding, checking the toilet tank, invading Rhonda's backpack. All in vain.

"See, what did I tell you?" Rhonda said as the King returned to the table. "I don't have it."

The King raised his index finger in correction. "You don't have it here. And it's a very big world out there."

"What do you want me to do?"

The King squeezed her hand again. This time, he exceeded the threshold of pain. "Very simple. Find it and give it back. You might want to confer with your boyfriend about this. Between the two of you I'm sure you can work something out."

"But he's locked up. He's in jail."

"Ever heard of visiting hours? I bet you have. And when you put your pretty heads together, be sure and tell him that bad things can happen in jail. In fact, they happen all the time."

The King let go of her hand, which pulsed from the pain of his grip. He produced a card with a handwritten phone number. "Here's how to find me. And don't worry, I know exactly how to find you. People like me, we own the streets, and the streets never lie."

He got up and stopped when he reached the door. "Forty-five thousand. All of it." He turned to leave, paused and looked back at her. "You know, there's something about you. You've played with the big boys, haven't you?"

"I don't know what you mean," she said.

His obnoxious smile returned. "Oh yes, you do."

Rhonda watched the door shut behind him. The room went silent, broken only by the distant flush of a toilet from the floor above. She surveyed the wreckage caused by his search. Disturbing, but not nearly as troubling as his departing words. He saw right through her. He was right. She had no place to hide, at least not for long.

She began to gather up her things. She was out of here. This time for good.

25.

PARK POLICE STATION

Stone knew something was wrong has soon as he pulled off Kezar Drive in Golden Gate Park to enter the police station. Two armed officers stood guard at the gate to the parking lot. The first made him state his business, which was to meet with Detective Sergeant Linehan. The second got on a handheld radio and relayed his intent to someone inside. After a few moments, the radio squawked an all clear and he entered the parking lot. What the hell had gone wrong here?

Two more officers guarded the front entrance. They instructed him to wait for an escort from inside. A moment later Linehan appeared and shook his hand. "Mr. Stone, come on in. Sorry about all this."

Linehan offered an explanation as they walked down the hall to his desk in a common area with several others. "Hope you don't mind, but we had you checked out."

"I assume that went well," Stone said.

"Indeed it did. The folks down in Bakersfield speak very highly of you."

"Good to hear. So, what's all the fuss about?"

"When I told you about Sergeant Burke, you only got part of the story. He was chasing someone who attempted to blow this place sky high. We found a bomb with enough explosive power to level the whole building. It was rigged for remote detonation but never went off."

"Lucky break," Stone said.

"Very lucky. We've kept it out of the papers. I assume we can count on you to keep it that way."

"Yes, you can."

"There's a lot of nut cases in this town, and we don't want anyone to take a hint," Linehan explained.

"Absolutely," Stone responded. "How's Sergeant Burke?"

"The good news is he's going to pull through. The bad news is that it's going to take a while. Like I told you, we've prioritized his cases with the DA. The Larry Boyd case has dropped down the list. We've got the suspect in custody and plenty of evidence."

"That's probably just as well. I came by to update you on the suspect's girlfriend. I've lost contact with her."

"Too bad," Linehan said. "Know where we can find her?"

"Not right now. But I think it's a pretty good bet she's out on the street somewhere in Haight Ashbury."

Linehan had to chuckle. "Her and a few thousand of her new best friends."

Stone shrugged. "Could be."

Linehan looked at his watch. "I gotta go." He paused. "I think you should know that there's other things going on with this case. Things you won't see on paper."

"Oh?" Stone said. "Like what?"

"Let's keep in touch," he advised Stone. "I get a little time, maybe we can talk about it."

"I'm around," Stone said.

"Good. See you later."

The white man shifted his weight on the park bench to better accommodate his bulk. "You know what I think?" he told the King. "I think the snake's going to take him out."

"You think so, huh?" The King said. They were both observing the conflict atop Rideout Fountain, a battle frozen in sandstone between the big cat and fanged serpent.

"The snake's got him coiled. All it needs to do is bite his head."

"Yeah, but when it goes to bite, the cat will have a clean shot at its neck."

"And so on," the man said. "It never ends, does it?"

"No, it does not," the King replied.

"You realize that I'm personally responsible for the investment we've made in your enterprise."

"I do."

"And that you are responsible for any losses that we incur in the process?"

"I do." In truth, the King could easily absorb a loss of fifty thousand dollars. His liability was more a point of pride, an insult to his business acumen. He also knew that, in this case, it was highly advisable to keep the hurt to himself. "The way I see it, we've had a temporary setback, but nothing that will compromise our overall strategy."

"I'm glad to hear that," the man said. "I truly am."

The King sincerely doubted that. But it didn't matter. They had a history of overlapping interests that kept them on a common track. The payoff promised to be substantial, maybe even global in scope.

26.

THE PANHANDLE

Rhonda sat cross-legged on the freshly mown grass midway through the Panhandle. A girl named Sunshine sat opposite and passed her a dying roach for one last toke. They had met a few weeks back in the meadow at the bottom of Hippie Hill. Several bands were performing a free concert, none of them very good, but a few puffs of premium-grade weed fixed all that. The groups played atop a makeshift plywood stage, with the Hell's Angels guarding their PA system because of previous rip-offs at this same venue. The music, the sun and the gentle marine breeze cast the scene in a most pleasant light. Sunshine swayed to rhythm and spoke freely of her origins.

She had arrived last month from a small island in Puget Sound, where her dad fished and her mother drank. With her fair skin, blues eyes and natural blonde hair, she looked to be of Scandinavian extraction. She'd taken off on a whim with her boyfriend, who planned to play in a band. He didn't know which instrument yet, but that was a petty detail compared to his grand vision of ascendance to a nearly mythical level of artistry. They'd hitchhiked down the interstate, but a few weeks after their arrival, had somehow lost track of each other in a dense cloud of drug-induced ambiguity. No matter. They were both beautiful people in a beautiful world.

'So, where's your boyfriend?" Sunshine asked.

"He's not around anymore," Rhonda volunteered.

"It's okay. You're beautiful. It always helps to be beautiful."

"Thanks," Rhonda said. She found it encouraging. Sunshine was maybe eighteen; she herself was going on twenty-four. A little doubt was starting to intrude.

Sunshine took one last toke and stubbed the roach. She wore sweatpants and a T-shirt underneath a thin cotton jacket. "It's almost time," she said.

"Time for what?"

"Time to eat," she replied.

It reminded Rhonda of her precarious financial situation. "I'm gonna pass," she said. "I'm a little short on bread right now."

"Not a problem," Sunshine said. "It's free."

"Free?" Rhonda asked skeptically,

"Yeah, free. Everything's free. Only most people don't know it yet."

Rhonda passed this comment off to the fact that Sunshine had just smoked a little dope. "So where do we go for this?"

Sunshine came to her feet. "Follow me."

They walked two blocks west through the Panhandle. A block ahead, Rhonda saw a small crowd assembling on the lawn. Upon arrival, each person stepped through a yellow wooden frame of some kind. It stood upright and looked large enough to accommodate people of any reasonable size.

"What's that yellow thing?" Rhonda asked.

"It's the frame of reference," Sunshine said. "If you want to eat, you have to step through it."

"How come?"

"It's supposed to change your point of view," Sunshine answered. "Once you go through, you can see the world in a different kind of way."

"Who built this thing?" Rhonda asked.

"The Diggers. It's totally their trip."

"Does it work?"

Sunshine shrugged. "It works for me. That's all that counts, I guess."

Rhonda abandoned her line of inquiry as they approached the frame. It seemed a small request for a free meal. She followed

Sunshine to where a ragtag line had formed. A second smaller line ran parallel, backed by an assortment of boxes and containers. It was populated by people doling out various food items to those in the receiving line.

A slender bespectacled man handed her a paper plate and some plastic utensils. She moved on to where a teenaged girl was ladling a stew of meat chunks and beans out of a large metal pail. Further on, a young man fished pieces of day-old bread out of a cardboard box. In all, maybe a hundred people were being fed.

Rhonda and Sunshine found a vacant spot to sit and consume their meal. Around them little was said. Hunger carried the moment. It made Rhonda realize how famished she was now that her nerves had abated. When finished, they tossed their plates and utensils into a waiting garbage pail.

"Let's go check out the scene," Sunshine said.

"What scene?"

"You'll see," Sunshine said with a knowing smile. They threaded their way through the diners to the curb at the edge of the park. An old Ford pickup sat parked at the curb, with two women in the bed arranging boxes and large steel milk cans. One looked up at their approach. "Hey Sunshine," she greeted them.

"Nicole," Sunshine said. "How's it going?" Nicole looked to be in her late twenties and wore a paisley print dress that exposed a very shapely pair of legs. Communal sexuality, Rhonda thought, a real contradiction in terms. An air of authority hung over the woman.

"Just hangin'," Sunshine replied. "This is Rhonda."

"Rhonda, hello," Nicole said. "We're going to make a run by the store. Want a ride?"

"Yeah, sure," Sunshine said and turned to Rhonda. "You coming?"

"Yeah, I guess so." Rhonda decided it was one those times when it was best just to go with the flow.

Nicole and the other woman hopped out of the bed and into the cab, leaving room for Sunshine and Rhonda. "Pretty groovy, huh? Free ride, free everything," Sunshine remarked.

As Rhonda attempted to make sense of this cockeyed proposition, a young man showed up and opened the door on the driver's side. He had Jesus-like hair parted in the middle that fell to his shoulders. "Sunshine!" he said. "Hey babe. Peace."

"Crazy Johnny, same to you," Sunshine replied. He climbed into the cab, started the engine, and they took off. Seated backward in the bed, Rhonda watched the blocks recede behind them, and took comfort in it. It suggested that she was putting ever more distance herself and the King and Speedo. They cruised down Oak Street for a few blocks and turned south onto Clayton. After about a half dozen blocks, they stopped and backed into the driveway of an apartment. Crazy Johnny hopped out and opened the garage door, which exposed the distinctive odors of fresh cooking. "Alright, let's get this stuff into the garage," Nicole said as Rhonda and Sunshine jumped out of the bed.

"You don't have to if you don't want to," Sunshine whispered to Rhonda. "Everybody's free to do their own thing. That's the way the Diggers work. It's really far out."

Rhonda had to agree, but figured that she was in their debt for the free meal and pitched in. When the boxes and cans were stowed, Crazy Johnny took off back to the Panhandle and the women climbed the stairs from the garage to the first floor. They entered a kitchen area that verged on utter chaos. A dozen women had taken on the task of converting assorted boxes of produce into edible meals. Peeling oranges, skinning potatoes, dicing raw meat, paring apples, cutting peppers. No one seemed in charge, but the entire scene had a sense of direction and purpose. Two women stuffed a brownish dough into coffee cans and placed them in a waiting oven. "Whole wheat bread," Nicole explained to Rhonda. "It's actually good for you." Others poured meat chunks, cut vegetables and beans into big pots of boiling water. Rhonda guessed correctly that they were prepping the essence of tomorrow's handout in the park.

A large open space lay beyond the kitchen, what once might have been a living room. No longer. A random sprawl of sleeping gear covered the bare wooden floor. Pads, cushions, sleeping bags, air mattresses. They formed little islands inhabited by people talking, smoking, staring, singing, playing guitars.

"You heard about crash pads, right?" Sunshine said to Rhonda. "Well here you go. Pretty cool, huh?"

In fact, it reminded Rhonda of scenes from refugee camps somewhere on the far side of the world. However, it did offer the benefit of safety in numbers, something of prime importance to her right now.

They threaded their way through the room and a thin blue haze of pot smoke to a hallway beyond. Rhonda had no idea where they were going, and it no longer mattered. All she could do was surrender to the moment and ride the waves of probability that rolled out endlessly in front of her.

Sunshine turned into what must have once been a bedroom but now held a maze constructed of cardboard partitions. Wild swatches and strokes of color decorated many of them and gave each space its own character. The maze defined a series of sleeping spaces filled with cushions, mattresses and the like. Sunshine led them though to a space with two old cushions and a brown wad of blanket. "We can hang here for a while," Sunshine announced. "Have a seat."

Rhonda sank down onto a cushion and looked at the red and yellow splashes on the cardboard. Were they Sunshine's? Who knew? Who knew anything anymore? She looked up to the ceiling and the naked bulb that shone down from an ancient fixture of scrolled bronze. Its light fell in a dismal cast that left her anxious and sad.

"Want to crash here tonight?" Sunshine asked.

"Why not," Rhonda answered. Where else was there? Nowhere.

"Hang tight. I'll find you some stuff." Sunshine left their partition and drifted to some other part of the floor beyond view. Rhonda closed her eyes and let the room talk to her. It spoke with a soft buzz of dialogue, a trickle of laughter and a few rogue guitar notes. Sunshine soon returned with a worn pillow and an inflatable air mattress. "Here you go," she said.

"Where'd this come from?" Rhonda asked.

"Somewhere over there," Sunshine said, pointing to the left.

"You mean from someone else's space?"

Sunshine's face took on an odd mixture of patience and exasperation. "Nobody owns any space. It's all free. All the time."

"What about this stuff?"

"Same thing."

"What are they supposed to do when they find it's gone?"

"They just go and find more stuff, free stuff. That's the way it works. Can you dig it?"

"I'll try," Rhonda promised. This was someone else's world, someone else's rules. Best to just go along.

"Groovy." Sunshine reached into her jacket pocket and pulled out a small pipe. "Let's have a little hit so we can get settled in."

They did just that and Sunshine reclined onto her cushions in blissful repose. Rhonda looked out over the tops of the cardboard partitions to the other inhabitants, who were only partially visible. Many heads rocked and swayed to an inaudible rhythm. As she speculated on how that might be possible, a male figure appeared in the doorway and calmly surveyed the scene with pale blue eyes. He looked to be in his mid-twenties, with an angular face topped by a tidal wave of dark brown hair that broke to the right. He took a drag on an unfiltered cigarette and exhaled a thin blue fog. The buzz in the room subsided by several degrees in acknowledgement.

Alpha. Rhonda knew it immediately. She had a nearly flawless instinct for detecting it, all the way back to Bakersfield. The nexus of power, the focus of influence, the magnet of attention.

"Who's that?" she asked Sunshine.

Sunshine propped herself up for a look. "Oh, that's Emmet."

"Emmet?"

"Emmet Grogan," Sunshine answered. "He started all this."

"He did?" She knew intuitively that beneath this supposedly classless society a submerged hierarchy existed, the same one found throughout the entirety of human existence. Emmet was the unspoken, undeclared leader, but the leader, nevertheless. From lizards all the way up the evolutionary ladder to humans the game remained the same. Everyone here might do their own thing, but in some intangible way it also happened to be Emmet's thing.

Emmet's hooded eyes caught hers. They lingered only for an instant, but long enough that she knew he was hers for the taking. Rhonda turned to Sunshine. "Does he have an old lady?"

"We're all his old lady if we want to be," she answered. "He's for free."

Rhonda sincerely doubted this. "Where did he come from?"

"From New York. They say he used to be a burglar there. He ripped off rich people who had way more than they needed. Even back then he knew that everything was supposed to be free."

Grogan took one last drag on his cigarette and walked off. Rhonda considered her options. She was on the run, and he was a highly visible figure whether he liked it or not. If she became entangled with him, she would share this visibility. And as her pursuer had said, the streets don't lie.

Things might change, but for now it seemed best to go hunting elsewhere.

27.

HUNTERS POINT

"Pig Eye," the good cop said. "That's what they call you, right?"

"Yeah, that's what they call me," Pig Eye affirmed. Sweat trickled down his back under his dirty T-shirt. It pooled in the crease of his belly overhang. Was it some kind of cop trick? Is that why they cranked up the heat in the interrogation room here at Hunters Point?

"You know what Pig Eye means?" the bad cop said. "It means you're a bullshitter. So just how did you wind up with a name like that? I gotta wonder."

"Now look," the good cop said in a reasonable tone, "we just went through that Miranda shit with you. All that crap about having a lawyer here. But you know what the problem is with that?"

"What?" Pig Eye asked. He had no idea. All he knew was that the gun dealer ratted him out.

"If you want a lawyer here, we know exactly what's going down," the good cop went on. "You're guilty as hell. And then the DA is going to smell blood. And then you're in truly deep shit." He paused and smiled sympathetically. "But it doesn't have to be that way. Maybe we can settle up with you right here."

"You better hope so," the bad cop added. "We're not talking about just any old gun. We're talking about a genuine combat weapon. And you know what? That brings in the feds. And when it's all done, that means federal prison and no parole. Real hard time. You ever done any real hard time, Pig Eye? I bet not. You're just a little punk with a big bike."

"Your patch says Hells Angels," the good cop added, feigning genuine interest. "That who you're riding with?"

"That's right," Pig Eye confirmed.

"They have anything to do with this?" the bad cop asked.

"They didn't have shit to do with this," Pig Eye said defensively. They were starting to fuck with his tribe.

The good cop sensed his mood shift. "Okay let's back off and go over this thing from the beginning. You meet this guy at the bar. Says he's a Vietnam vet. You make some kind of deal with him and wind up with a real honest-to-God M16 rifle. How am I doing?"

"Yeah, that's about it."

The good cop sighed. "I gotta tell you, Pig Eye, it's a little thin."

"What do you mean?" Pig Eye asked.

"He means, like, how much did you pay for it?" the bad cop intrudes. "And just who was this guy and how did he wind up with it. Stuff like that."

"Yeah," the good cop agreed. "Stuff like that."

Pig Eye feels the heat, feels the pressure. The room contracts. His breath grows short. His heart labors. He fights to stay on top. It should have never come to this. He was just another guy on his bike in the park, listening to some of that hippie music shit. Then he started talking with this guy about Vietnam. Turned out the guy had an M16. Very cool. A deal was cooked up. And now here he was, in the Hunters Point Police Station, looking at God knows how much hard time. Worse yet, these guys were holding all the chips. He had nothing to bargain with.

But wait. Maybe not.

"What if there's something else going on?" he asked the good cop.

"What do you mean, something else?" the bad cop asked.

"I mean there's things I know about another case, a big one. Way bigger than this one. Maybe I could help with that one and this one could kind of go away," he ventured.

The two cops looked at each other. The good one spoke first. "Let's just say we're reasonable men, Pig Eye. You help us and we'll help you. As best we can."

Pig Eye didn't like the qualifier on the end, but sensed it was the best he could get. "Okay."

The cops visibly relaxed. "How about a little water?" the good one asked.

"Sure."

The good cop left the room. For the first time, the bad one smiled at him. "You're doing the right thing, buddy."

Pig Eye thought so, too. Fuck Hank and Adam. His singular loyalty was to the Hells Angels and Sonny Barger. Anyone else didn't really matter.

The good cop returned with a paper cup full of water. Pig Eye gulped it down and sat back.

"A big case, huh?" the bad cop said. "And just what case might that be?"

"There was this thing on the news about a murder in Marin County. It said they found this dead acid dealer in a sleeping bag hanging off a cliff."

"Go on," the good cop encouraged.

"There's a couple of guys that hang out down at The Ball and Chain. Small-time dope dealers. Hank and Adam."

The good cop scribbled on a note pad. "Last names?" he asked without looking up.

"Don't know. Never asked. Anyway, a couple of days ago I went over to their pad to hang out. We got a little high on speed and did a little talking. I noticed that Adam was wearing a big flashy gold ring. It was new."

"How'd you know that?" the bad cop asked.

"I used to watch him play pool. I would've seen it."

"This is good," the good cop said with an affirmative nod. "Go on."

"I asked him where he got it. He said it was a kind of bonus for this job they'd done up in Marin County."

"Job? What kind of job?"

"Didn't say. All he said was that it was for some big-time spade here in the city."

Silence. The cops stared at him expectantly.

Pig Eye shrugged. "That's my tale, man. That's the whole deal."

"You got an address for these guys?" the bad cop asked.

"It's this dump at the end of Hudson Avenue. You can't miss it."

The cops both got up. "We'll check it out. If you've been straight with us, we'll talk to the DA and see what we can do. Deal?"

"Deal," Pig Eye responded. As if there were some choice.

"You're kidding me," Jerry Garcia said to Stone. "You hung out with Merle Haggard and Roy Nichols? That's fantastic! Those are some heavy dudes, man."

Stone found Jerry's reaction amusing. A lot of people would have been shocked that someone out on the far electric edge would be so enamored of a couple of shitkickers from the San Joaquin Valley. But not Stone. In a time when most players were following the screaming path of distortion blazed by Jimi Hendrix, Garcia mostly stuck to a clear, bell-like guitar sound very reminiscent of Haggard and Nichols. He'd obviously been a student of these guys.

Stone and Garcia were standing backstage at the Fillmore Auditorium, where Stone was a guest of promoter Bill Graham. The Grateful Dead had just finished an extended set that included a twenty-five-minute version of "Dark Star" that sent the audience into transcendental rapture.

"Haggard and Nichols, yeah. It was a long time ago," Stone explained to Garcia. "They were kicking around in a bunch of honky-tonks down in the valley. But even then, you could hear something special. They had that certain sound, and it was definitely all their own."

"Just imagine what it would be like if those guys got stoned on acid," Garcia said. "You couldn't touch 'em. They'd blow you away, man."

"Maybe so," Stone said diplomatically. He had his doubts. Alcohol reigned supreme in the country scene, along with a sprinkling of amphetamines. No one was looking to blow on through the doors of perception.

"Sorry I missed a chance to work with you," Stone added. "You happy with Warner?" The Grateful Dead was one of his major regrets. Warner Brothers had snapped them up late last year and already had an album out.

"I dunno," Garcia said. "I mean, how happy can you be with a big record company?"

Stone nodded. The Dead's resistance to big-time capitalism was well established. He was surprised that they hadn't struck out on their own. In the end they probably would do just that. To these guys, Capitol and Stone were just another big record company.

Bill Graham, the Fillmore's owner, walked up. He always seemed to be in a hurry, and right now was no exception. "Five minutes," he said to Garcia. "You're on again in five."

"Right on," Garcia said with a knowing smile. "Let me see what I can do about that."

Graham turned to Stone. "Know what? I was just out front and saw some stoners hanging on the sidewalk. Now I'm okay with that, but then one of 'em starts to hassle me about why I charge money for the music. And you know what I tell 'em? I tell 'em if wasn't for me and the money, there wouldn't be any music." He paused and scratched his thick curly hair. In truth, he looked more like a prizefighter that an impresario of the avant garde. He sighed. "I love this fuckin' music. I really do. And I love the people who make it. But that's got nothing to do with paying the electric bill. Know what I mean?"

"Yes, I do," Stone said.

"Enjoy the show," Graham said, and went off to whatever the next crisis might be.

Stone stepped forward and peeked around the curtain at the audience. For no good reason, he wondered if Rhonda was out there. With this Speedo maniac locked up, she was in no immediate danger and could start getting on with her life. But what kind of life would that be? He hoped it was a good one. After all she'd been through in her formative years, she deserved it.

But his forty-plus times around the sun had taught him a sad lesson. People didn't get what they deserved. People got what they got. Life was basically a roulette wheel.

Out on the stage the Dead launched into "Viola Lee Blues," and he let it take him to a better place.

In the end that's what good music was all about.

28.

CLAYTON ST.

"It's really easy," Morning Dew told Rhonda. "You don't have to say anything. All you gotta do is be hot."

The communal pickup truck had just pulled to the curb on the block occupied by a company called United Produce Distributors. Morning Dew was a friend of Sunshine, or so it seemed. She had joined them to form an expeditionary force into the south Mission District on this dull, overcast morning governed by a pewter sky. Crazy Johnny rounded out the group and remained behind the wheel in the cab, discretely out of sight.

The three women hopped out of the bed and started down the block toward a ground-level shipping dock. Morning Dew and Sunshine both wore short dresses that generously exposed their youthful legs. They giggled fitfully as they approached the open dock.

A man in his forties appeared at the opening, wearing an apron and a hard hat. Behind him Rhonda could see stacks of produce boxes filled with all manner of vegetables. His dark hair and olive skin suggested he was of Italian descent. His eyes immediately strayed to the exposed flesh before looking back up.

"Good morning, ladies!" he exclaimed. "So good to see you."

"And it's good to see you," Morning Dew said. "It's always good to see you."

"Know what?" he said with hybrid grin and leer. "I bet I got what you want."

"You sure about that?" Morning Dew teased.

"Want to find out?" he asked.

"Maybe some time," she said. "But right now, we need a little help feeding the poor." Rhonda noticed she didn't refer to the hippies. They remained something less than venerated in the blue-collar universe.

The produce man looked back toward the stacks of boxes. "Well, let's see what we got here." He moved to a stack toward the wall. "Oh yeah. This stuff's a little on the rough side. Edible but ugly."

"That would be just perfect!" Sunshine exclaimed with girlish enthusiasm.

"Well then let's do it," the man said. He lifted the top box off the stack and moved it to the edge of the loading dock. Rhonda could see the pale purple of beets. The man looked down the block to the parked pickup and knew exactly what the score was. "Let's cut the bullshit. Tell your buddy to come around and back in."

"You are so nice," Morning Dew told him.

The man ate it up. "Nothing to it. Let's move along."

Ten minutes later, the three women squeezed themselves in between cardboard produce boxes as Crazy Johnny drove on out of the Mission. Warped beets, wilted iceberg lettuce, deformed potatoes, flaked onions, and drooping celery. All dying, but not yet dead.

"Who does the recipes?" Rhonda asked.

"Nobody," Morning Dew said. "We just make it up as we go along."

Crazy Johnny backed the pickup into the driveway at the Clayton Street house, and they all carried the boxes of produce up the steps and into the kitchen. Nicole, the oldest of the kitchen crew, nodded in approval. "Nice haul," she said.

Rhonda noticed that while much sleeping gear remained in the main room, many of the owners were absent. "Where did everybody go?" she asked Sunshine.

"Wherever they want," she said. "Everybody does their own thing."

Rhonda found that this slogan was beginning to grind on her. She'd just have to bear it until she found some way forward.

"If it's a nice day, they probably hit the park to score a little weed or acid," she added. "Then they make it to the Panhandle to eat around four. After that they hang out on Haight Street and then come back here to crash. It can be a really beautiful life if you let it."

Rhonda thought otherwise but turned her attention toward the kitchen, where a dozen or more women were starting to process the incoming produce. "I don't see any guys around here," she commented.

Her remark caught the attention of Nicole, who said "No, you don't. They're all out thinking higher thoughts. Isn't that nice?"

Rhonda sensed a generous portion of vitriol in her remark. Once again Sunshine's utopian model of everybody doing their own thing didn't seem to apply. Your thing apparently depended on your gender.

"You mean you don't have any say in what's going down?" she asked. The question caused several of the women to look her way and then turn to Nicole, their apparent spokesperson.

"Oh yeah," Nicole said. "We got power, and it's not just pussy power."

As if on cue, a group of small children toddled down the stairs from the second story.

"It's called Aid to Dependent Children," she went on. "When the welfare checks show up, they're not made out to John Doe. They're made out to Jane Doe. We let the money do the talking."

"Is that how you pay the rent?" Rhonda asked.

"Sometimes," Nicole said. "We also got some trust fund people."

"How does a trust fund work?" Rhonda had heard the phrase, but it always dwelled in some vaporous legal domain far removed from her daily life.

"It means you've got rich parents or relatives or something. They take a bunch of bread and put it in this thing like a bank account. You get to take it out, but not all at once, so you can't do anything really stupid."

"Sounds pretty cool," Rhonda remarked.

"All depends on what you do with it. If you help out with the rent here, then that's pretty cool."

Rather than wander around exposed on the streets, Rhonda decided to stick around and help in the kitchen. Nicole had a bit of hard edge that she could relate to, and other women told her assorted tales of their pre-Digger lives. Most came from elsewhere, some all the way from the east coast. They told of relationships gone wrong, abusive fathers, errant mothers and alcoholic uncles. Also of unadulterated wanderlust, the liberation of pure adventure and the quest for some undefined utopian ideal.

As evening approached and twilight graced the windows, she grew restless and decided to venture out for a bit. She stepped onto the porch and looked across the street to the west. The glow of sunset cast the houses across the way into partial silhouette. She started to descend the steps, which looked down on the communal pickup parked in the driveway. From this angle she had a view into the passenger seat, and it took her back ten years. It held a plastic bag of white powder, rubber tubing, a charred spoon, and a hypodermic needle. All the major players in the life of a confirmed junkie.

She slowed her descent and her eyes adjusted to the fading light, which revealed a limp forearm resting on a thigh dressed in worn corduroy. A few more steps gave her a clear view of the person in the driver's seat. Emmet Grogan. His motionless head tilted backward, his eyes closed and his mouth partially open sucking in the evening air. An alpha addict. An ideal archetype of the high brought low, of the precipitous fall from grace. Still, she sensed a mythical air of dignity about this magnificently flawed man. It only heightened her attraction to him.

Stone and Christine sat atop a shallow rise of dunes between the highway and the beach near Judah Street, a short walk from their rental. The sun had left a thin splash of high cloud after its descent into the ocean.

"So, what have we heard about Rhonda?" Christine asked.

"Nothing," Stone said.

They lapsed back into silence. Near the water's edge a woman walked a small dog, which tugged energetically against the restraint of its leash.

"There's something I have to know," Christine said.

"What's that?"

"Are you attracted to her?"

"No." It was the truth. If it had been a lie, he would've had to pause and think about it. "Did you think I might be?"

"Of course. She's not thirteen anymore. She's a fully realized woman."

Stone shook his head. "That's not the way I see her. To me, she's still a child. Probably always will be."

"Well, James Stone, that's very good to hear."

Stone always marveled at Christine's grace under pressure. Tonight was no exception. He leaned over and gave her a kiss. "Sorry. You're in a league of your own."

"I damn well better be."

"So, what do you think?" he asked her. "Should we just write her off?"

"Depends. I mean, what else can be done?"

"She could still be in a jam on account of this Speedo character. If she gets the wrong guy at the DA's office, they might try to tie her in as an accomplice."

"You really think so?"

"Not likely, but definitely possible."

"So, what can you do?"

"I don't know. I guess I could find out who Speedo's attorney is and check on how he sees this thing going down."

"Well then, there you go."

"Yeah, there I go," he said with a wry smile.

29.

DOWNTOWN

"Mr. Stone, right? Okay, tell me again about your interest in the Dalberg case."

Stone sat in a very small meeting room with one Gerald Rifkin, an attorney with the San Francisco Public Defenders Office. He wore a tweed jacket with a knit tie around a scrawny neck topped by a dour face and partially bald head. Before showing up here at the Hall of Justice on Bryant Street, Stone had read all the press accounts of Mr. Eric Dalberg, aka Speedo, he of the now famous severed arm. The Office had appointed Mr. Rifkin as the public defender in the case. He seemed none too happy about it.

"I'm a friend of a woman named Rhonda Savage," Stone started out.

Rifkin cut him off. "Ah yes, Rhonda Savage. The police report states that she was in a domestic relationship with Mr. Dalberg at the time of the alleged crime. So what?"

"I know this may seem a little odd, but she's very concerned about him. I have a background in law enforcement, so she asked if I could find out how he's doing."

"Law enforcement? What kind of law enforcement?"

"I was a homicide detective in Bakersfield."

"Homicide, huh? Good. Then you know what I'm up against." Rifkin leaned forward. "Okay here's the deal. First, my client is a hippie. Strike One. Second, my client was a stoned hippie at the time of the crime. Strike Two. Third, my client admitted his

complicity in the murder to two reporters from the *Examiner*.
Strike Three and Out. Got it?"

"Got it." Stone responded. "Tell me this. What are the odds
that the cops will charge Miss Savage as an accomplice?"

"Zero. They want her as a friendly witness because of the
arm and the money. Besides, the whole thing has slid back to the
caboose because of that cop's heart attack out at the Park Station."

"I assume you've met with Mr. Dalberg, right?" Stone asked.

"Yeah. He's either crazy or the best actor in years. Either way,
we're looking at an insanity plea, which is a real pain in the ass."

"Yes, it is," Stone said. Insanity pleas often became long drawn-
out affairs, with tons of testimony and reams of paperwork. Rifkin
clearly thought his time better spent elsewhere.

He leaned back and lifted his arms in resignation. "Find out for
yourself. Go see him. Talk to him. You can't do any more damage
than what's already been done. Good luck."

Hank could see the cat perched up on a joist in the old garage next
to their rental on Hudson Street. It stared down at him in con-
tempt with yellow eyes set in a large head with tufted ears.

"Go get the fuckin' slingshot," he ordered Adam, who stood
behind him on the oily dirt.

"Yeah," Adam grinned. "Now we're talkin'!'"

While he waited for Adam's return, Hank examined the red fur-
rows plowed into the back of his right hand. The cat had fucked
him up. And for no good reason. All he'd wanted to do was see
how far he could throw it across the yard. As soon he picked it up
and cocked his arm, the cat went nuts and cut into him.

And now the wounds had turned angry and burned and itched
at the same time. A very unpleasant combination. Revenge was
called for. So said the major hit of amphetamines they'd consumed
a short time before.

Adam returned with the slingshot. "What you gonna use for
ammo?" he asked.

Hank hadn't thought that far ahead. The speed had shrunk
his time horizon to almost zero. That and a few beers to balance

things out. He took a quick look around the garage, where the door was open to the cloudy morning. "There's some ball bearings over in the cabinet," he told Adam.

"Right on," Adam said and went to fetch them. "What do we do when we get it down?"

"We're gonna skin the fucker," Hank said. "We're gonna skin it alive."

"Wow," Adam said. "Never seen that."

"Well now you're gonna," Hank replied as Adam handed him a ball bearing. "Here's what you do. Go get the garbage can. Put it under the cat. Take the lid off. I'll shoot the fucker and knock it off its perch into the can. Then you slam the lid back on."

"And then what?"

"Then we let it go nuts for a while. When it's all done in, we take a baseball bat to it. That'll soften it up so we can tie it up and go to work."

"Hey, good plan dude," Adam said. "Let's have another hit first, okay?"

"Yeah, sure," Hank said. "But let's get the fucker into the can first. Then we're all set up." The throb from his wounded hand kept creeping ever higher up his arm. "Go get the can. I'll keep him cornered."

Adam walked out into the daylight and took the lid off a nearby garbage can made of galvanized metal. "There's already some shit in here," he yelled back to Hank.

"Well then dump it out and we'll deal with it later. Let's get going."

Adam dumped the contents onto the rear of the gravel driveway and brought the can into the garage. "This is gonna be pretty cool," he said as he placed it under the cat's overhead perch.

"Yes, it is," Hank agreed as he planted the ball bearing in the leather patch on the slingshot. He stretched the rubber tubing to test the tension. "Okay here we go."

A sudden crunch of gravel caught their attention. Two cop cars pulled into the driveway, one of them unmarked. A pair of detectives got out, sports coats open and shoulder holsters exposed.

"Aw shit," Hank said. He dropped the slingshot. The ball bearing rolled loose and dug a little track in the dirt. In a blur, the cat shot along the joist, leaped down and disappeared outside.

Two patrolmen with shotguns now backed up the detectives. "Adam Wren and Hank Foster," the first detective said. "We're placing you under arrest on suspicion of murder." He pulled out a small book and read them their Miranda rights. It was a new routine, and he needed to make sure they got it right. "Now step forward with your hands up."

As the detectives came closer, the second one noticed the nasty red gouges on Hank's hand. "Jesus!" he exclaimed. "How in the fuck did you do that?"

"Nuthin'," Hank mumbled. As the pain burned on up his arm, the dead black guy in Marin burned up to the surface of his thinking.

You didn't have to be a lawyer to know that they were in really big trouble.

30.

FREDERICK ST.

"Timing is everything," Crazy Johnny told Rhonda. "You watch, you listen and then you move."

They sat in the cab of the communal pickup, which smelled of stale tobacco smoke baked into the headliner, a legacy inherited from previous owners. Moments before, a delivery truck from a meat distributor had pulled into a service area behind the grocery store across the street. Now it came to a stop beside a loading entrance with a steel rolling door. The driver got out and pressed a button in the wall.

"Okay, now we go," Johnny ordered Sunshine, who was driving. As he spoke, the steel door rumbled open and the driver headed to the back of the truck.

Sunshine started the pickup and pulled it across the street to the edge of the service area. As she stopped, the delivery driver pulled his truck's rear door open. Inside, beef carcasses hung from hooks in the roof. Big slabs of red meat embedded in white bone. The floor held boxes full of smaller cuts.

The driver stepped in and hoisted a carcass onto his back, which unhooked it from the roof. He moved back out, his knees slightly buckled from the load, and started toward the loading door.

"Right now," Crazy Johnny said. He got out of the cab and sprinted toward the loading area. By the time he arrived, the driver had disappeared inside. Johnny yanked a sizable cut of meat from one of the boxes and ran back to where they were parked. He pitched the meat into the bed, vaulted in behind it and delivered a single thump on the rear window. Sunshine took the cue and pulled away. The deed was done.

Rhonda started to relax. When she came along for the ride, she assumed it would be like yesterday's produce run, where a small investment in charm yielded a sizable cache of free food. No one had told her that this trip would involve outright banditry. She turned to Sunshine, who pushed the floor shift up a gear on the way back to Haight Ashbury.

"That was a rip-off, it was a pure rip-off," she said. "We could've been busted."

"There is no such thing as a rip-off," Sunshine explained with a dreamy smile. "You can only have rip-offs when people own things. And nobody really owns anything, you see. We're way past that."

"You might be," Rhonda retorted. "But not the cops."

"Emmet says that the cops are the soldiers of greed," Sunshine responded. "So they don't count."

Rhonda didn't reply. In her world the cops counted in a very big way. Especially given the mess with Speedo and Larry the dead acid dealer.

"You may find yourself falling into a tunnel, a place of darkness where all hope is extinguished. But if you truly surrender to the power of your reordered synapses, a light appears, distant but unmistakable. You see it as a beacon and are drawn inexorably toward it. But the light at the end of the tunnel is not the true light, and now we come to the essence of your journey. Because beyond the light you enter into infinite space and all of its multiple manifolds..."

Rhonda and Sunshine sat cross-legged on the floor of the Fredrick Street Free Frame, with dozens of Diggers and non-Diggers alike. The distinction was minimal because all points of view were embraced without bias in any given direction. Folding tables with great heaps of used clothing lined the walls, free for the taking as well as the giving.

The speaker was Timothy Leary, he of local renown as the supreme prophet of LSD. A necklace of small shells hung around his neck and a solitary flower pieced his gray hair. He wore a shirt and pants of loose cotton, in the style of an Indian mystic. He spoke with a calm conviction and mildly amused manner that suggested he was the keeper of a vast store of spiritual knowledge slightly beyond mortal reach.

"...And so, at some point, you start to realize just how vapid life has become within the modern American empire. The TV screams at you to buy and buy. The corporations yell at you to work and work so you can buy and buy. And on it goes, like the mythical snake consuming its tail. A circle of mindless consumption..."

The poet Allen Ginsberg sat in the lotus position behind Leary. Unmistakable with his prolific beard, black-frame glasses and pale dome with waterfalls of descending black hair. He nodded in silent assent to Leary's words.

Rhonda did not. To her, Leary came off as a clever salesman pitching a new and novel brand of snake oil, but snake oil, nevertheless. She was not alone. A quick scan of the audience revealed growing discontent. They had decided that in the end, this man was probably a martini-swilling carnivore, just like their dads. A product of Johnny Walker Black and premium tenderloin.

From next to Sunshine a young girl cut into Leary's silken delivery. "You don't turn me on!" she shouted.

Leary, ever the facile pitchman, kept his cool. "Ah, but you see, that's not the point," he told her. "The real question is whether you turn yourself on, whether you..."

The young girl fired back and switched from the singular to the collective. "You don't turn us on! You don't turn us on! You don't turn us on! You don't..."

The crowd caught both the substance and rhythm of it. Soon, the entire room reverberated with the chant. Leary lapsed into silence, desperately searching for a graceful exit. Finally, he raised his arms in concession with an amused grin that seemed to say: When you finally reach my level of personal awareness, you'll come to understand the folly of your ways.

Then he turned to Ginsberg, murmured something and headed for the door, maintaining the same omniscient smile all the way out.

After Leary's ignominious departure, Ginsberg stood and spoke briefly of love and compassion and understanding for all, with the "all" part obviously aimed at Leary. The poet had a pleasing way about him, but the audience was saturated with all the cerebral musing and gradually leaked out the door onto Fredrick Street. Sunshine announced that she was walking over to the Panhandle with some of the others and invited Rhonda, who declined. Digger life afforded little in the way of privacy and she needed a few minutes of quiet repose.

She soon found herself alone on the bare, dusty floor with her future in tatters. She needed breathing space, a respite where she could regroup and find her way. While she found certain aspects of Digger life appealing, it wasn't going to work. She considered going back to Stone and Christine, but that seemed like admitting defeat in her quest for independence. She thought of her dead fiancé and the life she would never live, but she cut it short. Self-pity was okay in small doses but soon turned corrosive.

In the solitude she heard voices. They came from the rear of the building, through a door left slightly ajar. She stood up in alarm and trained her ears toward the sound. Two distinct voices wafted out. One sounded all too familiar. A black voice. The King's voice.

Her pulse headed for the moon. Was it really him? Of all places, why would he be here?

An alarming parade marched through her mind: The King at Larry's. The cash on the table. Dope money for sure. Big time dope money. The paraphernalia in the pickup. The comatose Emmet in the driver's seat. Shot up to the max.

The King was Emmet's connection. One major player to another. Only their context differed. The name of the game was the same. Heroin with a capital H.

Rhonda knew she should flee. Straight out the door and into a cab to Stone and Christine's. But she couldn't. She had to know if the second voice was indeed Emmet's.

She walked quietly across the empty floor to the rear. A table with giant heaps of clothing afforded a view through the door and into the room. She slid in between the wall and the clothing and found a position where she could look in unobserved.

Emmet sat slumped on a metal folding chair facing a small table. The telltale rubber tubing and charred spoon rested on its wooden surface. She couldn't see the King's face, but his hand was visible resting on the table's edge.

"You shouldn't be charging," Emmet said with eyes at half-mast. "It's not about money. You know that, don't you?"

"You mean, hand it out for free?" the King asked.

"Right on."

"Free? Okay, let's talk about free," the King said. "Sometime back, my people came here from Africa. And you know what? They got a free ride! Didn't cost 'em a dime. Just one problem. They never asked for the ride in the first place. And when they got it, they paid for it forever. So maybe free isn't free at all, know what I mean?"

"Things are different now," Emmet protested.

"Yeah, maybe for you," the King countered. "But not for me. Can you dig it? I just work with what I got, and what I got ain't free. So, go figure."

"I'll do that," Emmet promised as he drifted. "Yeah, I'll do that."

Rhonda had heard enough. She slipped out from behind the table and headed for the door. No more Diggers. With Emmet's junk habit, the King would always be hovering in close proximity. She couldn't take the risk.

She walked down Fredrick to Clayton and the crash pad. Once inside, she headed for the cardboard maze in the bedroom and the small space she shared with Sunshine.

Her stuff was gone. All of it.

And why not? It was for free.

31.

SAN BRUNO

San Francisco County Jail #3 was dying. Leaking pipes, crumbling cement, arcing electrical, rusting cells, broken heating and scuffed linoleum. All symptoms of terminal rot and budgetary decay.

Stone did not penetrate far enough to see these flaws. The visitor's center was on the first floor a short distance from the entrance. As a public relations ploy, the county kept it in reasonable repair.

The same could not be said of Eric Dalberg, aka Speedo, who sat on the far side of the glass from him. He was a dirty, disheveled mess, both inside and outside.

Ironically, his first words to Stone were "You don't look good, man. You don't look good at all. What the fuck's wrong?"

"Nothing. I'm fine," Stone answered.

"I knew you'd say that," Speedo said.

"You did? How?"

"Because The Black Angel always lies through his teeth. And you know what? His teeth are made of lead, pure lead."

"So, you think I'm The Black Angel? Is that it?"

"I don't think you're The Black Angel. I know you are." Speedo leaned back, crossed his arms and smiled in utter conviction.

"Well then, why don't you tell me a little bit about myself?"

"You come from the deepest bowels of hell, where the light is totally gone. That's how you got your name."

"But I don't look very black, do I?"

"That's because you put on a people suit. You have a giant closet full of them. Everyone who ever went to hell is hanging there."

Stone decided to play ball. "I could take it off, but it would scare the crap out of you. And that's not what I'm here for."

Speedo warmed to this line of thought. "Then what are you here for?"

"I got a message from up above, where the light is. It's from Capitol Records. They've heard about you and they want me to talk to you."

Speedo softened considerably. He leaned forward. "Capitol Records? About what?"

"They think you've got big potential. They want you to put together a band."

Speedo's wattage now doubled. "I've been writing, you know. All kinds of stuff. I've been writing in my head."

"I know you have," Stone said. "That's why I'm here. You just need a little help to get it where people can hear it. We've got some really good players who've heard about you and they want in."

"Of course they do," Speedo said. "I've got things to say."

"Yes, you do," Stone agreed. "So, we need to start on a plan to get you going."

"Like what?"

"We need to talk about what you're writing, your material."

Speedo squinted suspiciously at Stone. "What for?"

"You know what happened when Johnny Cash took his original stuff to Sam Phillips, the guy who produced the first Elvis records?"

"No."

"He told him it just wasn't good enough. He told him you've got to write from the heart. You're got to write about what's close to you. And we all know what happened, right?"

"Johnny Cash is a fuckin' genius."

"You got it. And so it goes. When you write, stick close to your real life. In your case, that's doubly true. You're a sensation right now. People want to hear your story."

Speedo grew agitated. A twitch developed below his left eye. "Of course they do! It's a story of the devil loose in the world, and how he tried to spread his seed through my woman. It's about a great struggle and how I won out, and how I stole the history in the man's hand."

Stone wasn't sure about the historical hand part, but they were moving in the right direction. "It was about a battle, huh?"

"It was about a battle on a scale you can't even imagine. The stakes were huge."

Stone decided to chance it. "And what went to the victor? The money?"

"It does really matter. In the presence of the universal truth it has no value. None."

"I know you're right, but people will want to understand why you're thinking this way."

"Ink and paper. That's all it is. A big pile of ink and paper."

"Of course, but most people aren't like you." Stone said. "They want to be, but they're not. They're tiny and greedy. So they're going to want to know what happened to it."

Speedo smiled. "And the answer is so very simple. I gave it to God. All of it."

"All of it?"

"All of it. I was told he keeps an incinerator for this very purpose, to burn the evil out."

"Did you help him?"

Speedo shot to his feet. "Don't fuck with my story, man!"

Stone raised his right hand in concession. "Sorry. Won't happen again." He felt a hand on his shoulder. The guard. Time was up. "We'll talk again later, okay?"

"Not okay," Speedo said. He turned and stalked off into the darkened innards of the jail.

Stone stopped on the steps outside. The sky seemed so brilliant and clear, the hills so lush and beautiful. He smiled to himself. His years as a cop told him why. The world always put on its best face when you stepped out of a jail and into the perpetual light of freedom.

He reflected on his time with Speedo. A madman, but a fascinating one. Was he capable of cutting off someone's arm? Most certainly. More disturbing, he would do so with the best of intentions, with the moral force of all creation behind him. He was probably due for a "mental health assessment," but Stone also knew about bureaucratic inertia in the justice system. At some point he would most likely be declared criminally insane; however, that point was still out in the indeterminate future.

So much for Speedo. What about Rhonda? His concern for her was what brought him to this dank and depressing place.

He built a timeline in his head to try to make sense of what was going on: Rhonda sleeps with Larry, the acid dealer. She sees a black guy there and a big stack of money. Speedo somehow knows what Rhonda did. He murders Larry and shows the arm and the money stash to Rhonda, then splits. The cops bust Speedo and find the arm, but most of the money is gone.

The money. Why did it always come down to the money? Maybe Speedo had it right. May it should all be burned in God's incinerator. But in the meantime, it had the power to put Rhonda in a real jam. And what was the deal with the black guy at Larry's? He was obviously a drug dealer and, judging by the quantity of cash, way up the food chain. It was also a good bet that the money was part of some deal between him and Larry. But then Speedo crashed the party, and Rhonda was Speedo's girlfriend, which put her right smack in the middle of it all.

Two seagulls flew over the top of the jail. Bright white against deep blue. Their wings beat in a lovely synchronous rhythm that propelled them toward places unknown.

Stone started toward his car. The birds paid him no heed.

32.

GOLDEN GATE PARK

By now Rhonda knew the east end of the park quite well. She crossed over Kezar Drive, walked the paved path through the trees and wound up in the big meadow below Hippie Hill. She took a seat on the thick lawn and stared at a little patch of white clover, a tiny herd in search of sustenance on a vast plain of green. Would they find it? Probably not. They would fall beneath swirling blades of steel during the next mowing cycle. Such was life. Sooner or later, the swirling blades would find you.

She had nothing, nothing at all. No money, no gear, no clothes, no friends to speak of. She should have felt utterly alone and devastated but she didn't, and she knew why. She had always been utterly alone. It blew through her life like the chronic wind over an open prairie. As the years passed, it had transformed from an affliction into a given.

She put her ruminations aside, closed her eyes and tilted up to the afternoon sun, whose warmth shone on all with equal measure. Geese squawked in the distance. A small dog yapped. A child squealed in mysterious delight. The world settled.

A bell tinkled nearby, a small bell by the sound of it. A triple drumbeat followed, fingertips impacting stretched hide.

Rhonda opened her eyes. Two hippie women had seated themselves a couple of meters away. Both wore dresses of stained cotton and dilapidated sandals. One held a bell suspended from a leather shoelace. The other cradled a small drum not unlike a tambourine. Their hair ran long and wild.

"Hey," the bell lady greeted Rhonda. "Want to turn on?"

"Sure," Rhonda said. "Why not?" She got up and moved over so the three of them formed a triangle.

The bell lady reached into a leather pouch slung over her shoulder and pulled out a matchbox and some rolling papers. "I'm Sasha and that's Melody."

"Hi," Rhonda responded. "I'm Rhonda."

"You mean like Rhonda Fleming, the movie star?" Melody asked. She had a sweet way about her that Rhonda found appealing. Like one of those people who viewed the world in a perpetual state of amazement.

"Yeah, like her," Rhonda said.

"Far out," Melody said. "I never met anybody with that name."

"Well now you have," Sasha said. She spread a paper out on top of her pouch, pinched some marijuana out of the matchbox onto the paper, and deftly rolled it into a joint. "Got a match?" she asked Rhonda.

"Sorry," Rhonda said. "I don't. As a matter of fact, I don't have anything. I got ripped off."

"Wow!" Melody exclaimed. "Bummer."

"Yeah. Bummer," Rhonda agreed.

"Hey, here's a lighter," Sasha said as she fished around in the pouch. She had an ancient symbol of unknown origin tattooed on the back of her right hand.

"So, where you going to stay?" Melody asked.

"I don't know. I haven't thought about it. Haven't had time."

Sasha lit the joint, took a deep puff, and passed it to Rhonda, who did likewise and passed it to Melody.

Sasha exhaled and sighed. "Good shit. You don't have a place to crash?" she asked Rhonda.

"Not yet."

"Well maybe you should come with us. We got a family scene, sort of." Melody said.

"You sure that's okay?" Rhonda asked.

"Yeah, at least for tonight," Sasha said. "We got room. If you like what's happening, maybe you can hang for a while."

"Maybe so," Rhonda said. She had no idea what kind of scene they were talking about, but right now, anything was better than the street.

They finished the joint and headed east through the Panhandle. Between the warm afternoon and the pleasant buzz from the joint Rhonda felt somewhat refreshed. Soon they came upon the big yellow Frame of Reference and the Digger feed just beyond.

"Wanna get something to eat?" Melody asked Rhonda. "It's for free."

"Don't think so," she said. "I'm not really hungry right now."

"Me neither," Sasha interjected. "Anyway, we're not really into the Diggers. We got our own thing."

Rhonda had to wonder just what that thing might be. Despite their domestic anarchy and a junkie leader, the Diggers had an offbeat charm that Rhonda found appealing. But given what she'd seen on the street, she wasn't so sure that the same charm applied to other living arrangements in the vicinity.

They continued east, past Rhonda's previous apartment and toward the fringe of the district. Along the way the two women spoke of their origins. Sasha came from Roseburg, Oregon, where her father stacked framing studs in a lumber mill and told nigger jokes every night at dinner. Her mother dispatched taxis and prepared hateful little meals because she loathed her husband. Sasha made light of her mother's revenge and considered it cutting off your nose to spite your face. They made enough to afford an extra refrigerator in the garage, which contained nearly one hundred bottles of Schlitz beer. On the weekends Sasha let young loggers diddle her in the back of hot rods, but they never got to finish. She liked to come, but she didn't want any logger babies.

Melody came from Idaho, from a farm way out on the Snake River plain. Her father tended to a flock of farmers in a small church with a very narrow interpretation of the Bible. Melody learned that to be a nubile young woman was slightly sinful in and of itself. Her mother reinforced this notion and mandated dresses that minimized any exposure of the flesh, which was ever so weak and fallible. Earlier in the year, Melody let her boyfriend persuade her to join him on a grand exodus to San Francisco, where love and hope would conquer all. The Greyhound left at 10 PM, only half full. Melody made up for lost time by giving him a blowjob in the rear seat.

Both women were seventeen years of age.

They continued east into the Mission District, where apartments mingled with auto repair shops and storage depots. They came to a two-story brick structure with a paint warehouse on the bottom and a rambling apartment unit on the top. Someone had painted aggressive splashes of color on the walls of the staircase ascending to the second floor. They gave Rhonda a mild case of vertigo by the time they reached the top and entered the apartment space. A pair of stereo speakers oozed Moby Grape and blanketed numerous people in an open space filled with pads and cushions, the staple furniture of the Love Generation. Rhonda immediately picked up on a lopsided gender ratio. Twice as many boys as girls. Not a good sign.

A stratified haze of blue smoke hung in the air from candles, pipes and cigarettes. The whole place reeked of cat urine, bad plumbing and patchouli oil, a supremely offensive combination. A young girl, maybe fourteen, came up and gave Melody a hug and wandered off, as if treading on cloud tops. An oppressive heat filled the room, and most of the males were shirtless. They pulled on pipes, puffed on joints or simply closed their eyes and nodded to the music. A spontaneous sculpture of glued egg crates rose near the center of the room, with cobwebs hanging from its edges.

"So, this is it," Sasha declared to Rhonda. "Far out, huh?"

"Yeah, far out," Rhonda said. And in its own repulsive way, that's exactly what it was. It made the Diggers place look like a suite at the Fairmont. Two women stood over an ancient electric stove in a kitchen area to the left. They stared at something boiling in a big pot. Random food items sat on the counter, including open cans of vegetables with tin lids rising in serrated salute. A half loaf of bakery bread spilled out like a deck of cards. A mangled head of iceberg lettuce rested nearby.

"I'll show you where we crash," Sasha said, and led them to a hallway at the rear of the room. Its length held four rooms, two on each side. Three small children ran out of the first room, one with a disposable diaper, two naked. The open door revealed a half dozen people clustered near a TV tuned to a cartoon show. They passed a joint as they watched Deputy Dawg gesticulate wildly in dull color.

Rhonda followed Sasha and Melody into the far room on the right, which held stained mattresses, piles of clothing and cardboard boxes full of personal items. Sasha pointed to a vacant mattress in the far corner. "You can have that one. Cat Girl left and I don't think she's coming back." Tiny brown foxholes from cigarette burns dotted its surface.

Rhonda began to regret that they hadn't eaten with the Diggers in the Panhandle. "What about the food?" she asked Sasha. "How does that work?"

"You just do your own thing," she explained. "You take what's there and make it up."

"Where does it come from?"

"People chip in. They get little day gigs, make some scratch and put it in the kitty. It's a beautiful thing to do. I think Zinger probably covers the rest, but I don't know for sure."

"Zinger?"

"Yeah, he's the main dude." Sasha pointed toward the wall. "Got his own pad right across the hall."

"For himself?"

"Yeah, but he's the one who makes the rent, so that kind of makes it okay."

"Where does he get the money?" Rhonda asked. "Does he have a job?"

"No, but he's from a rich family back east. He has a trust fund."

"Oh yeah?" Rhonda remembered Nicole at the Diggers talking about the trust fund people.

"He's doing a really righteous thing. He's taking from the rich to feed the poor. Kind of like Robin Hood."

"Kind of," Rhonda said and let it go. A goopy cough filled the room. A girl of about ten lay shivering under a blanket on a nearby mattress. Her glazed eyes and shiny forehead indicated that she was wandering alone through the secret world of the sick.

"She doesn't look too good," Rhonda observed.

"Oh no, she's healing," Melody said. "Her inner spirit is showing her the way. We all have an inner spirit. Did you know that?"

"I guess not," Rhonda said. She wasn't the most compassionate of people because it triggered inner storms she tried to avoid. But the girl looked like she should probably be in the hospital. A dried pool of vomit lay a short distance from the mattress. "How long's she been like this?" Rhonda asked.

Melody shrugged. "For a while. It's all part of life on this earth."

Another hunger pang hit Rhonda. "I think I need to eat a little."

"The kitchen's wide open," Sasha said. "Let me show you."

As they left the room, the door to Zinger's room opened. The slender man who came out looked like he came off the Nevada desert at the turn of the last century. Black cowboy hat over long stringy hair. Droopy outlaw mustache. Leather vest hanging from narrow shoulders. Blue denim shirt right off the rodeo circuit. Hand-tooled western boots with almost no mileage.

"Zinger," Sasha declared.

Rhonda had never considered that there might be dilettante hippies, but that's what she now beheld. He looked ridiculous. A copy of a fabrication of a forgery.

"Hey babe," Zinger said to Sasha, all the while casting predatory eyes on Rhonda. "Who's this?"

"This is Rhonda," Sasha said. "We met her in the park. She got ripped off and needs a place to hang while she gets it together."

"No problem," Zinger said. "I mean, that's our whole trip, right? So, where you from, Rhonda?"

"Los Angeles." Rhonda kept her delivery flat and devoid of subtext. The guy was obviously an asshole. Not a trace of the alpha male she observed in Emmet Grogan. This one sat atop a little kingdom papered together with family money that made him the Boss Hippie with no substance to back it up.

"Far out," Zinger responded. "I know some people down there. Music people. Pretty trippy. You part of that scene?"

"Not really."

Zinger stuck his thumbs in his belt next to a heavily engraved buckle. "Well let's talk about it sometime. I gotta split, but I'm sure I'll see you around."

"Right," Rhonda said, with no hint of favor.

Zinger strutted on down the hall in a clumsy swagger that just didn't work. Not now, not ever. Rhonda knew that he would probably be trouble but put it aside. Her stomach carried the moment.

33.

GOLDEN GATE PARK

A walk in the park. It was Detective Sergeant Linehan's idea, and Stone immediately read the narcotics cop's intent. A few minutes earlier he'd sat in Linehan's office and expressed his concern about Rhonda's safety. The cop had nodded thoughtfully and suggested that they take a little stroll. Some things were best discussed in a distinctly unofficial setting.

They walked along a paved path through the meadow below Hippie Hill, and Stone commented that the crowd seemed thinner than usual. Linehan pointed to the sky with its thick gray overcast. "No sun," he said. "They're like reptiles. They like it warm." He smiled and sighed to himself. "No offense. After a while you either love 'em or you hate 'em. It's hard to stay in between. Know what I mean?"

"I know," Stone said.

"So, you want a little help with this Savage girl, right?" Linehan asked.

"Right. Like I told you, I think she might be in a real jam over this Speedo thing."

"How come?"

"It all comes down to the money," said Stone.

Linehan snorted cynically. "Doesn't it always?"

"She saw it twice. Once was when Speedo showed up with the arm. That's not the problem. The other time was when she was leaving Larry's. It was all out on the table in big stacks of hundreds in front of this older black guy. If he knows she's connected to Speedo, he probably figures she's in on it. What makes it worse is that it's a lot of money. Not a good situation. By the time they busted Speedo he only had a few grand. So, where's the rest? It all points toward Rhonda. She can run, but I'm not sure she can hide."

Linehan didn't immediately answer. His face took on a gloomy cast. "Tell you what," he finally said. "I want to take this conversation up to about ten thousand feet, so we get a better view. Only thing is, we never had it. You okay with that?"

"Absolutely," Stone said. Now they were getting somewhere.

"I've got a pretty good idea who the black guy is, but we'll come back to that. For starters, let's look at why he's here at all. In this city you've now got two dope markets. The old one is heroin and speed and all that kind of stuff. The new one is psychedelics, like LSD, mescaline and so on. Somewhere in the middle you've got pot and hashish, but we'll leave them out of it for now. Anyway, the psychedelic market is growing like crazy, especially since Reagan outlawed LSD. And guess what? The heroin and speed guys aren't going to just sit in the bleachers and watch. They're bad guys, but they're not stupid guys. They want in. We're getting word off the street that they're starting to become players right here in la-la land. And that brings us back to the black guy and the money. If I got it right, and I think I do, he's Willie Mather, and he's major trouble."

"How come?"

"He's a big-time heroin and speed dealer. Way big. Our pals at the Federal Bureau of Narcotics have been tracking him for years. They see him as a genius-level player. He's put together a national distribution network, and not a pretty one. Lots of guns and dead people all the way from Seattle to Miami. Last few years he's even developed his own supply lines from overseas."

"So, what's he doing here?"

"He's an opportunist. He's always ahead of the curve when it comes to the next big deal. Like I said, the market for stuff like acid is exploding. Not just here but all over. He wants to be sure he beats the competition to the punch."

"Right in your own back yard," Stone observed. "You going to let him get away with that?"

Once again Linehan lapsed into silence. "We're going to go way off the record here," he finally said. "You okay with that?"

"You have my word," Stone said. "That's the best I can do."

"That's good enough for me. There was a murder a while back, an acid dealer they called Superspade. You read about it?"

"I did. They found his body hanging off a cliff up north of here."

"That's him. He did most of his dealing here in the city, and had a pad over on Page Street, so we took jurisdiction. Burke worked on it, but he came up empty. So did everybody else. No leads. So, we put it on the back burner and waited for a break, and then we got one."

"What happened?" Stone asked.

"This idiot biker called Pig Eye tried to sell an M16 combat rife to a gun shop in the Mission. The owner reported him, and the cops over in Hunters Point put the heat on him. He tried to make a deal to wiggle loose. He knew these two lowlife dope dealers who said they'd made a big score from a job they'd done for this big-time black guy. So they busted these guys and found them in possession of some of Superspade's jewelry. The DA loved it, and the cops leaned on them really hard until they broke. Pretty soon they had a lawyer and a deal was cooked up that would keep them out of the gas chamber. They sat them down and took 'em through a set of mug shots, and both of them fingered the same guy: Mr. William Mather. Murder for hire, pure and simple."

"None of that made the papers," Stone said. "So, I assume something blew up on you."

"You assume correctly," Linehan said. "The deal was made, the DA was locked and loaded, and we were all ready to haul Mr. Mather in. A major score for sure."

"And then?"

"And then we get a call from the DA's office. It's all off. No go."

"With no explanation?"

"None. But people talk. They always do. I have a backdoor connection into the DA's office. It seems that the feds intervened. I don't how or why, but the bottom line is that Mr. Mather is no longer fair game."

"Wow. You think there's a payoff involved?"

"Probably, but somehow I don't think it's that simple."

"Then what do you think?"

Linehan stopped and faced Stone. "I think you should drop this whole thing. It involves people way up the food chain, people with no public accountability. You become a problem, you just might be the next Superspade."

34.

SUTRO DISTRICT

"It's going to be really hard to help her if she doesn't want to be helped," Christine said. "And it's going to be even harder when you don't have any idea where she is."

"I know," Stone admitted. He gazed out the view window at the vastness of the Pacific as seen from Louis' Restaurant, which sat on a grassy bluff above the shoreline. Only a half hour walk from their rental, it helped peel off the burden of the day.

"It's a tough one," he added.

Christine tentatively spooned her bowl of clam chowder. "So where do you go from here?"

"I keep going back to what I got from the narcotics cop today at the Park Station. Most of what he said was off the record and it's not good news."

"Which is usually the case when things are off the record," Christine observed. "So, tell me the deal. I'll keep mum, I promise." She held up her right hand. "Girl Scout's honor."

"It turns out to be a lot bigger game than I realized. Larry the dead acid dealer may just be a preview of coming attractions. When all this summer of love stuff first fired up, the hippies had their very own kind of dope, their own dealers and their own users. But now the hardcore guys are moving in, people peddling heroin and speed. If psychedelics are the new drug of choice, they want to be in on the action."

Christine nodded. "We're starting to see signs of that at the clinic. People with infections from dirty needles. Very nasty."

"And it's probably going to get a lot nastier. Speedo is in way over his head, or what's left of it. Even in jail. Which means Rhonda's along for the ride, too."

"How's that?"

"At Larry's, she crossed paths with this big-time smack dealer called the King. For reasons unknown, he seems to be immune from prosecution. They went after him, but the feds stepped in and said keep away."

"That's pretty scary."

"Yes, it is. Something else is going on here. Something totally off the books."

"Speaking of the books, I had an odd thing happen today at the clinic."

Stone had to smile. "Everything that happens at the clinic is odd."

"True. But this is a little different. A guy came in, a young guy, nicely dressed, not a hippie. He was from a research institute. It was private but funded by a federal research grant. I was busy, so I don't remember the name, but I kept his card."

"What did he want?"

"He said they were doing a study on psychotic reactions to drugs, especially psychedelics. He wanted to know if we might share our records on LSD overdoses. All anonymous, of course. The names aren't important. It's the medical data that they're after."

"Are you going to do it?"

"Probably not. It would be a real pain in the ass to go through all the patient records and redact the personal stuff after we copied it."

"Weird." Stone commented. He looked back out at the Pacific. "I wonder how long it would take to swim to Hawaii."

The scientist in Christine took over. "Let's see about that." She retrieved a ballpoint pen from her purse and started scribbling on a napkin. It didn't take long. With Christine, it seldom did.

"Just a guess," she said. "But somewhere around seven weeks."

"Too bad," Stone said. "I just don't have the time. Maybe later."

"Okay then, back to Rhonda. What might your next move be?"

"It's turned out to be a different game than I thought it was," Stone said. "First thing I need is to learn the new rules."

35.

SAN BRUNO

The man seemed quite pleased with himself when he let Rhonda out in the parking lot of San Francisco County Jail #3. He gave her a big smirk and a little wave as he drove off in his late model Cadillac. A clever businessman who'd just concluded a highly favorable deal. The negotiations had begun shortly after he'd spotted her hitchhiking in the Mission at the onramp to the freeway south. He'd intended to travel on down 101, so the jail was definitely not on his way, but perhaps something could be worked out. After a brief negotiation, it was agreed that she would jack him off in lieu of a blowjob. She did so with expert precision and timing. It ended just as they pulled off Highway 35 toward the jail. Otherwise he might have dumped her far short of her destination.

She felt no guilt, no anger, no remorse over the incident. Given that she was destitute, it was simply a means to an end. No moral deficit was accrued, no justification required.

She climbed the steps, entered the reception area and signed in at the front desk. After waiting twenty minutes in a chair of molded plastic, she was motioned through security and down a featureless hall to a room full of partitioned visiting areas. She sat down on her side of a glass window and took the phone off the wall. While waiting for Speedo, she mulled over how she might approach him but got nowhere. It all came down to one simple question: Where was the money? Unfortunately, the journey to the answer was anything but simple. It involved steering a madman without losing control, which might push him past the point of no return.

Speedo arrived and sat down while she was still deliberating. He looked awful, with darkened eye sockets, gaunt cheeks and a strange twist to his mouth. His fingernails had grown long, and the little finger on his left hand twitched wildly. He said nothing and stared at her intently as he picked up the phone.

"How are you?" she said. She waited for a response, but none came. His stare became more disconcerting with every passing moment.

"I said, how are you?" she repeated.

"How do you think I am?" he hissed. "You have the devil's baby in your belly. And every moment it grows bigger and stronger. You've become the vessel of evil on a scale we can scarcely comprehend."

Rhonda wasn't sure where to take things. Maybe an apology would help. "I'm really sorry, Speedo. I know I did a bad thing. I know I betrayed you. So, tell me, what do I have to do to make it better? Just tell me."

"There is nothing to tell. There are no words. We've traveled way beyond words. They have very little purpose anymore."

"But they're all I have," Rhonda said. "So please let me try. There is no baby. Not from the devil, not from you, not from anybody. I was bad. I admit it. But there's no baby."

"Can't you feel it?" Speedo asked. "Can't you feel the talons scraping against your innards? Can't you feel the heat of hell itself coming off its scales?"

"It's all in your head," Rhonda said. "You took way too much acid and you took it way too many times. You're not seeing things like they really are."

"My vision is perfect," Speedo countered. "It sees past the veil that the world has pulled over us. All has been revealed. I see past the four corners to places beyond imagination."

It wasn't working. No amount of verbal stealth was going to get her what she needed. Time to attack head on. "Look, we're both in really big trouble," she told him.

"Ah yes. But we've always been in big trouble, you see. All the way back to the darkness itself."

"The money you took at Larry's wasn't his," Rhonda explained. "It belongs to this black drug dealer who came and leaned on me. He's really pissed and wants it back. Forty-five thousand. When they picked you up, you only had five thousand. What happened to the rest? What did you do with it?"

"The answer is so very simple," Speedo said. "And that's why you can't see it. The fetus has released its toxins, and there are many. They have blinded you with complexity."

"Then help me," Rhonda pleaded. "Help me to see what happened to the money."

"I gave it to God."

"You what?"

"I gave it to God. With no strings attached."

"If we don't give the money back, he'll kill us. Both of us. It won't matter that you're in jail. He'll get you. Do you understand?"

Speedo shook his head. "He will not get me. He will not get you. You carry the perfect heart of evil within you, and the devil will not hesitate to bring his shield to bear. Not even the biggest of fools would mount an attack on you now."

"And just who's going to protect you?"

"Ah yes, me. There is no me. Not anymore. What you see is only a shadow. The rest has moved on into the eternal light. How do you kill a shadow?"

Rhonda felt her reserves run dry. "You kill it with a gun, or a knife or a baseball bat and it hurts really bad. So where is the money?"

"Where it always was and will always be." He put his phone receiver back in its cradle and stared at her with an idiot grin. End of conversation.

Rhonda dropped her phone and leaned in close to the glass between them. "You're fucking crazy!" she yelled.

Her declaration prompted an officer to remove her from the room and escort her to the entrance. Out on the steps she sat down and went limp. It was hopeless. He really was crazy. She dredged up her concerns about the head injury he'd received in the racing crash. She didn't know all the details, except that he was comatose for a while and spent months in "recovery" – whatever that meant. What happens when you follow an episode like that with massive amounts of LSD? Who knew? Probably no one.

She and Speedo might be the very first to find out.

36.

THE TENDERLOIN

Stone knew he couldn't keep this up. He'd always been a man of his word, as was his father before him. He made a deal with Capitol Records to prospect for new talent up here, sign them and get them in the studio before their musical moment had come and gone. To his credit, he'd started off with the best of intentions, even though he was late to the game. By the Monterey Pop Festival the brightest stars in the firmament of love were already under contract, and he was left to chase the second string. Which would have been good enough if Rhonda hadn't suddenly shown up and disappeared just as quickly under very disturbing circumstances. No matter how he tried, he couldn't shake his sense of obligation to her. And now that sense was consuming major chunks of his time that were really the property of Capitol.

All that said, he felt he owed her something, but not the entire balance of his music career. After all, it was her choice to take off, good idea or not. In truth, he might have already abandoned his search if it wasn't for his last visit with Linehan in the park. It brought the cop in him to a rolling boil. How could a national-level drug dealer manage to buy his way under the radar like this guy had? Who would let such a thing happen? And why?

A de facto grant of immunity for a criminal of this magnitude was a big deal and Linehan's sources tied it somehow to the Feds. So, the logical place to start was with federal narcotics enforcement right here in the city. Which brought him to this under-stuffed green Naugahyde couch in the waiting room of District No. 17 of

the Federal Bureau of Narcotics. Stone had to wonder how the
FBN had escaped the political tentacles of J. Edgar Hoover at the
FBI, but so it had. It hung suspended under the Department of
Treasury on the federal org chart.

Stone watched the office secretary thread some stationary into
an electric typewriter, which issued a series of sharp mechanized
clacks as she hit the keys. He'd decided to use the same entrée
here that he'd used with SF cops and see where it took him: An
ex-cop, now in the music business. He'd noted that nobody had a
problem with the "ex-" part of his cop story, especially when the
payoff was landing in something as flashy as the record industry.
This time he planned to use his music man credentials as cover for
a fishing expedition of sorts.

An intercom on the secretary's desk buzzed and a light flashed
on its console. She switched it off without answering and went to
open a door behind her. "Mr. Larkin will see you now."

A corner office. Of course. After all, the occupant was the
District Supervisor, who merited premium office real estate. Roy
Larkin rose from behind a clean desk and moved around to shake
Stone's hand.

"Agent Larkin, thanks for the taking the time," Stone said.
"I'm sure you've got a lot on your plate."

"Not a problem, Mr. Stone. Good to meet you." Larkin moved
back to his seat and waved Stone to a chair opposite. His build
suggested a background in football or rugby, full of power and
bulk. It pushed aggressively at his white shirt, gray slacks and tie.
His face was more of the same, full and broad with a pug nose. His
hair had retreated to nearly the top of his head, save for a desperate little island centered high on his forehead.

"So, you were a cop, huh?" Larkin asked as he settled back.

"That I was. First with Vice in LA, then Homicide in
Bakersfield."

"Wow," Larkin said soberly. "You know what that'd make me
want to do?"

"What?"

He broke into a broad smile. "It'd make me want to get into something like the record business."

"Well, that's my story," Stone said with a modest grin. Larkin had obviously had someone check on him.

"It's a good story," Larkin said. "I like it. So, what can I do for a fellow officer?"

"I'm with Capitol Records now. We're looking for new talent. It's a great time for music here in the city. But you probably already know that."

"I do know that. It's also a great time for narcotics," Larkin said.

"And that's what brings me here," Stone said. "At Capitol, we're really pumped about a lot of the music that's coming out of here. It's a whole new wave and they're doing some really amazing things. But we've got a real problem with the drug side of it. It's kind of out of control. I mean, if we saw a little weed and a few pills it would be business as usual. We're used to that."

"I'm sure you are," Larkin said with a cynical overlay.

"But anymore that seems to be just the start. Like this acid thing. It's everywhere around here. You've got a lot of these players wandering around stoned out of their gourd. Do we want to invest in them? Hard to say. They seem to get whacked out but then they bounce back, so maybe we can live with it. But the real problem is the old-school stuff. Heroin and speed. We're seeing more and more of it, and that we can't live with. It always goes from bad to worse. Believe me, we've been there."

"As have we," Larkin said.

"So, where's it coming from?" Stone asked. "From what I can tell, the music scene here used to be a closed system. Hippies selling pot and acid to other hippies. What went wrong?"

Larkin's cool smile returned. "We ask ourselves that very same question every day." He stopped and pulled a pack of Marlboros from a desk drawer and offered one to Stone. "Smoke?"

"No thanks."

Larkin produced a lighter and lit up while Stone continued his judicious probing.

"It's kind of funny," Stone said. "When I was with Vice in LA, the same thing was going on in the movie business. Big-time stars shooting up and being carted off under the radar to rehab. After a while I started seeing a pattern to it. You had a hierarchy of dealers with a few kingpins at the top, and these guys thought it was super cool to be hooked into the film industry. Big-time dope meets big-time celebrities. Both sides were addicted to each other, but in different ways. I have to wonder if maybe the same thing is going on here."

Larkin exhaled before responding. It caught the sunlight streaming through the window and curled into a swirling palette of thin blues.

"Nice theory, but you gotta remember that every city is different. That's why they're District 18 down there, and we're District 17 up here. The film biz in LA is a mature industry and set in its ways. That's not the case here in the city. The SF rock scene is a work in progress and so is the drug scene. It's a moving target. Know what I mean?"

"I do." Stone knew his fishing expedition was over. "And thanks."

"No problem." Larkin paused to exhale more smoke, then smiled in amusement. "Homicide cop becomes record producer. I like it. It's a great story. You ought to sell it to the movies."

"I'll work on that," Stone promised.

Larkin stubbed his cigarette in a glass ashtray and stood to indicate the meeting was over. "Let's stay in touch. I'd like to hear more about your adventures in entertainment."

"By all means," Stone said.

Stone took the Geary Blvd bus to get home. Parking downtown was always problematic, and this bus provided a most entertaining means of conveyance. It cut all the way across to the beach through a succession of ethnic neighborhoods, each a world unto itself. Chinese, Irish, Japanese, Russian and so on. The bus's interior resonated with multiple languages as it moved west out of downtown.

The meeting with Larkin had produced some intriguing over-tones. It was more what he didn't say. He had dodged any direct discussion about who was peddling hard drugs in Haight Ashbury and how they went about it. To get to his current post in the fed world, he had to be a master political manipulator and know precisely what to say and when to say it – all in synchrony with his personal agenda, whatever that might be.

Oh well. One thing at a time. Stone settled back into the multi-lingual chaos and let it carry him away.

37.

SAN BRUNO JAIL

I feel each drop and the power within it. They crash down onto my head and my shoulders. They slither down my arms, my belly, my legs, my feet. They fall an immense distance, from a place lost in the commotion of the churning clouds so far above. They start to pierce my body. I feel the rain in my heart, my gut, my cranial cavity. It washes away all that has come before. I regress into a purity of blinding intensity. I stand newly delivered beneath a perfect sky.

A short distance away, a prisoner walks along the corridor on Level Six of San Francisco County Jail #3. His flip flops smack the concrete floor as he walks past fifty-eight cells on his way to the showers near the middle of the building. Only one cell interests him, a solitary cell near the shower area. Most of the cells hold two inmates, but this cell holds only one. A particularly difficult one.

And right now, this cell is empty, because its occupant is in the showers. Precisely as planned. Just like the guard said, the same guard that had approached him a week before. It turned out that the officer knew many things about him, such as his conviction for assault, armed robbery and attempted murder. He was also aware of the prisoner's addiction to heroin, a difficult habit to maintain within the confines of the jail. Supplies were limited, contested and expensive. But perhaps, under the right circumstances, something could be worked out.

All my brothers in the Order of the Deluge stand alongside me. Mostly pink, some black. Their skin shines and glistens in the torrent from above. Their limbs twist and bend in the ritual cleansing. We gather here to consecrate the city below and bathe ourselves in the sacred waters gifted to us from on high. We form an army of infinite proportion and the Head Devil cowers at the very thought of us.

The prisoner enters the shower area and places his flip flops and towel on a bare wooden bench. The men bathe under the hiss of running water and a cloud of steam drifting near the ceiling. The walls are in a hopeless state of disrepair. Cracks, peels and flaking reveal crumbling layers of plaster and paint. The piping and shower fixtures run exposed along each wall, with rust and leakage all along their length.

The prisoner spots his prey at the far end. Unlike the others, he stands motionless with eyes closed and head tilted back into the water stream. Just as the guard predicted. During their previous encounter the guard had passed the prisoner a bag of high-grade China white and guaranteed a continuous supply for some time to come. Only a single favor would be asked. The prisoner initially hesitated, but not after he snorted the fine white crystalline powder. A beautiful and familiar feeling set in, like he was finally home. The deal was sealed.

The inundation has begun. Miles below our feet, the water advances through the city, block by liquid block. It charges down the avenues that crisscross into perfect squares. It erases centuries of construction and upkeep. It dissolves history. It obliterates cherished tales. Its surface reflects pinpoints of white light. They streak by me and up into a stratosphere of deep blue going on black. But wait. They've changed course. They now streak right through me and carve out great spaces where none should be. No matter. I surrendered long ago.

The prisoner enters the showers and takes his place at the near end. Down the line men rinse soapsuds off their bodies and rinse their hair. They are the last batch for the day. When they leave, solitude will return, broken only by the drip of leaky plumbing.

"Okay, that's it!" a guard yells, the very same guard who retained the prisoner. The men file out, all except the one at the far end. He remains motionless, eyes closed. The others ignore him. His craziness is well known. They towel down, remove their uniforms from wooden pegs and file out.

The prisoner lags back and waits until the last man has left. He must move quickly now. The knife awaits him in an eroded pocket of masonry behind the cold-water pipe. He pries it loose and advances on his prey, who remains oblivious to his presence. He brings the blade up and slashes both carotid arteries in a single motion. The man collapses onto the tiled floor, hitting his head on the wall as he falls.

The fire in my throat lasts only an instant. It quickly burns itself out. A distant impact follows, a collision of some kind. I rise on up out of myself and float to the ceiling. I see my body crumpled on the floor. The water still flows and guides a river of red into the drain.

I feel no fear, I feel no pain.

The prisoner returns the knife to the pocket in the masonry and hurries out. He soon catches up with the others returning to their cells. He knows that a bag of China white awaits him under his mattress.

He can hardly wait.

"Excuse me, Mr. Mather, you have a message, sir."

The King had to smile at the perky young woman behind the counter at the St. Francis. Given that he was black, her attentiveness had a lot more to do with his generous tipping than his sterling character.

She handed him the message, which didn't identify the caller. It simply said "Done." He rolled it into a very small ball and flicked it into a wastebasket on the far side of the counter. The young woman was impressed. "Nice shot," she remarked.

"Thanks," the King said, and started toward the elevators. A very special kind of justice had been done, and it was absolutely necessary. No one, no matter how insane, could steal his money and get away with it. His personal balance scales simply would not allow it. But that left the matter of recovery, and the key to recovery was the girl.

38.

NOB HILL

"I've gotta be honest with you," Rick Ponytail told Stone. "I have this material out with three other labels. The group is really concerned about finding the right relationship."

"Yeah, we'd all like to find the right relationship," Stone said. He had already forgotten Rick Ponytail's real name. He wished he could forget that he'd ever agreed to this meeting. He'd only done it as a favor to a promoter he knew over at Family Dog. But here he was, in the Tiki Bar at the Fairmont, surrounded by bamboo, palm fronds, thatched roofs, green water and festive lighting.

Ponytail pushed a demo cassette a across the table in Stone's direction. "You have to understand that the recording quality isn't that great, but it doesn't really matter. It's the essence of what they're doing that counts, and it's really pretty amazing. I put it right up there with the Airplane and the Dead. It's really deep but spontaneous at the same time."

Stone found many things about Ponytail annoying. His carefully pulled-back hair, his neatly trimmed goatee, his hip pendant, his pullover turtleneck. In short, an LA promo man recently converted to hippiedom because it was the flavor of the moment. But what bothered him the most was the man's accent, an odd pseudo-British affectation, sort of like LA meets Liverpool. He would have bet big money that Ponytail had no such accent a year ago.

Stone abandoned his higher self and decided to fuck with the guy a little. He picked up the cassette and examined it. "Okay, I'll give it a listen. We'll see how it goes." He ambushed Ponytail with a sudden stare. "I don't think you told me about your other clients. Who else do you represent?"

Ponytail instantly tightened up and began to fidget. He started to blather on about "several other acts he had in development," whatever that meant. In a desperate search for a way out he finally looked at his watch and excused himself to go to another meeting. He was, after all, a busy man.

Stone watched him stride nervously toward the exit and smiled. He'd stuck Stone with the bill, but the entertainment was worth it. Stone pocketed the cassette. He was an honest man. He would dutifully listen to it and it would be terrible. All part of the job.

A clap of thunder rolled out of some concealed speakers, followed by a sprinkle of rain on the large shallow pool in the center of the room. Trouble in paradise apparently. It subsided as Stone paid the bill and headed toward the exit.

"Officer Stone!"

Stone knew the voice. Deep and gravelly. It belonged to none other than Roy Larkin of the FBN. He turned to see Larkin sitting by the pool with a second man.

"We meet again!" Larkin said and motioned to an empty chair. "Join us."

"Why not?" Stone said. He had an hour or so to burn before taking a taxi on home.

"James Stone meet Hal Olsen," Larkin said as Stone sat down. "We were just discussing the war." Olsen appeared about the same age as Larkin but had a wiry build and a full head of salt and pepper hair.

"Which war?"

"World War Two. The last honest-to-God war," Larkin said. "Hal here bombed Italy while I was right below him on the ground. Thank God he missed me." They both chuckled and took a sip of their drinks.

"And what do you do now, Mr. Olsen?" Stone asked.

"I'm a publisher and an author," Olsen replied. He opened his wallet, which was out on the table, and handed Stone a business card that read Vixen Press.

"My wife's a big reader," Stone said. He often referred to Christine as his wife to dispense with lengthy explanations about their relationship. "Maybe she's seen some of your stuff."

The two men smiled knowingly at each other. "Maybe, but probably not," Olsen said.

"His work is a little on the naughty side," Larkin explained. "Lesbians, high heels, spanking, that kind of stuff."

"Not for everyone," Olsen added. "But it does pay the bills."

"I'm sure it does," Stone said.

"So, what are you drinking?" Larkin asked as he motioned to a passing waitress.

"Gin and tonic," Stone said.

Olsen and Stone continued to chat while Larkin ordered the drink. "So how many books have you written?" Stone asked.

"Lost count. About a book a month. I use different author names, so it doesn't look like I'm a factory. And what about you, Mr. Stone? What are you up to?"

Larkin rejoined the conversation. "Officer James Stone quit the cop business a while back and became a producer for Capitol Records." He raised his glass in salute. "Good move."

"Excellent move," Olsen added. "I know the gig. I've got a degree in musicology from Bowling Green."

"You've also got a degree in lesbian sax players with handcuffs in their horn cases," Larkin said.

Olsen took no offense. "Come on, Roy. I'm an artist. Give me a break."

"Okay tell us about the Beach Boys," Larkin said to Stone. "They're on Capitol, right?"

"That they are."

"I know some people in LA and they told that those guys are good singers, but they can't play for shit," Olsen declared. "They bring in all these heavy-duty studio players to do the instrumental tracks. That right?"

"Let me just say that I'm not at liberty to say," Stone replied.

Larkin put his hands together in mock applause. "Well put, Officer Stone!"

And on it went. The conversation ricocheted around between the war, popular music and softcore porno. A second round of drinks produced more of the same. Stone noticed that Larkin never regressed into shop talk. The drug scene, criminal escapades and law enforcement all failed to surface. Tall women, shapely bottoms and spiked heels seemed to carry the day, along with carpet bombing and Bill Haley and the Comets.

Stone felt a mild buzz after the second drink and decided to call it a day. "Gentlemen, you'll have to excuse me. It's time to get on home."

Larkin raised his glass in farewell. "Always good to see you, Officer Stone. To be continued."

It was about four o'clock, so Stone's cab driver avoided the heavy traffic on Geary and took California Avenue, which cut across town all the way to the beach. They traveled due west, and sunlight streamed directly in through the windshield, prompting Stone to shield his eyes whenever he looked up.

When sifting through the impromptu encounter with Larkin, he kept arriving at a major paradox. FBI and FBN agents usually came across as models of Midwestern propriety. Conservative suits, wingtip shoes and sterling manners. Churchgoers one and all.

But not Larkin. He presented himself as a barhopping swashbuckler, openly discussing kinky sex with his pornographer buddy. Not exactly the fast track to the District Supervisor's office in a city like San Francisco. Stone wasn't sure what to make of it, but experience had taught him that a great many investigations start this way. You accumulate facts that seem unrelated but come together somewhere down the road.

A funny feeling hit him a few blocks before they reached 25th Avenue.

His stomach turned slightly queasy and he felt lightheaded, but in a very odd kind of way. No faintness, no dizziness; just a general sense of detachment from normality, whatever that was. The cab stopped for a light and he looked through the Plexiglass barrier between himself and the driver. Its surface contained various scrapes and smudges, and they abruptly took on the form of clouds, all gray and misty. Stone might have accepted this as a routine trick of the mind, as a matter of subjective interpretation, but then the clouds begin to move in a lazy drift.

A bolt of panic shot through him. Something was wrong. No, everything was wrong. His primal wiring drove him to the only possible conclusion. Time to flee, time to get out. He slid the barrier window open and instructed the driver to pull over. While doing so, he felt a curious sense of bifurcation. Even as the world began to wobble and weave, he was able to conduct business with the driver in a very routine manner. After paying his fare, he opened the door and stepped out onto the sidewalk.

The city exploded.

39.

MISSION DISTRICT

"Trooper Jim, Trooper Jim, Trooper Jim, Trooper Jim...."

The shirtless male occasionally flipped a greasy strand of hair out of his face as he sang his song of two words in endless repetition. Rhonda couldn't decide which was worse: His singing or his strumming on a bargain basement guitar as he sat cross-legged on the commune's dirty wooden floor.

She finally settled on the singing. From where she sat propped against a brick wall in the far corner, it verged on unbearable. She expressed this opinion to Zodia, the woman sitting next to her, and Zodia agreed. Rhonda had just met her and sensed an affinity. Zodia was about her age and had a frank sexuality about her. She'd been a resident here for a few weeks, and Rhonda guessed that she'd slept with Zinger as a personal contribution to the communal kitty. Yet in all this squalor Zodia somehow managed to keep up her appearance, with peachy skin, dark brown hair and full sensuous lips. She also knew her way around the politics of this supposedly apolitical place.

Zinger came out of the back and swaggered past them with an arrogant nod and a tip of his pseudo-cowboy hat. Zodia managed a tepid wave. When he'd passed, she turned to Rhonda.

"You fucked him yet?" she asked in a tone stripped of any emotional baggage.

"No."

"Well don't, unless you have to. He's a lousy lay."

"I'll remember that," Rhonda replied. In fact, Zinger had already made a move on her last night when she got back from the jail in San Bruno. He caught her in the hall, grabbed her arm and tried to steer her toward his room, all the while murmuring the usual platitudes about her being a stone fox, a groovy babe, and so on. In response, she told him she was right in the middle of her period. It worked. Sometimes, men would demand a blowjob as a consolation prize, but not this time. He simply gave her a disgusted look and wandered off.

A loud, insistent voice rose over the Trooper Jim song. Rhonda turned toward the source across the room near the entrance. It belonged to a diminutive man locked in verbal combat with Zinger. The man had an abundance of thick black hair and a beard to match. His small hands gesticulated wildly to reinforce whatever his point was. A slender woman with lank brown hair stood silently beside him in an earthen sun dress.

"Who's that?" Rhonda asked.

"Charlie Manson," Zodia answered. "He's fucking bad news."

"What's his problem?"

"He thinks Zinger should let him move in and Zinger thinks otherwise. Typical male bullshit. He who wins gets the pussy, or so they think."

Manson did an angry pivot and stalked off down the stairs, followed by his woman. Zinger waited a safe moment and flipped them off once their backs were turned. Someone passed him a joint to take the edge off.

"I think I know a way out of here," Zodia announced.

"What kind of way?" Rhonda asked.

"I heard about this exclusive club up on Telegraph Hill. Rich guys, big money. They're looking for hostesses – whatever that means. You wanna guess?"

"Don't have to." A circle formed inside Rhonda, a circle ten years in the making. She was nearly back to the beginning, a source of both repulsion and fascination.

"Well I'm in for sure," Zodia said. "Why don't you think about it?"

"I'll do that," Rhonda promised. Out on the floor the ballad of Trooper Jim dragged on and on. Three small children ran out of the hallway and stopped to behold the scene. They looked to be about two years old, and only one wore a diaper. One of the others, a girl, stood naked and deposited several loads of excrement onto the floor.

Rhonda turned to Zodia.

"Okay I'm in."

40.

VISTA DEL MAR

The blast sent Stone reeling. The noise, the light, the heat.

He recoiled into his very center, a place where the rest of him watched the movie of his life rolling by. From this nexus of self, he gazed out upon a nearly overwhelming spectacle, terrifying yet irresistible. He knew he couldn't stay in this dark and quiet place. He had to go back out.

The traffic roared and bellowed, a mechanized roll of thunder that had no end. It verged on unbearable, but then again, what did unbearable really mean? What harm was there in it? His resistance dissolved and the great tide of noise began to transport him down the sidewalk. Its cement surface came alive and took on a slow boil but continued to hold him up. Tiny beachheads formed around the edges of his shoes.

Should he be terrified? Should he declare a personal emergency? Should he call out for help? Maybe so, but probably not. What good would it do? His voice of reason told him it had to be a psychoactive drug of some kind, but it no longer mattered. Whatever had been set in motion had a will of its own and would roll on toward its inevitable conclusion, regardless of outside intervention. He was sure of it. Better to move forward than succumb to raw panic.

The traffic became a river of calamitous color, with the brake lights stretched into brilliant streaks of red. The flow of it generated a subtle wind that caressed his exposed skin.

A bubble formed inside him as he moved along, a dense sphere full of power and warmth. It reached out and saturated him all the way to his furthest extremities and became the engine that powered his flotation through time and space.

He stopped and took in his surroundings, the cars, the buildings, the people, the bushes, the trees. What city was he in? He had no idea. It no longer mattered.

He quickly lost track of his path through the streets. His travel now put him on a large boulevard lined with a bewildering array of shops. Their window displays beckoned to him in silent persuasion. Medicines, perfumes, stationary, appliances.

Appliances, yes, appliances. Six vacuums stood at attention in a perfect row, a domestic army waiting to march. Their hoses expanded and contracted in a synchronous rhythm, sucking the essence out of the world below. So be it.

A bus stop loomed up with a transit map posted on its side. Red streets marked the route, and they rose and floated above the map's surface in a dimension all their own. Meanwhile an electric bus pulled up, a great metal beast done in orange and white. It sprouted twin antlers that thrust up into a maze of overhead wires. The doors folded open with a rude hiss, but no one escaped. They folded shut and the bus moved off with a powerful hum and a surge that tickled the hair on his arm.

An eruption of color clawed at his peripheral vision and he turned to take it in. A painting appeared, a work of exquisite beauty, a convocation of fantastic color. It stood before him in the window of a small gallery and he moved ever closer until his nose nearly touched the glass. The work was abstract yet somehow organic. Its slashes and swirls and dabs moved in a lazy dance and invited him to merge and bathe with them. Color became sound. Sound became color. It held for him eons.

When he emerged, a second piece presented itself. A mask, a primitive carving of the kind he associated with shamans in far-away jungles. Long strings of tattoo marks snaked along over its wooden surface. The facial features were brutally simple, with a hollowed-out mouth and vacant eyes. And within these vacancies, he saw a darkness, a blackness beyond redemption. They depicted death and decay with an absolutely horrifying power. And in that instant Stone realized that he saw the mask precisely as its creator intended. All pretense of civilization and reason gave way to a display of utterly raw emotion, a potent combination of horror and wonder.

He reluctantly let it go and drifted among passersby, each with a face etched in almost unbearable detail. If he stopped one, would they let him scrutinize the furthest reaches of their identity? He doubted it and let them swim by like creatures in a great urban sea.

A block further, he came upon a church, and it stopped him cold. Six frescoes of saintly figures adorned its front of pure white. The figures within these paintings begin to move as though acting in miniature movies. Above them five onion domes of brilliant gold sat atop the roof, each with its own cross pointed heavenward. All these features merged into a mystical whole inside Stone, and he realized that the church itself was praying. It called out to the sky in a silent stream of incantations describing the joy of all who sorrow.

On he went, in the direction of the late afternoon sun. Eventually the ocean came into view, an infinite expanse of slate blue. He left the main street, the traffic, the pavement, the noise. A portal of deep emerald presented itself, framed by squat trees shaped by an eternal wind. The grass beneath glowed in a saturated green that squirmed with life. Stone entered this magical glade along a narrow, paved path. The constructs of man receded; the work of God took over. He could see delicate signs of motion, the kind he'd never before noticed. A slight bend to a blade of grass, a certain slant to a slender twig. They formed the tracks of birds and animals now departed.

The path opened out onto a viewpoint where the enormity of the ocean seized him and held him transfixed. The afternoon sun spilled fire onto its surface. Millions of sparks danced and dazzled their way across the pulsating waters.

He came upon an old wooden bench of deep brown facing the sea. Two boards served as a backrest and strings of white graffiti ran along their surface in a chaotic scrawl. Loops and curls and slashes in a forgotten language. Stone came in closer and examined their flow, and they begin to speak to him. Simple tales of love, loss and conflict.

After they had their say, he sat for a moment and became enveloped in the ocean breeze. In front of him large blocks of granite sat between lengths of pipe to form a barrier between the bench and the beach below. They obstructed his view and robbed it of its purity. He felt compelled to regain it, so he hopped up onto one of the blocks. From a squatting position, he brought his hand up to shade against the sun and looked down upon the surf. Its white froth patiently devoured the sand along twisting wave fronts that intersected in endless patterns.

In this moment and posture, he regressed thousands of years. He became a hunter, clad only in a loincloth, who had finally reached the sea and found himself lost in the wonder of it.

The moment retreated and the breeze stiffened. He wandered down a series of pathways until he reached the level of the beach and the coast highway. Rush hour had set in, and a thunderous stampede of traffic blazed by. Given the motorized violence, he refrained from crossing to the shore and followed a path along the inland side. An occasional bicyclist swooshed by, like a ghost gliding on a pair of wheels spun into a mad blur. The sun sank ever lower, and the light turned golden.

He reached a major intersection where a small cluster of people waited to cross to the beach. Safety in numbers. They would not be run down by the pitiless metal insects massing against them. The light changed and they all crossed to the beach side, where a set of shallow dunes rose. Clusters of dry grass crowned their tops and the breeze bent their stiff blades shoreward. Stone removed his shoes and started to climb the nearest one. The cool sand caressed his feet on the way up.

He reached the top just before the sun touched the horizon. It pitched brilliant splashes of color at him. Pinks, yellows, reds, golds and even a hint of green. He sat motionless and thoughtless as the remnants of the day drained away.

Dusk still hung overhead when he descended the dune and put his shoes back on. He had his bearings now. He wasn't that far from home. He headed back toward the highway.

Nothing would ever be the same.

41.

TELEGRAPH HILL

The woman's black hair hung in a severe cut an inch above her neck. Her white skin and cherry lipstick made it seem the color of coal. To complete the look, she wore a black lace garter belt and nylons with seams running up their backs to her naked bottom. She brought one knee up onto the king-size bed and arched her back slightly to show off her ample breasts. The nude man on the bed reclined into a stack of decorative pillows and appeared more relaxed than enthused. He did manage an appreciative smile and the woman immediately reciprocated. She knew the game well.

"Yeah, she's a hot one. How do you find 'em?"

"Not a problem. Word's out that we pay top dollar. They come to us."

"What about the cops?"

"You're kidding, right?"

"Yep, just kidding."

The woman completed her climb onto the bed, revealing five-inch spiked heels, each secured by a thin leather strap. She started kissing the man's midsection and worked her way toward his flaccid penis. He closed his eyes and crossed his hands behind his head and smiled. She continued her journey south and grasped his wilted organ with her thumb and middle finger and twiddled. Still no go.

"How much did you slip him?"

"Three hundred mics. Pharmaceutical grade. We mix it into their drinks."

"Kind of like a Mickey Finn, huh?"

"Kind of. Only this time, I think old Mickey would've seen the Second Coming."

The woman reached the man's soft member, wrapped her lips around it and started to suck. Still nothing. He maintained the same distant smile. Behind him, empty shackles hung from eyelets in the large oaken headboard.

"Damn! I'd have a fucking telephone pole by now."

"Oh yeah? You wanna give it a go?"

"You mean with the dope?"

"Yeah, with the dope."

"Don't think so."

"You have to remember that the dope is whole point of it," Larkin explained to the King. "It's not what they do when they're straight, it's about what they do when they're high. That's what we're after."

The pair sat in front of a two-way mirror looking into the erotic tableau in the next room. Beside them, a 16-mm Bolex movie camera rested on a tripod and hummed as it captured the action. To their rear was a counter and a long rack full of film cans.

"I know goddam well what happens when people get high," the King said. "They feel better than when they're not high. And the better they feel, the more they're willing to pay."

"That's just the economics," Larkin said. "There's a lot more to it than just the money." He looked through the window at the encounter on the other side. "Looks like we're stuck in low gear. Let's take a break."

They left the room and walked down some stairs to a large room with low lighting and sleek furniture. An attractive woman in her forties stood behind a small bar in the corner. She nodded at the pair as they walked through and out onto a balcony with a stunning view of the bay. The lights of Treasure Island and the Bay Bridge shone in the distance. The heat rising off downtown warped the air and caused them to twinkle.

Both men rested their elbows on the railing and Larkin lit a cigarette. "We picked this place because it's on a dead end," he said. "No though traffic. No nosy neighbors."

"It also happens to be way uptown," the King added. "That's gotta help."

"Definitely," Larkin said. "We want people to feel they've come to someplace special." The house stood at the far end of Montgomery Street, up above downtown. It dated from the twenties but had undergone substantial remodeling to meet Larkin's requirements. He referred to it as a "luxury club" to give it some status and legitimacy and told his female contractors to do likewise. They themselves were to always be "hostesses."

"You might make 'em feel special on their way up here," the King said. "But what about on their way down?"

Larkin smiled. "Think about it this way. You're a guy from Cincinnati here on a business trip, a young guy. You've got a great little wife and a couple of kids back home. You've also got a major hard-on for a little fun. So, you run into this hot chick that can make it happen. You get here and it turns out to be more like Alice in Wonderland than the Playboy Club. Who you gonna tell? The cops? Your family? Don't think so. You're gonna keep this one to yourself and you're probably gonna keep your dick in your pants for the foreseeable future. End of story."

"Maybe for him, but what about you?" the King asked. "What do you get out of all this? What's the FBN want all his shit for anyway?"

"And what about you?" Larkin countered. "We're talking quid pro quo. So, what's your side of it?" He paused and exhaled through his pugnacious nostrils. "You know what quid pro quo means, right?"

"Don't insult my intelligence, Agent Larkin. I know exactly what it means and what I get. I get the market, a whole new market, along with a hands-off from you guys while I'm putting it together."

"Yeah, that's the deal," Larkin said. "All you have to do is keep the quality consistent, just like you've done with your other product offerings back east."

"That I can do," the King said. "But who cares? Are all you guys going to go to chemistry school or something?"

"Let's just say it's part of our planning process," Larkin answered.

"Okay, so be it." The King knew that Larkin was never going to come clean with him about what they were up to. And it didn't matter, because neither was he. In fact, he had no intention of providing a clinically consistent supply of LSD any longer than he had to. Over time he would start to introduce hybrid doses containing amphetamines or opioids. The old and the new markets would merge into a single market of unprecedented proportion.

Larkin put his hand on the King's shoulder and looked back toward the bar inside.

"Forget about all this dope stuff. Let's have a drink."

42.

OUTER SUNSET DISTRICT

Stone took a seat on a wooden bench at the far end of Judah Street. He removed his shoes and shook out the sand accumulated during his walk up from the beach. It fell in a silent earthen snow onto the pavement under the streetlight.

Dusk had passed and the urban sky glow had set in with a slight tint of rose. A little dog yapped in the far distance. A car door clunked shut somewhere nearby.

The drug was departing. It was delivering him back into the world of the tangible, the logical, the familiar. He should have been relieved, but he wasn't. He'd witnessed a mode of being with a power and beauty all its own and, in truth, he would miss it.

He put his shoes back on and started down Judah Street He smiled and thought of all the kids in the park and their entanglement with this phenomenon born of chemistry gone rogue. He hadn't understood what Jimi Hendrix meant when he sang "Are you experienced?" but now he did.

A streetcar rumbled past on its way into the heart of the city. Its interior lights shone brightly on the advertisements lining its upper walls. They stretched in a long parade of loud type and persuasive color.

Stone knew he should gather his wits. But for a little longer he'd let them roam free and easy.

The blocks rolled by. Few people were out right now. They were in behind those little rectangles of house light, finishing dinner, watching TV, trading barbs, laughing at the joke of the day.

They held great mysteries within them. They filled the world to the point of bursting.

He came to 39th Street and turned right. His rental was just a few houses down. The porch light cast an anxious glow as he ascended the steps and unlocked the front door. Christine rushed up before he was even all the way through.

"Oh, thank God! You're safe. Thank God!" Her eyes turned wet and she threw her arms around him. "I was just going to call the police. Are you alright?"

He wrapped his arms around her. "I'm alright. I love you."

"And I love you." She led him over to the couch and they sat down holding hands. "What happened to you? Are you sure you're okay?"

He was okay, but not in any way he could easily articulate. "Yeah, I'm okay, I guess. I think somebody drugged me."

"Then we need to get you to the hospital. Right now."

"You're a doctor. Isn't that good enough?"

"I'm a doctor, but I love you way, way too much. We need to have somebody look at you."

Stone understood. "Okay. But I think you better drive."

"Of course, I better drive. Let's go."

Christine managed to contain the urge to speed on the ten-minute trip to St. Mary's hospital. Along the way Stone related his experience in a sketchy kind of way but left out the poetic side. She was worried enough, and he didn't want her to think he'd had some kind of psychotic break.

When they arrived, Christine pulled rank as a doctor and got Stone right in. In no time at all he sat with his legs dangling off the end of an examination table. A nurse had taken his pulse and blood pressure, followed up by a lab tech drawing a blood sample. All under Christine's watchful eye.

The curtain swung open and a doctor entered, an older man with a weary face and gray beard. "Good evening," he said to Stone. "I'm Dr. Quinn. How are you doing?"

"Doing well," Stone answered and nodded at Christine. "This is my partner, Dr. Harmon."

"Nice to meet you, doctor." Quinn seemed unperturbed by the presence of another physician, and a female one at that. He looked down at the admission report on a clipboard. "So, it looks like somebody got you high without your consent. Do you remember when you first felt something?"

Stone gave Quinn essentially the same rundown he gave Christine. The doctor listened attentively and took a few notes as they talked. When Stone finished, Quinn sat on a stool and reflected for a moment before responding with slight smile.

"Congratulations, Mr. Stone. You're now an experienced acid tripper." He looked to Christine. "Would you concur, doctor?"

"Yes, I would," she said.

"As you know, we're right next to Haight Ashbury, which has made me sort of an authority on the subject. We deal with LSD cases on a daily basis – sometimes an hourly basis. Toxicology will confirm it, but I'd say you absorbed a dose of somewhere around 300 micrograms. The good news is that it will be completely out of your system by tomorrow. And the bonus prize is that there seems to be no long-term damage from this kind of thing."

"That's good," Stone said. "I like my brain just the way it is."

"It's also good news that you didn't go off the deep end. Cases like this can turn a little rough when there's an underlying psychosis involved, like schizophrenia or manic-depressive disorder. It speaks well of your mental health."

Quinn stood up. "I think that about does it. My recommendation is that you go home and watch Johnny Carson." He turned to Christine. "And if I may ask, where do you practice, doctor?"

"Right down the street, at the Free Clinic."

"Ah yes, then you know precisely what I speak of."

"I do." Christine liked Quinn. He was a great model of grace under pressure.

"A good evening to you," the doctor said and left.

Stone turned to Christine. "Well I guess there's nothing left but Johnny Carson."

"It must have happened at the Fairmont," Stone remarked to Christine on the way home. "In the bar. It was the first time I ate or drank for several hours."

"I'd say that's a pretty good bet," Christine replied. "So where does that leave you?"

"Four possibilities. First, someone behind the bar did it, but that seems like a real long shot. Why me out of everyone else? And why me at all? Getting customers stoned on hallucinogens isn't exactly good for business."

"And next?"

"This manager guy who was pitching me on some new band. A sleaze ball for sure, but the last thing he'd want to do is piss me off with a surprise acid trip. Not him. He's out."

"And then?"

"I ran into this guy I just met the day before. He's the local head of the Federal Bureau of Narcotics."

"Not a likely candidate," Christine remarked.

"No, he's not. But he was there with this other guy, a real odd-ball. He writes soft core porno and runs a little publishing company that puts it out."

"Now we're getting somewhere," Christine said.

"It would seem so," Stone said. "But the question becomes, what do I do about it?"

43.

TELEGRAPH HILL

"Wow!" Zodia exclaimed. "Check out the view. This is way uptown."

Rhonda had to agree. They stood on the porch of the elegant house at the end of Montgomery Street, waiting for someone to answer the bell. They'd taken the bus into downtown and the cable car up the hill, which put them within walking distance of their destination.

An elegantly dressed and well-preserved woman of about forty answered the door. Pulled-back hair, bright red lipstick, dark complexion, short skirt, high heels. "Good evening. Can I help you?"

Zodia took the lead. "Hi. A friend of mine told me that you were looking for hostesses, so we thought we'd come by and see what it's all about."

"I see. And what's your friend's name?"

"It's Scarlet. I don't know her last name. She never used it."

"Ah yes, Scarlet. How is she?"

"I don't know," Zodia responded. "She split. She's down in LA somewhere."

"That's the word," the woman confirmed. "Why don't you come in?"

They entered a spacious room with a bar off to one side. Recessed lighting shone down onto stylish furnishings and plush carpeting. The woman gestured to a couch made of soft brown leather. "Have a seat," she said as she sat in a chair opposite them. "So, what did Scarlet say about us?"

"She said that this is a very exclusive club," Zodia replied. "Very expensive and very private. She said you offer a variety of services."

"Did she say what kind of services?"

"She said you offer companionship to businessmen visiting from out of town. She said that you cater to their individual needs."

"She's right about that," the woman said. "And if you want to work here, that's what you would be called upon to do. Do you have any problems with that?"

"No," Zodia said.

The woman turned to Rhonda. "And you?"

"No problem," Rhonda said. As long as the money was right.

The woman seemed to read her mind. "Good. I'll let the manager explain your compensation and terms of employment, but first let's have a drink."

They crossed over to the bar where Zodia and Rhonda sat down on high stools padded with a very soft leather of deep gray. The woman slipped behind the bar and said, "What can I get you?"

Zodia and Rhonda both ordered a glass of Chardonnay, and the woman poured herself one as well. "By the way, I'm Grace and you are...?"

"I'm Zodia and this is Rhonda," Zodia volunteered.

"Good to meet you," Grace responded. "You like the stools you're sitting on?"

"They look like they're on the expensive side," Rhonda commented.

"You're absolutely right," Grace said. "Want to know what they're made of?"

"Sure," Rhonda said.

"They're made from the foreskin of a whale penis." Her bright red lips curved into a lascivious grin. "That big enough for you?"

"Plenty big enough," Rhonda shot back.

Their exchange was interrupted by a man who appeared from a nearby hallway. He wore a tropical sport shirt over a bullish figure topped by a squat face and a big balding forehead with a single patch of hair holding out in the center.

"Rhonda and Zodia," Grace said. "This is our manager, Mr. Johnson."

Roy Larkin, aka Mr. Johnson, took a stool next to Rhonda. "Ladies, pleased to meet you. I assume Grace has told you what we're all about and what our expectations are. That right?"

"Right."

"Okay, let's go for a little tour and we can discuss the details. Follow me."

Grace excused herself, and the three of them ascended a staircase to a hall that traversed the length of the upper story. Larkin guided them to the second door on the left and opened it.

"This is the main suite," he said. "Fully equipped."

A king-sized bed with an oaken headboard faced a large wall mirror positioned for maximum voyeurism. Twin cabinets flanked the bed, and undoubtedly held the tools of the trade. Rhonda noticed the shackles on the headboard. "So what's with the bondage stuff? How does that work?"

"We find that some of our clients liked to be secured as part of our service," Larkin explained. "So we provide the necessary means."

"And what if they want to secure us?" Zodia asked cautiously.

"That's entirely up you. We don't promote it, and we have a security system to prevent people from breaking the rules. It's seldom been a problem. Truth is most clients are so loaded by the time they get up here that they can barely perform at all."

He steered them back out into the hall. "We have two backup suites in case there's a full house."

"And where do all these clients come from?" Rhonda asked.

"That's your job. First thing, we advance you enough to dress with a little class. Then you go to the better bars and clubs downtown and pick out men who can afford you. You bring 'em back here and do the deed and you're done."

"Not quite," Rhonda said. "How much do we get?"

Larkin grinned. "Thought you'd never ask. We pay well. You'll receive one hundred dollars cash for each episode. All off the books."

Zodia's mouth dropped. Rhonda somehow managed to keep her cool. It was a lot more than she expected. All her reservations evaporated.

"So what do you say?" Larkin asked.

"Fine be me," Rhonda said. "Me too," Zodia added, still in shock.

"Well, all right then!" Larkin said. "Let's go down and have a drink to seal the deal."

Rhonda spied the door open to a bathroom across the hall. "Sure. Mind if I use the restroom?"

"Be my guest. See you in a minute," Larkin said. He took Zodia by the arm and they headed to the stairs.

Rhonda walked into the bathroom and shut the door. It was well-appointed, and the toilet was actually a bidet, which seemed quite appropriate. But she didn't need to use it. What she needed was about thirty unobserved seconds outside. During their tour she'd noticed that there was another door right next to the one entering the master suite. What was that about?

After a brief interval she opened the bathroom door slightly and listened. Voices floated up from downstairs, but none came from nearby. She stepped out into the empty hall and crossed directly to the door in question. Its knob contained a keyhole, but it was still worth a try.

She twisted the knob and the door opened. A two-way mirror framed one wall and looked into the master suite. Two chairs faced the mirror, along with a movie camera mounted on a tripod.

She'd seen enough. Larkin's hundred dollar per gig offer had seemed quite generous; however, it now seemed only reasonable. But in the end it didn't break the deal. She'd been photographed countless times before.

She shut the door and headed downstairs.

44.

MISSION DISTRICT

Stone found an open spot on 10th Street about two blocks from his destination and grabbed it. Parking was at a premium down here and he didn't want to gamble on winding up further away. Besides, it gave him a little time to frame his upcoming conversation with Mr. Hal Olsen of Vixen Publishing. He had no hard evidence that Olsen had spiked his drink with LSD. It was more a process of elimination. Olsen aside, the only remaining possibility was Roy Larkin, who seemed a most unlikely candidate for any number of reasons. Why would the local head of the FBN take the insane risk of drugging innocent people? It would constitute incredibly risky and reckless behavior, especially on the part of a career federal bureaucrat.

He plugged the meter with a couple of quarters and started down the sidewalk under a slight drizzle. He had left the more elegant part of downtown. Debris littered the sidewalk and indigent men sat propped against grimy walls riddled with graffiti. The address for Vixen Publishing turned out to be an aging three-story brick structure just off the corner with Folsom Street. As Stone climbed the stairs to the second floor, he decided that an oblique approach was the best option. To go at the writer head-on might prompt him to clam up completely.

Halfway down the hall he came to a door labeled Vixen Press and opened it. Sure enough, there was Hal Olsen sitting behind a cluttered desk in an equally cluttered room. Framed book covers lined the walls and presumably represented Olsen's output. The titles ranged from *Gold-Plated Sin* to *Sweet and 20* to *Carnal Cargo*. All were illustrated with long-legged women in various stages of undress.

"Well, if it isn't Officer Stone!" Olsen said as he looked up from an old Remington typewriter. "Come on in."

Stone realized immediately that he'd guessed wrong about this guy. Olsen failed to show any sign of the alarm normally exhibited by the guilty.

"Good to see you," Olsen said as Stone took a seat across the desk. A thin blue band of smoke rose from an ashtray by the typewriter and broke into lazy waves near the ceiling. "What's happening?"

"I was downtown, and it seemed like as good a time as any to look you up," Stone said.

"Glad you did. You know, I'd like to pick your brain about your cop experiences. Same for the record business. I'm always looking for new material."

"Well I might have something interesting for you, but it's not being a cop. It's about being stoned."

Once again, Olsen showed no sign of alarm. "Stoned? You mean stoned as in martinis, or stoned as in something else?"

"As in something else," Stone said. "After I left you guys at the Tiki Room, I started feeling a little strange."

"Oh yeah? And then what?"

"And then I started feeling really strange. Not exactly hallucinations, but something pretty close. It went on for hours. I couldn't even find my house until after dark."

Olsen gave him an incredulous stare that lingered for moment before he burst into laughter.

"Roy! He did it again."

"Did what?"

"He slipped you a dose of LSD. Welcome to the club."

"The club?"

"Yeah, Roy has a habit of sending people on a surprise trip to la-la land. It tickles his funny bone, I guess."

"How long's he been doing this?"

"I dunno. A couple of years, maybe. A while back he slipped some to this cocktail waitress downtown who wanted to be a singer. She flipped out and wound up in the ER. Another time he dosed this hot actress chick in his apartment, and she damn near jumped off the roof because she kept seeing monsters."

"So why does he do it?"

"Hard to say," Olsen said with a philosophical shrug. "Why does anybody do anything?" He stubbed out the cigarette in the ashtray and leaned back. "Besides, it isn't any weirder than his sex life."

"What do you mean?"

"Roy has some pretty eccentric tastes. Some people might call 'em kinky, but I prefer eccentric – especially given the nature of my work."

"Such as?"

"He's got a real thing for high heels and nylons for starters."

"For starters. And then what?"

"One time my wife and I went with him to a hotel room. He'd hired a prostitute dressed in a garter belt and stiletto heels. We all had a couple of drinks and smoked a joint. After that, she tied him to the bed and whipped him. He loved it. I loved it. It was perfect for one of my books."

"Sounds like it," Stone said. "It just seems really strange that he can do all this and still be District Supervisor of the FBN. How do you think he pulls it off?"

All the levity left Olsen's face. "To tell you the truth, I don't have any idea. And I don't want to. And neither should you. Know what I mean?"

Stone knew exactly what he meant.

45.

TENDERLOIN DISTRICT

Rhonda spotted the mark within moments of entering the bar atop Loews Regency in downtown. He sat alone at the far end, all full of strut and swagger. The bartender nodded patiently at the man's officious patter. She put his age as early thirties, and he was definitely on the attractive side. Not necessary, but certainly a bonus.

She caught a glance of herself as she passed a mirror and decided that she'd done well with the advance Larkin had given her. She'd gone shopping at Saks Fifth Avenue and selected a black mini-dress, which came off as sexually daring, yet fashionable and expensive. To complement it, she chose a deep red clutch purse of Italian design. She also fulfilled a specific request from Larkin that she be fitted with spike heels of shiny black leather. She had her hair cut into a flipped bob in the style of wealthy women on the eastern seaboard. The net effect rendered her erotically charged yet sophisticated in a formidable kind of way.

She sat four chairs down, close enough to encourage an encounter but far enough off to not be a blatant come-on. The bartender, an older fellow in an immaculate white jacket, caught sight of her and came over to take her order. He seemed clearly relieved to escape from his obligatory banter with the mark.

She ordered a gin fizz and stared out the window at the spectacular view of downtown. She could feel the heated gaze of the mark but ignored it. It wouldn't take long.

"Pretty nice view, huh?"

There he was, right next to her, elbow resting on the bar top at a jaunty angle.

"Not bad," she replied with a faint, slightly bored smile.

And so the dance began. Little was required of her. Like most men, he loved to talk about himself and what he was up to. He hailed from Pittsburg and was in the industrial control valve business. A major player by his own estimation. That's why he was here at the top of the world in downtown San Francisco. He was meeting with executives from several major oil companies about their refinery operations. He had the latest valve technology at his fingertips, and they were chomping at the bit to get on board. A really big deal for sure.

When he'd finished constructing this monument to himself, the second phase of the encounter kicked in. Perhaps they could go "someplace else" for a drink or something. Rhonda closed in for the score. She knew about a very exclusive and very private club that he might find quite entertaining. As she finished her pitch, a smug look of cognition came over the mark. This was a commercial proposition. But he wasn't put off in the least. The implicit terms of the bargain were sealed. Let's go, he said.

In the taxi, he tried to work his hand up her thigh under her dress. She countered by telling him that all things would come in due time. They had the entire evening in front of them, so why rush? When they arrived at their destination atop Telegraph Hill, he was suitably impressed by the glittering panorama below.

"Wow!" he said. "How come I never heard about this fucking place?"

Rhonda explained once again that the club was very exclusive, and not for just anybody. He was in the Big Time now. He liked that.

He liked it even more when the lovely Grace mixed him his favorite drink at the bar inside. He launched into a political diatribe that held the two women entranced, or so it seemed. Ronald Reagan was a fucking genius. The government had to get off the backs of business and let it do its thing. Trickle-down economics was brilliant, because there was something in it for everybody.

Occasionally Grace would intervene with a question that extended his rambling discourse. To Rhonda it seemed like a deliberate move. But to what end? Why not get the deed done, dump the guy into a taxi, and get back to business as usual? Did it have something to do with the back room with the camera? Was it a blackmail scheme of some kind? It didn't matter. The ship had sailed, and she was on it.

Eventually Grace suggested that Rhonda show him the special suite upstairs. On the way up, he clumsily grabbed her and kissed her. He smelled of alcohol, cologne and tobacco. For some reason Rhonda wondered if he smelled this way to his wife at home or if she'd just grown used to it. She finally got him into the suite and told him to make himself comfortable while she changed into something more suitable. He didn't protest and flopped down on the bed, where he stared at the ceiling with a big grin. It's a beautiful world, he told her, a really beautiful world.

She told him she thought so too and retreated to the bathroom across the hall. A garter belt and black nylons lay neatly folded on the counter along with some very brief lace panties. She shimmied out of her dress and put them on. When she finished, she gave herself a long look in the mirror. Ten years. She'd come full circle. Back to sex with strangers. In an odd kind of way she felt quite comfortable with it. It put her in proximity to large measures of wealth, power and prestige. These people were her peers, her partners, her equals in a grand game beyond the understanding of ordinary people.

Suddenly she felt a great undercurrent churning within her. Pain and rage and despair. She quickly shut it down before it gained a real foothold and kept her from the task at hand. Do the gig. Get the money. Get out.

When she crossed back into the suite, the mark was under the covers and his clothes lay in a pile on the floor. He lifted the covers in invitation and revealed his naked self.

"Come in, come in," he said.

She tentatively crawled in and waited for his advance. It never came.

"See the sky, see the clouds," he said. "Can you feel them?"

Shades of Speedo. She knew it right away. He was stoned on some kind of hallucinogen. It explained why Grace had stalled them. She'd put something in his drink and and didn't want him up here until it took hold. It also explained the two-way mirror and camera. So what was this place? A laboratory of some kind? She envisioned Mr. Johnson – or whoever he was – on the far side of the mirror, watching them while he masturbated and the camera rolled. But to what end?

She wondered if they expected her to take the lead and jack him off or something. Given his current state, it hardly seemed worth the trouble.

"Uh oh," the mark said as he came upright and pointed at the ceiling. "Look at all the bats." He shrank back down under the covers. "There's way too many of them. Make them go away."

"I don't know how," Rhonda said.

Fear saturated his face. "Please. They'll eat me. I know they will."

"They won't eat you," she reassured him. It didn't work.

"Oh my God! The sky's curling up! Everything's falling." He clutched her hand. "Hold on."

He went rigid for a minute and then relaxed. He brought her hand up close to his face and held out her middle finger. "Your nails," he murmured. "They're like rose petals. There's never been anything so red."

Alternate waves of ecstasy and anxiety. They rolled over each other for what seemed like hours, leaving Rhonda both exhausted and bored. A quick bout of kinky sex might have been preferable. Eventually, Grace knocked on the door and called her out into the hall. The mark barely noticed her absence.

"Looks like he got a little goofed up," she said casually. "Don't worry. You did great. We'll take it from here. Get changed and come on down. I've got a taxi waiting for you."

To conserve her cash, Rhonda chose a mid-range hotel off Union Square. Top-end establishments had room rates of fifteen dollars or more, which would rapidly deplete her earnings. She looked up at the clock behind the front desk. It read a little past 2 a.m. The lobby was deserted, the adjoining bar shuttered for the night. A terminally bored clerk manned the front desk and ignored her until she stood right in front of him.

"Yes," he said impatiently.

"I'd like a room. A single."

He gave her a highly judgmental look through horn-rimmed glasses. "The rate is nine dollars a night. And how long will you be staying?"

Rhonda wanted to keep her options open. "Just for the night," she said.

"I see." He turned around to a wooden array of key slots and pulled one out. While he did so, a bellhop materialized from somewhere behind her. A red pillbox hat sat on his youthful head, and he wore a matching red jacket in the historical military style favored by his profession. He stared at her expectantly while the clerk plunked the key down on the desktop.

"And how will you be paying?" the clerk asked. His tone indicated that he already knew.

"Cash." Rhonda pulled up her clutch purse and extracted a twenty-dollar bill. While the clerk made the change, the bellboy approached. "Do you have any luggage?" he asked, knowing full well she didn't.

"No. I'm fine," she said while putting the change into her purse.

"Not a problem," the bellhop responded. A pair of slightly bulging eyes dominated his eager face. "Let me take you up to your floor."

Rhonda started to object but thought the better of it. She was tired. Better to play by the house rules. "All right."

The elevator stopped on the twelfth floor and the bellhop held the door for her. Once they were in the hallway, she followed him down to her room, where he stopped and gestured toward the door. "Here you are," he said and made no move to leave. Rhonda took the hint and gave him a dollar tip.

"Thanks. Have a good night." He was off down the hall at a brisk pace.

Rhonda unlocked the door and put her purse down on a small writing table. She went into the bathroom and examined herself in the mirror. She looked terrific. Maybe in some other universe this was the way it had turned out. Clothes, money, cars, college, trips, beautiful boyfriends. Maybe so.

Her musing was cut short by a knock on the door, which quickened her pulse. She waited. The knock repeated, only louder this time. She had no choice but to check it out.

"Who is it?" she asked through the door.

"Police," a male voice on the far side told her.

She looked through the peephole. A badge and ID filled the foreground with a cop trailing off behind.

"Can you give me just a minute?" Rhonda said. She turned and frantically scanned the room until she spotted the phone. Her finger started to shake as she dialed the front desk. No answer.

Another loud knock, followed by "Open up!"

She had no choice and opened the door and the cop bulled his way in. He wore a cheap suit and an aging fedora. His fiftyish face looked like a back-alley brawl. He shut the door behind him and looked her up and down.

"Well, look what we got here," he said with a parched smile. "Top of the trade. How much you fetch, sweetheart?"

"What are you talking about?" Rhonda said.

"I'm talking about what you get for that sweet little pussy of yours." He spotted her clutch purse on the desk, opened it and counted out the cash. "Not bad. Not bad at all." He stuffed the cash in his pocket and put the purse back down.

"In case you didn't know it, we just made a deal," he told her.

"What kind of deal?"

"I'm not gonna take you in. So have a good night – or what's left of it."

Before she could protest, he was out the door and gone.

In the elevator, the cop turned to the bellboy. "You done good, son." He gave the bellboy a five-dollar bill. "Keep 'em coming."

"Yes sir."

Rhonda undressed, pulled back the covers and crawled into bed. She was dead tired but at least not sitting in jail, which put her one step up from bottoming out. The rest could wait until tomorrow.

She dreamed she was at a zoo, looking into a large cage full of monkeys. They all applauded.

46.

CIVIC CENTER

Pay dirt. An old miners' expression describing a huge load of mud with a gem or two in the mix. Right now Stone was doing some mining of his own at a reading table at the San Francisco County Library. This particular gem dwelled in perhaps the most stultifying publication he'd ever picked up. With a little help from a kindly assistant, he'd retrieved it from the library's arcane depths. Entitled "US Directory of Institutions Engaged in Medical and Psychiatric Research," on page 237 it contained an entry reading "Madison Institute for Neural Science."

What made the Institute special was that its name matched that on a business card given to Christine at the Free Clinic. She got it from a young man seeking data on LSD overdoses, which fit quite neatly under the Institute's research umbrella. But Christine sensed something odd. When she asked around, nobody had ever heard of the organization.

Stone would have let it go at that – until his unsolicited acid trip, courtesy of Roy Larkin. It left him with a heightened curiosity about LSD, Larkin, the FBN and how they related to the hippie community, which was growing exponentially.

And now this: The entry on page 237 listed Roy Larkin as a member of the Madison Institute's board of directors.

Stone closed the book and looked down the cavernous length of the reading room. Apparently, there was more to Larkin and his agency than met the eye, at least the public eye.

It was time to go back to the people at ground level in this scene, the local cops. Time to talk once again with Officer Linehan at the Park Station, ground zero for local acid consumption.

Like the first time, Linehan suggested that they take a walk in the park, and the weather cooperated beautifully. The noontime sun stole its way over the zenith and cast a stunning light over the great sprawl of greenery. Linehan was on his lunch break, so Stone offered to buy him something from one of the vendors. He refused, saying that Officer Burke's heart attack had put him on the straight and narrow when it came to junk food.

Stone looked out at the clusters of hippies spread across the lawn. "I think I just got initiated into their tribe," he told Linehan.

"Oh yeah? How's that?" Linehan asked.

"Somebody slipped me a hit of acid," Stone said.

"Wow. Well at least you survived the experience. You got any idea who did it?"

"I do. But you may find this a little hard to swallow," Stone said.

"Try me."

"A couple of days ago, I was in the Tiki Bar at the Fairmont. I ran into Roy Larkin, District Supervisor of the FBN. He was having a drink with a friend and I joined them. A while later I took a taxi, and after a couple of blocks everything got really weird. It stayed that way for hours."

"That's the way it works," Linehan said. "What then?"

"At first, I thought that Larkin's friend might have done it. He's a very odd sort of guy. Writes kinky books for a living."

"Did you pay him a visit?"

"I did. And he just laughed. He told me Larkin has pulled this stunt before, and more than once."

"Do you believe him?"

"I didn't want to. I mean, why would anybody that high up in the federal law enforcement bureaucracy pull a trick like that?"

"Roy Larkin," Linehan said, and went silent for several steps. "A real asshole."

"You know him?"

"A little. And a little is more than enough. Did you know that he used to be a spook during World War Two?"

"That's what I gathered," Stone said. "He and his writer buddy kept swapping war stories at the bar."

"I know a couple of people over at the FBN. They're a pretty tight bunch, but people talk. They always talk. Especially when somebody's way out of line. Agent Larkin's extracurricular behavior has not gone unnoticed."

"And what do they attribute it to?"

"Word is that he's tied up in a lot of stuff that's completely off the books, which gives him a lot of room to move without getting in deep shit."

"What kind of stuff?"

"No one seems to know. But if I was going to bet, it has something to do with his spook background." Linehan stopped walking and faced Stone. "You know, I could live with all that. I really could. But now he's started fishing right here in my very own pond – without a license."

"Meaning?"

"Remember our little talk about a big-time smack dealer named Willie Mather?

"You mean the guy you nailed for murder for hire in the Superspade case?

"That's the one. And remember how I said that that the DA chickened out on taking him down after the feds stepped in?"

"I do."

"Okay then, tell me this: How could the Feds not be on to this guy? How could a murder case involving a national-level smack dealer not ring a few bells over at the FBN? It all comes back to Roy. He knows the deal. And somehow, some way, it gives this Mather guy a license to do whatever – right here in our backyard."

"And why would he do that?"

"Don't know. But what I do know is that you better start watching what you step in. It just might stick."

47.

OUTER SUNSET DISTRICT

Stone was still lost in a haze of speculation as he climbed the stairs of his rental and unlocked the front door. During his cop years he'd seen more than his share of corruption, both in LA and Bakersfield. But this thing with Larkin and the FBN topped it all. If Linehan had it right, they were shielding a criminal implicated in both murder and drug dealing on a national scale. How could an institution dedicated to bringing down the narcotics trade be conspiring with one of the biggest narcotics traffickers in the country? And conspiring to do what? Was it money? Maybe. Or was it something else? Larkin's previous connections to national intelligence presented endless possibilities but no definitive answers.

Stone opened the door, and there was Rhonda, sitting on the couch next to Christine.

She wore one of Christine's housecoats and slippers, with her knees together and hands folded neatly in her lap. She smiled sheepishly as Stone shut the door.

"Rhonda." Stone said. He wasn't sure what else to say.

"I'm sorry," Rhonda said quietly. "I didn't want to bother you, but I just ..."

"She called me from downtown," Christine explained. "I took a taxi and brought her back. It sounds like she's had a pretty wild ride."

"I just need a little time to get things together, that's all," Rhonda said. "Just a couple of days."

Christine put her arm around Rhonda's shoulders. "You can have as many days as you need. Don't worry about it."

Stone walked over and gave Rhonda an affectionate pat on the arm. "It's good to see you, Rhonda. It really is. I was getting worried."

Rhonda looked up at him in disbelief. "You were? Really?"

Stone nodded and smiled. "Yes, I was."

Rhonda burst into tears. They came on with a startling intensity. She buried her face in her pale hands. She began to rock gently in convulsive sobs. Christine hugged her close.

The Prodigal Daughter. Was there such a thing? Stone wondered. If not, there was now. But this time there was no need for forgiveness, only for compassion. He sat next to her and patted her knee while she cried. He felt close to tears himself. He was probably the only person left in the world who knew what she'd been subjected to in her earlier years. He didn't want her to feel alone in it all. Not then, not now.

Sometime later the ship's clock on the mantle chimed thrice. Rhonda's sobs died away. Her hands came down off her face and she took a deep breath to recover.

"I'm really embarrassed," she said while staring at the clock. "I'm so sorry to be this way in front of you. I'll get over it, I promise."

"You'll get over it when you're ready to get over it," Christine said. "So let's not worry about that right now. Would you like something to drink?"

"Just a little water."

"I'd like to know what happened to you," Stone said, as Christine went to get the water. "But only if you feel like talking about it."

Rhonda sighed deeply before answering. "I think I would." Christine returned with water and she took a sip. "Where do you want to start?"

"Where did you go after you left here?"

"I went back to my apartment. And this black guy shows up. The same guy that was at Larry's counting the money. He thinks that Speedo stashed it, and he wants it back. Forty-five thousand dollars. He says Speedo and I are dead if he doesn't get it. So I took off. I wasn't going to be safe if he knew where to find me."

"Where did you go?"

"Out onto the streets. I wound up at a crash pad run by the Diggers. You know about them?"

"A little," Stone said. "What then?"

"It didn't work. The head Digger is a smack freak and it turns out that this same black guy is his dealer. A real bummer. So I wind up at another crash pad, only this one's like something out of a bad dream."

"So what did you do then?"

"First thing I did was to go to the jail and try to get Speedo to tell me what happened to the money. But it didn't work. He was totally flipped out."

"He's dead. You know that, right?"

Rhonda nodded. "Christine told me on the way over. I haven't been checking the news, so it got by me." She smiled grimly. "Of course he's dead. They killed him because he wouldn't say where the money went."

"Do you feel any grief?" Christine asked.

Rhonda paused to reflect. "A little, but not much. It's like he was never really there to begin with. Know what I mean?"

"I do," Stone answered. She had a point. If you fatally stabbed someone, sliced off their arm and drove around with it, you might not be considered a person in the normal sense of the word.

"Anyway, after your jail visit, what happened then?" He asked.

"I met this girl named Zodia back at the crash pad. She knew where we could get work as hostesses at this high-end club up on Telegraph Hill. So we went up there to check it out and got hired."

"Oh yeah? Who did the hiring?"

"This really strange guy who called himself Mr. Johnson."

"What did he look like?"

"Kind of big and beefy. He was halfway bald with a funny little patch still on his forehead."

Roy Larkin. She'd just described Roy Larkin. Was it possible? Maybe, maybe not. A lot of other men fit the same description. But from here on he needed to proceed with care. He didn't want to push her toward any graphical descriptions of what went down.

"Did he give you any kind of job description?"

"We each got some money to get all dressed up. We were supposed to go into the bars downtown and bring rich guys back up. But then it got really weird and kinky. He had a two-way mirror set up to watch what was going on, along with a movie camera. And by the time the guys got into the room they were stoned on acid."

"Acid? You're sure?"

"Yeah, I'm sure. After Speedo, I know the deal."

It had to be Roy Larkin. What's more, it confirmed Hal Olsen's description of the rogue lifestyle led by the local chief of the FBN. On the surface it seemed utterly outrageous: A high-ranking law enforcement official running a whorehouse where the customers were observed and filmed while stoned on psychedelic drugs. Nevertheless, the facts all fit and pointed toward one enormous unanswered question: Why?

48.

TENDERLOIN DISTRICT

"The Cold War is a lot hotter than anyone wants to admit," Dr. Sidney Gottlieb told Roy Larkin. "We're locked in a struggle that most people can scarcely comprehend. Your service is greatly appreciated and won't be forgotten. I've made arrangements to have your contract with us extended indefinitely."

"Thank you, doctor," Larkin replied.

The Maître De at the House of Prime Rib had placed them at a table along the wall, which put other diners out of earshot. Larkin was halfway through his second gin and tonic and felt the glow coming on. "I know it's become tougher to shovel the money around," Larkin said sympathetically.

"The CIA takes care of its own, Roy. Always has. You have the full support of the Director, even if it's under the radar. Helms understands the big picture, unlike certain other people."

"You mean like that asshole, Earman?" Larkin said, referring to the agency's Inspector General.

"Among others," Gottlieb replied. "We've had to take MK-ULTRA off the books and send it underground. But don't worry. It still has a pulse. Besides, you still have your FBN job as a backstop."

"That I do," Larkin said. "And it's proven quite useful."

"I understand that your relationship with Mr. Mather is starting to produce some tangible results."

"Yes, it is. We've developed a very workable quid pro quo. He's well on his way to controlling the local market."

"I can't overstate how important that is from a scientific stand-point," Gottlieb said. "The entire project depends on maintaining a consistent dosage across a very large population. We can't have a bunch of street dealers peddling modified products. It destroys the integrity of the data and renders the results unusable."

"Of course," Larkin agreed. "And Mr. Mather has dedicated himself to making sure that doesn't happen. Anyway, that's the easy part. The hard part is keeping the local heat off him while he does it."

"I understand," Gottlieb said. "And I have assurances all the way to the top that, as long as Mr. Mather operates with relative discretion, we will intervene only when necessary. This is, after all, a matter of national security."

"Yes, it is." Larkin agreed. He flagged the waiter and ordered another gin and tonic.

Gottlieb nursed a whisky sour. He had a handsome, patrician face with a strong nose and receding white hair. "As we move forward, we need to keep the big picture in mind. Always," he proclaimed.

Larkin raised his glass in a mock toast. "Always."

"Just remember, Roy, it's all about mind control. It used to be nothing more than a political fantasy. Now it's very close to being a scientific reality. We know it, the Soviets know it. Whoever gets there first wins the game."

"Agreed," Roy said and drained his glass.

"It's all about scale," Gottlieb went on. "It's one thing to manip-ulate a single individual using things like hypnotic suggestion and psychological trickery. It's quite another to sway an entire army or political party or a nation. For that you need a pharmaceutical solution, and with lysergic acid diethylamide we finally have one."

"That we do," Roy said as he scanned the room for the waiter to order another drink.

"This whole thing here in the Bay Area gives us an unprec-edented opportunity. For years all our test subjects were anything but a representative sample of the population. Junkies, prisoners, prostitutes, gang members."

"That they were," Roy agreed as he signaled the waiter by pointing at his empty glass. "I remember it well."

"But now you have this mass migration. Tens of thousands of people, most of them young and middle class. Better yet, most of them are predisposed to taking psychedelic drugs. It's a fantastic opportunity. We just need ways to collect the data."

"We're working on that," Roy said.

"I know you are. Keep it up. Speaking of that, how are things with Midnight Climax?"

"Better than ever," Roy said. Gottlieb had periodically reviewed some of the film they shot through the two-way mirror.

"Well, have fun with that. It may prove useful. But keep your eyes on the big prize, okay?"

"You mean like ten thousand stoned hippies?" Larkin said in gin-fueled jest.

"That's precisely what I mean," Gottlieb replied.

He was, after all, a very precise man.

"I'm sorry. I don't want to keep bugging you about what happened," Stone told Rhonda, as they walked back home from Charlie's Market.

"It's okay," Rhonda said. "You're a cop and that's what cops do."

Stone had to grin. She was right. At some level he was still a cop and always would be. He also liked the way she said it, with a discrete dose of good-natured teasing. She must be feeling better. It would seem she had found the strength to pull herself out of a tailspin.

"Go ahead," she prompted him.

"Okay. I keep thinking about the black guy who leaned on you. Did Larry say anything about him before he showed up with the money?"

"Not really."

"How old do you think he was?"

"I dunno. Maybe late forties."

"And nobody mentioned his name?"

"Not that I remember."

Stone nodded. So why was a guy like this doing business with a white hippie kid? And a lot of business at that. Fifty thousand dollars' worth. Stone's experience told him that the whole deal pointed more toward heroin or coke than acid, at least in style if not substance. Which in turn pointed toward Willie Mather, who was already implicated in the murder of Superspade, another up and coming acid dealer.

Willie Mather. A big-time dealer of hard drugs, who was operating with impunity thanks to the local FBN office and their friends in DC.

Roy Larkin, a rogue FBN officer operating a whorehouse dedicated to stoning and filming clients high on LSD.

They knew each other. They had to.

Stone turned to Rhonda. "If you saw this guy again, could you identify him?"

"I could. But I'd rather not," Rhonda said. "I'd rather not see him ever again."

"Understand," Stone said. It didn't matter. He already had a workaround.

"Gotta make a call," Stone told Christine and Rhonda when a commercial came on during I Dream of Jeannie on NBC. He got out of his easy chair and went to the kitchen, where a phone hung on the far wall. He turned to check on the women. The commercial had ended, and Jeannie glided across the screen in her signature pink harem costume.

He dialed the SFPD Park Station and asked for Sergeant Linehan, who sounded as cynical and exhausted as ever.

"Working late, huh?" Stone said.

"Always."

"Sorry about that. I remember you saying that you saw somebody fishing without a license. I think I can help with that. You got a picture?"

It took a beat, but Linehan picked up on it. "You home at lunch time?"

"Yup."

"See you then."

By the time Stone returned to the TV Jeannie had a date lined up with somebody who was supposed to make Tony feel jealous. And so on.

49.

OUTER SUNSET DISTRICT

The knock came as Stone was listening to a bootleg cassette from a band called Fifty Foot Hose. They'd already signed with Limelight, which did a lot of jazz stuff, and Stone could hear why. Very creative but definitely outside the popular mainstream.

He turned it off and opened the door to Sergeant Linehan. "I owe you about a dozen lunches," Stone said.

Linehan pulled an envelope out of his sport coat. "Let's wrap it all up into one big dinner."

"Deal," Stone said as he took the envelope.

"You're lucky," Linehan informed him. "They told me they barely had time to snap it before his lawyer showed up."

"I'm not surprised" Stone said.

"Later." Linehan descended the steps without further comment.

Stone shut the door and opened the envelope. It contained a standard police mug shot of a black male in his late forties. Well groomed, short hair and a perfectly cinched tie – something Stone had never been able to master.

He took the photo down the hall and knocked on the guest bedroom door. Rhonda came out with her hair in some curlers that Christine had lent her. Stone handed her the photo.

"That him?"

"That's him."

Stone took the mug shot back. The last link now fell into place and the circuit was complete. Rhonda confirmed that her pursuer was Mather, the person behind the Superspade murder, the guy shielded by the Feds through some backdoor deal with the FBN, which pointed right to Larkin. In a word, Roy Larkin was complicit in letting a killer run loose on the streets of San Francisco – all under the blessing of those high above.

"That's a police picture," Rhonda added. "Is he in jail now?"

"No, but he ought to be."

"So what are you going to do?" she asked.

"I'm working on it.

50.

HAIGHT ST.

The Gold Cane held its own against the fever of the moment up and down Haight Street. It soldiered on as a booze bar amidst its newly minted psychedelic neighbors. It also happened to be just a short walk from the Park Station, which made it a convenient meeting place for Stone and several police officers. Two he knew, two he didn't, but all wanted in on the action as they partitioned a pitcher of beer.

"So you're back at it," Stone said to Detective Sergeant Burke, referring to his recent heart attack.

"Yup, I'm back at it. Good as new," Burke told him. He looked over to Sgt. Linehan. "Tom told me what you're up to. It just might work. I want in."

"Then you're in," Stone said. "It's not a sure thing. It won't work if Larkin doesn't take the bait, but I'm willing to bet that he will."

"I've got a judge who'll give us a warrant," Linehan said. "It's the same guy that signed the original one when Mather wiggled loose. He was pissed then, and he's still pissed now."

"Did you ask him about double jeopardy?" Stone asked. He was referring to the law of the land which states that if you're acquitted of a crime you can't be tried for it a second time.

"I did. Doesn't apply. He was never even arraigned, so there's nothing to stop us from busting him all over again."

"Good," Stone said. "Okay, let's go over this thing one more time."

And they did just that. When they were done Stone drained his glass and looked around the table. "One thing's for sure. It's gonna be really late when all this goes down, so you better sleep while you can."

"Got it," Burke said. The others nodded in agreement. They were on.

51.

CHINATOWN

"So you really think he'll go for it?" Rhonda asked Stone as he idly stirred his cup of Wonton Soup. The usual late-night outliers at Sam Wo's filled the tables around them. Aging beatniks, hip poets, jazz players, angry writers, grinning painters and failed film-makers, along with a generous dose of mainstream voyeurs.

"If I didn't, we wouldn't be doing this," Stone replied. He'd already recounted Hal Olsen's story of Roy Larkin being bound and whipped in a hotel room by a prostitute. "I seriously doubt that he'd do something like that just once. Most likely it's a fixation or fetish of some kind. All it should take is a nudge in the right direction."

"I hope you're right," Rhonda said.

"I hope so, too. But if I'm not, we haven't lost much. This guy's not a criminal in the usual sense. He's not going to hurt you. You have to understand that he's leading dual lives. He can't afford to get involved in anything where there's blowback from one side to the other."

"Let's say that he goes for it. How far do you want me to take things?"

"Nowhere. Try to keep it verbal. Make it sexual role playing. Know what I mean?"

"I know," Rhonda said. "You really think this will fix everything?"

"I do."

She stood up. "Alright. Let's go."

52.

TELEGRAPH HILL

"Slow night, huh?" Grace said as Rhonda approached the bar.

She took a seat on one of the stools. "Yeah, slow night. I picked up on a couple of scores, but they didn't seem right. Maybe vice cops or something."

"Don't want that," Grace said. "But don't worry if it happens. We'll take care of it. What are you drinking?"

"Just some soda water." Rhonda wore the same black mini-dress with the revealing hemline, along with the spiked heels.

"Actually, it's been pretty slow here, too," Grace said as she poured Rhonda's drink. "Sometimes it just works out that way." As before, she had her dark hair pulled back severely into a bun near her crown. A pair of gold hoop earrings offset her dark complexion and bright red lips.

"Yeah, I think you're right," Rhonda said. "By the way, is Mr. Johnson around?"

"I believe he is," Grace said. Her eyes sprung to attention. "Is there a problem?"

"No, I wouldn't call it that," Rhonda replied. "There's just something I wanted to ask him about."

"Really," Grace said in an inquisitive way.

Rhonda looked down at her glass as she answered. "It's kind of personal."

"I see," Grace said. Her lips twisted into a lecherous grin of tacit acknowledgment. "Let me check. I'll be right back." She disappeared down a short hallway off to one side of the bar.

Rhonda stared out the front windows, where a dazzling string of distant lights cut through the dark waters of the bay. A song by The Young Rascals drifted out of the stereo behind the bar and filled the deserted room. It occurred to her that this was her last chance to back out. But before she could work through it, Grace reappeared, followed by Larkin.

"Rhonda," he said with an expansive smile. "Why don't you come on back?"

She followed him down a short hall and into an office on the left. One look told her Stone had pegged the guy right. Garish photos and illustrations lined the walls, all depicting some form of bondage and discipline.

"Have a seat," he said and pointed to a chair in front of a bare desk. He wore a white short-sleeve shirt and gray slacks over his bulky frame, along with a narrow tie. He appeared completely unapologetic about the artwork as he sat down opposite her.

"Now what can I do for you?" he asked.

Rhonda calculated that it would take a few lines of patter before she pounced. "The new clothes worked really great when I went out for customers. Maybe we could add a few more."

Larkin shrugged. "Well yeah, I suppose we could. What did you have in mind?"

"Maybe a nice cocktail dress and another pair of shoes. Something with some extra high heels. You know what I mean?"

His narrow little eyes ignited. "Yes, I do."

That did it. She leaned back in her chair and propped her feet up on the edge of the desk. It brought her shiny spiked heels into full view and pulled her hemline up to expose her legs all the way up to her garter belt. "Of course you do. You're a bad boy. And you know what happens to bad boys?"

Larkin's hands had slid out of sight below the desk. He was obviously massaging his crotch. "Please tell me."

"They need to be punished."

"Yes," he muttered, "they do."

"I think we need some time alone, Mr. Johnson. Right now. I think you better tell Grace to close up and go home."

"Of course."

Rhonda pulled her feet off the desk and stood up. "Let's be quick about it."

"Right." Larkin nodded, got up and headed for the door. The baton had been passed. She was now in control.

Grace seemed to have anticipated what just happened in Larkin's office. She stood by the door with her purse shouldered and keys in hand as they entered the main room. "Have fun," she said. "I'm going to call it a night."

Rhonda took the lead and answered for both of them. "See you later." She watched closely and noted that Grace locked the door on her way out.

"Okay, big boy," she said to Larkin. "Let's get you upstairs and get to work."

She could almost feel Larkin shudder in anticipation as they climbed the stairs to the main suite. Once inside, he turned to her. "What do you want me to do?" he said quietly.

She put her hand against his chest and pushed him backward onto the bed. "I want you to suffer. Where do you keep the things I need for that?"

He silently pointed to a large cabinet beside the bed. She opened it to a large collection of bondage and discipline implements. Ropes, cuffs, paddles, whips, straps, dildos and chains. "Well look at this," she said. "You do come well equipped." She turned and glared at him. "Now get your clothes off."

While he undressed, she got out a set of ropes and leather cuffs. After tying a length of rope to each cuff, she threaded them through eyelets mounted on the wooden headboard.

Larkin now sat naked on the edge of the bed with an erect penis. She picked up one of the empty cuffs. "Don't just sit there. Put these on."

She watched while he meekly strapped himself into the cuffs. She could only hope that she would avoid anything that might break the spell. "Now lie down on your chubby white belly, Mr. Johnson, and put your arms out."

He did as commanded and she secured the ropes to the head-board. While doing so, she planted one of her high heels up next to his face. His breathing quickened and he made little thrusts down into the bed spread. She went back to the cabinet and selected a black leather strap with a braided handle.

"Perfect," she commented. "I'm afraid what happens next is going to hurt a little – or maybe a lot. I'm going to whip your lily-white ass until it's bright red. Understand?"

Larkin nodded silently. He squirmed and tugged against the cuffs while thrusting into the bedding.

"I'm going to the restroom now," she said. "And while I'm gone, I want you to think about what's going to happen to you. Let me give you little sample before I go."

She brought the strap down with enough force that it left a pink stripe on his pale haunches. He gasped and arched at the blow.

"Very good," Rhonda said. She put down the strap and left the room.

Once outside, she hurried down the stairs. There was no telling how long he'd remain immersed in his sadomasochistic fantasy. She reached the front door, turned the deadbolt and walked over to the entrance onto the deck. The air had turned cool outside and a thin layer of fog had settled in on the bay. Upon reaching the railing, she spotted Stone's car halfway down the block and waved. He immediately got out and waved back. It cued four men in the car behind him and they all came out onto the deserted street. One of them carried a large trash bag and another had a camera case slung over his shoulder. They joined Stone and started up the street as Rhonda went back in and up the stairs.

She found Larkin still writhing on bed in a fog of orgiastic anticipation. "Now let's see, where were we?" She picked up the strap. "Oh, that's right. We were going to light up your ass. Well let's get going on that, shall we?"

She brought the strap down a little harder this time and Larkin's buttocks twitched in response. Before she could ponder a third stroke, the door flew open. Larkin turned in alarm toward the sound.

Linehan followed protocol and flashed his badge. "San Francisco police. You're under arrest for operating a house of prostitution."

"What the hell?" Larkin managed to twist sideways while Linehan read him his Miranda rights. He appeared more angry than overwhelmed. A second cop with a flash camera came forward and popped off a series of shots that also took in Rhonda, the strap and the restraints.

Sgt. Burke joined Linehan. They both smiled contemptuously at Larkin's predicament. "Fun's over, buddy," Linehan said. He turned to Rhonda. "Cut him loose, sweetheart."

Larkin finally came uncorked as Rhonda removed his restraints. "What the fuck are you doing?" he screamed. "You know what this place is? Do you know who I am? You're way off limits!"

"Wait downstairs," Linehan ordered Rhonda as Larkin hastily pulled his shirt and pants on.

Burke pointed to the two-way mirror. "Cute trick with the mirror and the camera. Looks like you're in the porno biz as a side gig. We'll be bagging all that film as evidence. Sorry for the inconvenience."

Rhonda slid into her dress in the bathroom and walked into the viewing room on the other side of the wall, where Stone watched the scene unfold through the mirror. Larkin, now on his feet, gesticulated wildly, and they could hear his muffled voice yelling at Linehan and Burke.

Stone turned to Rhonda. "Congratulations. You pulled it off. I think we're going to get exactly what we need."

"I'm counting on it," Rhonda said.

Behind them a cop plucked the last of the film cans out of their wooden slots and tossed them into the trash bag.

Stone turned to him. "We're out of here. Thanks for your help. Good job."

The cop gave them a friendly nod and went back to work.

Larkin stood defiantly with arms out and fists clenched. "I'm gonna give you guys one last chance to get the fuck outta here."

Linehan turned to Burke and poked his chest in mock surprise. "Hey, now I remember where I saw this guy. He's Roy Larkin. He's the head of the Federal Bureau of Narcotics around here."

"You know, I think you're right," Burke agreed.

"It's really gonna stink when this gets out," Linehan said. "Boy, I dunno. Maybe we should try to work something out."

"Like what?" Larkin asked suspiciously.

"Here's the deal," Burke said. "Later today we're going to arrest your dear old friend, Willie Mather, for conspiracy to commit murder in the Superspade case."

"You already tried that," Larkin said defiantly. "It didn't work."

"Yeah," Linehan shot back. "And the reason it didn't is because you had somebody step in and kill it at the DA's office, somebody way up on high. We're going to play it a little different this time."

"What do you mean?" Larkin asked.

"We're going to bust Mather and we're going to book him. He'll duck and dodge through his lawyers, but the DA will get a clean shot. He'll get arraigned and he's off to trial. If that's how it goes down, we've got a terrific retirement present for you. You can have everything back that we just carted out of here."

"And if not?" Larkin asked.

"We send a little package of photos and film to the *Chronicle*, the *Examiner*, and most importantly to George Murphy and Tom Kuchel, US Senators for the great state of California."

Both cops watched Larkin's eyes go dead and his face sag in defeat. "You really think you can get away with this?" he asked weakly.

"Yes, I really think we can," Linehan said. "Goodnight."

Rhonda remained silent until Stone drove them across 19th Avenue toward the beach. She stared straight out the windshield when she finally spoke.

"I didn't want to stop," she said softly. "I wanted to beat him until he was dead."

Stone needed no further words, no more embellishment. He saw all the leering, predacious males of her past rise up and consolidate themselves into the person of Roy Larkin. He wasn't an expert on psychotherapy, but he knew it depended on break-through moments, milestones of self-realization on the path to healing. He had a strong hunch that he'd just witnessed one.

"Would you do me a favor?" he asked.

"What?"

"Would you talk to Christine about it?"

"I will."

"Good."

Nothing more needed to be said.

53.

TENDERLOIN DISTRICT

The King took his time going over the breakfast menu in the Oak Room at the St. Francis Hotel. He settled on eggs benedict with a fruit plate on the side. That way, the good stuff would cancel out the bad, he reasoned. The only items on his schedule for the day were a couple of calls to associates on the east coast. Otherwise, he was a free man.

"William Mather, I'm arresting you on suspicion of conspiracy to commit murder."

He looked up and over his shoulder. There stood Sgt. Burke, the same goddam cop he'd run into last time.

"Officer Burke," he said. "You can't be serious. We've been all through this. It's all settled up. Right?"

"Wrong," Burke replied. "Now stand up and turn around." A second cop stood behind him, holding a pair of handcuffs. All the patrons had turned and looked on. The trio had replaced the breakfast menu as the morning's main attraction.

"You know, I'm not a lawyer," the King said as he was cuffed. "But I don't think you can be tried for the same offense twice."

"You're absolutely right," Burke said. "But you were never even charged. Let's go."

The King felt his face burn with humiliation as he was marched out in the presence of his peers in the world of high commerce and professional services. Two Irish redneck cops hauling off a conse-crated member of the business aristocracy. Outrageous.

The phone rang as Stone was fixing lunch. Rhonda and Christine looked on expectantly as he lifted it from the cradle.

"Stone here."

"It's Burke. We got him. He was just booked downtown at City Jail."

Stone gave the women a thumbs-up while he listened to Burke. "Well done," he told the officer. "We're almost there."

"We'll know pretty quick," Linehan said. The arraignment should be scheduled by tomorrow. It's pretty much up to Agent Larkin at this point."

"That it is," Stone said. "Hang in there."

"You too."

Stone hung up and turned to Rhonda and Christine. "So they got him."

"But can they keep him?" Christine asked.

"We'll see," Stone said.

54.

CIVIC CENTER

The King hated the orange coveralls almost as much as the confinement. He'd always been a meticulous dresser and felt that his clothing was an extension of his true self. By that measure, his self-esteem was in serious jeopardy. To make matters worse, his back ached from sleeping overnight on the pitiful little bed in his jail cell.

The expression on his attorney's face didn't make him feel any better. As the man took a seat across from him in the visitors' center, the King noted his well-barbered hair, moderately expensive suit and stylish eyeglasses. By the look of it, he had to be a junior partner. Why had they sent a junior partner? They would hear more about this later. But right now the King's main concern was the scowl welded onto the man's face.

"Mr. Mather, I'm George Brinker. I'll be representing you." He proffered his hand, but the King did not reciprocate.

"So what the fuck's the problem? Why am I still here?"

"They can hold you up to forty-eight hours before they charge you," Brinker said cautiously.

"I know that," the King said. "And that's not what I asked you. Let me say it again: Why am I still here? Haven't you contacted Agent Larkin about this?"

"As per your instructions over the phone, I attempted to contact him at the FBN just before I came over here."

"And?"

"I was told he isn't available."

"And did they give you any hint as to why he isn't available?"

"He just announced his resignation and retirement. Effective today."

"You've got to be kidding."

"I'm afraid not, Mr. Mather. Right now, I think we best look ahead to the arraignment and preliminary hearing..."

The King switched him off. None of that mattered. Not anymore. Without Larkin, he was going down.

And going down hard.

55.

FILLMORE DISTRICT

The Paul Butterfield Blues Band came out swinging, and the crowd at the Fillmore responded in kind. The whole place rocked and swayed to a blistering rendition of "Born in Chicago." Fall was the warmest time of year here in the city and it lit the afterburners as the band moved into "I Got My Mojo Workin'."

Stone's vantage point from backstage gave him an unobstructed view of Mike Bloomfield, the young virtuoso guitarist whose soaring solos bordered on sublime. He turned to Christine. "It doesn't get any better."

"If you say so," she said with an amused smile.

He knew that he sometimes came off like a ten-year-old boy with a brand-new bike. Good music could do that to you.

Rhonda came up from behind and put her hands on both their shoulders. "So what do you think?"

"Perfect," Stone answered. "And how's things here at work?"

He was referring to her position as Bill Graham's personal assistant, which he'd helped engineer. Graham had been willing to give it a shot and found her to be both smart and capable, which was no surprise.

"It's going well," Rhonda told them. "I think I owe you dinner, or something like that."

"I've got a better idea," Christine said. "Why don't you come over and have dinner with us on Sunday?"

"Well yeah, maybe," Rhonda said. "Would it be okay if I brought a date?"

"You're seeing someone?" Christine instantly lit up in that special way that only women can at such news.

"Yeah, I guess I am," Rhonda said. "I mean it's not really serious or anything." She paused and smiled. "But it's nice."

"Well good for you," Christine said. "By all means bring him along." She took this to be a major step in Rhonda's emotional recovery. Just a few months of therapy were already paying handsome dividends.

Stone, of course, wondered about the guy's character. Was he good enough for her? By now he'd given up on resisting the fatherly role. They had coalesced into a family, albeit an unconventional one, and each was the better for it.

At the same time, his role as protector had subsided somewhat and no longer consumed him. The trial of Willie Mather was still a few months away, but the DA already had him nailed to a cross of his own making. Both the Superspade killers had formally cut a deal to testify against him. Since their alternative was to die gasping in a gas chamber at San Quentin, there was little doubt that the arrangement would hold up.

District Supervisor Roy Larkin was another matter entirely. Stone had expected that he would disappear into the impenetrable fog of national intelligence and resurface in some Third World outpost, where he could run amuck with little fear of reprisal. It didn't happen. In fact, upon retirement he moved to a small resort community on the coast up north, where he became the fire marshal. Stone found a certain measure of justice in this outcome. After careening wildly across the world stage for four decades, he would spend his remaining years in remote anonymity.

Only one dangling thread remained. The money. Forty-five thousand dollars. What had Speedo done with it? He claimed he gave it to God, but God cast a rather immense net, so Stone wrote it off as unsolvable.

Still, he would always wonder.

56.

DOWNTOWN

Some might behold the altar in the downtown Buddhist temple and think it ornate to the point of chaos. But not the young novitiate monk charged with maintaining it. He saw it as a garden rich in colors, textures, icons and offerings, each with a life of its own.

A large golden statue of the Buddha held him in its serene gaze as he went about his prescribed duties of cleaning, dusting and arranging the three platforms that comprised the altar. He worked his way from the front to the back, where the highest platform held the Buddha himself, flanked by a cheerful assortment of smaller statues, plants and flowers.

A small anomaly caught his eye, where the embroidered altar covering extended down to meet the polished wooden floor. A small piece of dark material protruded from underneath, perhaps a strap of some kind.

He gently tugged on it and a black backpack slid out. It felt heavy and had a bulky appearance. He was tempted to unzip it and inspect the contents but refrained. It was a matter to be handled by the dai-oshō, the resident priest.

The elderly monk had long ago mastered the art of appearing simultaneously stern and kind when dealing with the younger members of the order. As resident priest, he practiced it on an almost daily basis and did so now as the novitiate handed him the backpack.

After the younger monk had bowed and departed, he unzipped it. Inside, he beheld numerous bundles of hundred-dollar bills stacked at random, like paper rafts upon a stormy sea.

It ignited no fire within him. His age and cumulative wisdom saw its value as transitory at best, like the flight of a small bird through a winter sky. Instead, he wondered about the nameless benefactor.

Who would do such a thing?

1969

LATE FALL, SAUSALITO

Epilogue

Matt Carson feels the slosh from a passing wave that rocks the houseboat moored on one of the main piers in Sausalito. It reminds him of the lurch he felt when the choppers veered to avoid enemy gunfire in Vietnam. But that time has come and gone, along with the Summer of Love and all its trappings. A new dawn has risen, not a psychedelic one centered on love, but a political one focused on rage. And this houseboat, painted a cheerful pink, stands close to its smoldering core.

Carson feels centered here, welded into the moment. At last, his time of wandering is behind him. His two companions seated in a cramped living room resonate with his troubled worldview. One, a tall blonde surfer type, gesticulates emphatically with his long hands as he speaks.

"Can't you feel it? We're approaching the ignition point. The proletariat will rise up. Our revolution will become the people's revolution. The government will come down. They won't see it coming until it's way too late. Castro did it. Mao did it. Che did it. Now it's our turn. We'll burn the old order to the ground and build ourselves a righteous future. We're close, so very close. All those people out there, they're just waiting for a wakeup call, a catalyst."

The second man, a curly-haired caricature of a graduate student, speaks up. "Yeah, the time for all the chickenshit protest stuff is over. We need some really decisive action against the pigs and all they stand for. It's time for bombs. They're the alarm clock everyone's been waiting for."

Just outside the open door, a young woman descends an iron ladder from the roof, where she's been sunning herself. Carson can feel her sexual magnetism as she enters, topless and shameless. She glides on through in silence to a bedroom at the rear and shuts the door. During her brief excursion she holds them firmly within her libidinous sway.

"I've done a little planning," the second man continues. "I've sent people out around the city, always in pairs. A guy and a girl. Nobody suspects lovers. I've got a list of pig posts that look like fat targets." He pulls a folded paper from his coat and spreads it on the coffee table.

"Okay let's take a look," the first man says and scans the list. "Hunters Point is out. The black brothers have already taken way too much shit. And downtown won't work. Too much collateral damage."

He stops at the third entry. "Park Station at Golden Gate. That just might work." He turns to Carson. "You're the technical guy. Can you do it? Can you make it happen?"

Of course he can.

Made in the USA
Middletown, DE
28 October 2020